# Jay enjoyed watching her

It was a heady feeling, a powerful feeling, to find herself the focus of attention of one very handsome and charming man. Sometimes his eyes flickered with appreciation at something she said, and Lisa fought the impulse to become reckless with wit, to laugh louder, bat her eyelashes— anything to impress him. But that would be a mistake. He *was* impressed; she knew it.

Almost ceremoniously, he put his arms around her and kissed her.

"You really know how to kiss," he said after a few minutes.

"Only when I'm kissing the right person," she said.

"You must have had lots of practice."

"Not with the right person."

"What makes me so right?" he asked, his mouth close to her ear.

"Oh," she said, striving for a lightness of tone, "some kind of undefinable something, I guess."

"A good way of putting it," he agreed, and turned out the lights....

# ABOUT THE AUTHOR

Pamela Browning grew up in Lake Park, Florida, and spent much of her childhood in Jupiter on the Loxahatchee River, near the setting of *Sunshine and Shadows*.

## Books by Pamela Browning
### HARLEQUIN AMERICAN ROMANCE

237–SIMPLE GIFTS*
241–FLY AWAY*
245–HARVEST HOME*
287–FEATHERS IN THE WIND
297–UNTIL SPRING
354–HUMBLE PIE
384–A MAN WORTH LOVING
420–FOR AULD LANG SYNE

*THE HEARTLAND SERIES

# PAMELA BROWNING

## SUNSHINE AND SHADOWS

# *Harlequin Books*

TORONTO • NEW YORK • LONDON
AMSTERDAM • PARIS • SYDNEY • HAMBURG
STOCKHOLM • ATHENS • TOKYO • MILAN
MADRID • WARSAW • BUDAPEST • AUCKLAND

This book is for Melanie and Evan,
who bring sunshine into my life

Published May 1992

ISBN 0-373-16439-4

SUNSHINE AND SHADOWS

# Prologue

*June, 1969*

The shadowy refuge of the banyan tree in the park across the street from their neighboring houses was an oasis in the simmering heat of a South Florida summer; Megan O'Rourke and Lisa Sherrill, both age nine, found a grassy niche among the cool curving roots where they could sort through the basket of flowers they had just picked in Megan's backyard.

"One for you, one for me," chanted Megan as she doled out the pink-and-white phlox and the larger cerise hibiscus blossoms. The hibiscus flowers with their long fluttery petals were especially prized; Lisa's mother had given rare permission for them to pick them from the tall hedge between their houses.

"There's one hibiscus left," Megan announced. She thrust it toward Lisa. "Here, Lisa, you can have it."

Lisa accepted the flower and added it to the heap in her lap. Then, tongue held firmly between her teeth, she strung the phlox on long weedy stems that they had picked for the purpose. Three stems twisted together made a crown, and four made a necklace. They draped themselves extravagantly with the necklaces; Megan's crown swooped rakishly over one eye, and her hair sprang up through the center in a fluffy red pouf.

"I love pink-and-white," Megan confided, her earnest face dappled with sunbeams streaming through the leaves overhead.

"Me, too," Lisa said dreamily. "When I get married, I'm going to have a big wedding. My bridesmaids will all wear pink dresses and pink hats and pink shoes." The vision flowed out of her head and off her lips with no trouble at all; a born daydreamer, she could see every detail of her wedding in her mind's eye, and it was beautiful.

"Oh, I want a big wedding, too," Megan said. "Say, I have an idea—let's have a wedding today. We can make bride and bridesmaid dolls, and the hibiscus flowers can be their skirts." She twirled a hibiscus flower this way and that, critically examining it with an eye to its suitability.

Lisa pushed baby-fine strands of blond hair out of her eyes and painstakingly dug a dozen wood Popsicle sticks out of the pocket of her shorts. "I've been saving these all summer," she explained to Megan. "They can be dolls' bodies."

"And we'll draw faces," Megan said in delight. She held up a stubby, tooth-marked pencil.

Lisa, who at nine was possessed of a baby face that was still endearingly round, was twisting a piece of thread around the waist of her second bridesmaid doll, when her lower lip began to quiver.

"I just thought of something, Megan," she whispered. "We won't get to come to each other's weddings."

"Oh," said Megan, her face falling. "I almost forgot you're moving to Stuart."

"Maybe it's not too far," Lisa said, mostly to console Megan. "It's only fifty miles. Anyway, Daddy said we might move back someday." This was another dream, a more serious one.

"Fifty miles isn't next door, and someday may be never," was Megan's mournful reply.

"Well, no matter how far away I live, you'll always be my very best friend. I promise," Lisa replied with an air of forced cheerfulness.

Megan brightened. "I promise, too. In fact, let's swear that we'll be in each other's weddings. I want you to be my number-one bridesmaid."

"Maid of honor, you mean. And I would never have anyone but *you* for *my* maid of honor, Megan. I will never ever have a best friend as good as you as long as I live."

"Okay, it's a promise. Do you cross your heart and hope to die?" Lisa asked.

Megan, whose grandmother had died recently, looked unsure. "Well, I cross my heart. I don't like the other part," she said uncomfortably.

"I cross my heart, too," Lisa said.

The two friends beamed at each other, never noticing that a cloud momentarily obscured the sun.

*June, 1979*

"Don't you love the way the train on my dress swishes when I walk around corners?" Megan asked Lisa as they stepped out of the West Palm Beach dressmaker's shop into the humid half-light of an impending thunderstorm. Megan took a few mincing steps and twitched an imaginary train.

"You drove Mrs. Pogue crazy when you kept parading back and forth from the fitting room to the sewing room. She was afraid your heel was going to pierce a hole in the fabric," Lisa said.

"I have to learn to manage my train. The wedding's only two weeks away," said Megan in her own defense. They headed toward the parking lot, speeding up at the sight of the threatening thunderclouds scudding out of the west.

Lisa thought about asking Megan if she wanted to wait out the storm at the doughnut shop across the street, but Megan seemed to be in a hurry. It was past time for dinner, so she dismissed the thought and kept walking. It wasn't so easy to keep up with Megan; her long legs had always been able to outstride Lisa's short ones.

"You look gorgeous in pink, Lisa. Remember the day under the banyan tree when we swore we'd be in each other's weddings? Did you think we really meant it?"

Lisa smiled and hitched her steps in order to catch up. "Of course I did. And you've always been my best friend, even though I've moved away to Stuart and moved back to West Palm Beach and gone away to college and—well, I can't imagine having any other best friend. Ever."

Megan, more radiant than any bride-to-be Lisa had ever seen, impulsively stopped in the middle of the sidewalk and hugged her friend. "Me, either. Are we still going shopping tomorrow?"

"Sure. We both have things to buy, and we might as well go together."

"Shall I pick you up in the morning? Or do you want to stop by the house?"

"I'll come over. I want to see your handsome groom before the wedding and impress upon him how lucky he is to have found you."

"He knows. Hey, we'd better run before it starts to rain. I don't know how to put the car top up. Bye!" Megan took off at a fast clip, her skirt plastered to her legs by the rising wind.

Lisa considered offering to help with the convertible top, but Megan was already in the car, so she only waved back before climbing into her own blue Mustang. The last she saw of Megan was when Megan rounded the corner in her fiancé's vintage MG, her red hair streaming behind her.

That night, long after the rain had stopped, Lisa was awakened from a deep sleep by the ring of the telephone beside her bed. She squinted at the lighted dial of the clock. It was almost eleven o'clock; she scooped the receiver off the hook before the ringing could wake her parents.

"Yes?" she said. She heard a silence, then something that sounded like a sob.

"Who is this?" she asked sharply as she pulled herself to a sitting position.

"Megan..." said the voice.

But it wasn't Megan. She recognized the voice of Megan's fiancé, Barry.

"Megan? What—"

"She's dead, Lisa. She's gone. I'm at the hospital. I got here right after the accident. It—it happened in my car on the way home from the fitting at the dressmaker's. She never made it."

"No," Lisa said distinctly. "It isn't true."

Barry fought to control himself. "I'm afraid it is. Some high-school kid got drunk at an all-day graduation party and ran a red light in the drizzle. He hit Megan broadside, and the car rolled over twice with the top down. And he wasn't even hurt."

Megan . . . the rain . . . Barry's convertible. If only she had helped Megan to put the top up, it might have provided some protection, or if she had asked Megan to wait at the doughnut shop until the storm passed, the accident might never have happened! For a moment Lisa heard the blood rushing in her ears and then she felt violently ill. The unavoidable mental picture of Megan lying broken and bleeding on a slick pavement was fundamentally horrifying.

"Lisa? Lisa, are you there?"

Tears began to stream down Lisa's face. She felt so guilty. "I don't believe it," she sobbed. "I can't."

She didn't know what Barry said in reply, and the rest of that night would forever remain a blur, but eventually she did believe when at last she stood in front of Megan's flower-draped casket at the grave site, listening to the priest intone dry words that seemed meaningless in the face of senseless tragedy.

Barry, his face a mask of anguish, wept audibly throughout the service, and Adele, Megan's mother, collapsed afterward. Only Lisa exhibited no emotion at all; she sat as expressionless as a stone throughout all the formalities. A heavy cold weight had settled against her heart, and her grief had solidified into anger.

After the funeral, one bitter thought surfaced: *Somewhere that kid who killed Megan is going on with his life, and Megan's is over. I hope he goes to jail until he's very, very old. I wish he had died instead of her.*

But James M. Watkins, the boy who was responsible for the fatal accident, was sentenced by a lenient judge. For killing Megan, he was required to spend one year of nights and weekends in the Palm Beach County Jail and to provide one hundred hours of community-service work.

The last thing Lisa heard of him, he was attending the University of Florida in Gainesville, where, by arrangement of the authorities, he could conveniently serve his time in the Alachua County Jail, instead.

Lisa was glad that she had chosen to attend Florida State three years before; the two universities were a hundred and fifty miles apart. She knew with chilling certainty that if she ever laid eyes on James M. Watkins, she'd kill him. Which wouldn't bring her friend back to life, but would certainly make her feel as though justice had finally been served.

# Chapter One

*January, 1991*

Lisa Sherrill steered around a huge pothole in the main street of Yahola, a small community at the edge of the Florida Everglades, and eased her car to a stop in the Faith Mission School parking lot. Children swirled around her as she stepped out into the bright sunshine, beautiful children with eager faces. Brown faces, black faces, white faces. Somehow she had not expected the children of migrant workers in this labor camp on the edge of the Everglades to be so outgoing.

"Lisa, welcome," called Sister Maria Francisco as she rounded the corner of the chapel, her abbreviated dove gray habit a solemn contrast to the riotous beauty of the bougainvillea vine climbing the white brick of the chapel wall.

"Sister Maria," Lisa said, hurrying forward with a smile. The nun clasped both of Lisa's hands in hers and grinned at her. They were on the same eye level, and neither of them was much taller than the children who gathered around and clamored for attention.

"I'm glad you're here," Sister Maria said, her plump cheeks dimpling. "You're going to be exactly what we need. What the *children* need. Or maybe what the children's *stomachs* need." She laughed, a deep throaty chuckle.

A slim dark boy tugged at Sister Maria's arm and whispered to her in Spanish.

Sister Maria spoke to him rapidly, and although Lisa understood some Spanish, she could make out no more than a few words of this particular exchange.

"What did he say?" she asked Sister Maria after the boy scampered away.

"That was Pedro. He said his stomach needs ice cream instead of a pretty lady who smiles," replied the nun.

"Perhaps we can arrange for the ice cream someday," Lisa said, and this remark was greeted by shouts of approval from the four or five boys and girls who trailed after them as they stepped into the welcome shade of the covered walkway leading from the church to the school.

"We'll have no ice cream today, so run along and leave us in peace," Sister Maria informed the children as she shooed them away, and Lisa heard several disappointed groans.

"As I mentioned last time we met," Sister Maria went on as they resumed their walk, "we can't teach these children effectively if they're hungry. Your qualifications as a dietitian are excellent, and we're happy to have you aboard." She led Lisa through a cool breezeway where Lisa's footsteps echoed off the concrete-block walls.

"This is probably the most interesting job I've had," Lisa answered, slowing her step outside the lunchroom as she took in the colorful mural on the wall. It fairly burst with exuberance, a masterful mélange of colors and shapes.

"That's to remind some of the children of their culture," Sister Maria said. "We have a good number of

Haitian students at the school, but even more of them come from Guatemala or the Yucatán Peninsula in Mexico with their parents, who work the fields here in the winter. The stepped pyramid in the middle of this mural is similar to what they have seen at home, and the little boy with the burro in the foreground could be a friend they left behind."

"Who painted it?" Lisa asked as they continued walking.

"Most of the credit goes to our good friend Jay, who teaches art here on Monday and Wednesday afternoons. Oh, Jay is a godsend—a lawyer who volunteers his time to our children. What we'd do without him I don't know. Here's my office—come in, come in."

In the cool haven of the small cluttered cubicle, Sister Maria plucked a folder from the stack on her desk and handed it to Lisa.

"Here's a map of Yahola. In the envelope inside the folder is your key to our mission's community center, a small house that we have remodeled into a kitchen and dining hall where the children and their families will eat."

"Do the people here know about your program yet?"

"The children carried the bulletins home from school last week. Some of them have to read them to their parents, can you imagine? After five years at this mission, I still find it hard to believe that so many parents are illiterate in every language. Ah, well, we're making a difference. So will you. Sister Ursula, Sister Clementine, please come in. I'd like you to meet Lisa Sherrill. Lisa, here are your cooks."

Lisa looked up from the map as two nuns swept into the room. Sister Ursula was short, dark and dour with what appeared to be a permanent furrow between her eyebrows; Sister Clementine was tall, spare and had a smile that split her wedge-shaped face from ear to ear. Lisa shook their hands, well aware that they were sizing her up.

"I wonder if I'll have to do any public-relations work. You know, beat the drum to sell the advantages of good nutrition," Lisa said, turning to Sister Maria.

"Our balanced meals will be popular beginning from the very first day," said Sister Clementine with great conviction.

"*If* anyone comes to eat them," Sister Ursula said.

Sister Maria walked around her desk and sat down. "The men and women work in the fields all day doing stoop labor," she said. "They're usually too tired to put much more than a cold pot of rice on the table when they come in."

Lisa and the two nuns sat down across from her. "That's why this is such a worthwhile project," Sister Clementine said, leaning forward in her enthusiasm. "I'm happy to think that starting tomorrow on Mondays, Wednesdays and Fridays the children will be assured of a hot dinner three nights a week."

"Three nights. It's hardly enough," Sister Ursula said curtly.

"I agree," Lisa said. Her troubled eyes met Sister Maria's.

Sister Maria's lips fixed themselves into a grim line. "Nevertheless, for now it will have to do."

"Oh, but Sister," Sister Clementine said, her voice gentle. "We should be grateful that we can afford to feed the families properly three nights out of the week. I'm sure we can spark the parents' interest in learning nutrition so they can cook better meals for their children."

"Are all the parents negligent?" Lisa asked.

"Oh, don't get the wrong idea," Sister Maria said hastily. "The bonds in migrant families are often stronger than the ties among families who live in one place year after year. Families who move around the country have only each other, you see. However, many of them don't understand how important it is to eat a balanced diet."

Sister Ursula turned to Lisa, and when she spoke it was brusquely but not unkindly. "Some of the parents are unable to do their best for their children. A single mother like Pedro's, perhaps, abandoned by the father of her eight children, and who works all day bent double as she picks beans—how can she manage? A family where one parent is an alcoholic and spends the food money on his habit—how can they cope? These are the ones to whom we minister," she explained.

Lisa closed the folder decisively. "Tomorrow we'll begin," she said. She stood and held out her hand to Sister Maria.

Sister Maria's grip was warm. She clasped Lisa's hand a moment longer than necessary.

"I see that I was right. You are a special person. I see love and kindness in your eyes, and the children warmed to you immediately. I'm glad you're part of our team, Lisa. You'll be good for us, I know."

"I hope so," Lisa said, gripping Sister Clementine's and Sister Ursula's hands in turn.

After Lisa said goodbye to the nuns, she hurried to her car and headed back toward the highway. As always, the fragrance of the Everglades was sharp in her nostrils; it was intriguingly composed of the rich odor of the fertile black muck in the nearby fields overlaid with the fresh pungent green scent of growing things.

She swerved to avoid a pothole in the road; the hole was as big as the bathtub at home. The fields looked lush and prosperous, but weren't the roads here ever repaved? And didn't anyone ever complain about the rotting garbage in the streets in front of the houses?

Probably not. Yahola wasn't a place designed to command much attention. It existed solely because it was ideally located at the edge of a huge agricultural district where the mild climate made it possible to grow tomatoes and cucumbers, peppers and beans all winter long. An influx of migrants every year provided the stoop labor necessary to work the fields; most of them left during the spring or summer to travel to the next job. Yahola was a place that most people wanted to forget about, to pretend didn't exist.

So why was Lisa here? The newspaper advertisement of a full-time job at the mission had intrigued her, and the job interview had gone well. Planning nutritious meals for migrant laborers and teaching elementary rules of nutrition sounded more interesting than working as a dietitian in a hospital, which had been her last job; she had left it because she had been frustrated by unnecessary rules and all-day confinement in a dim closet of an office.

At the Faith Mission, run by the good Sisters of the Order of Perpetual Faith, every day promised to be different. She would plan menus, supervise the cooking of the meals and teach nutrition classes to the migrant workers.

She dodged another pothole and waved out the window at the boy she recognized from the school, the one named Pedro, who had commented that he didn't need a smiling lady, he needed ice cream. He was, according to Sister Maria, a prime candidate for her nutrition program.

First he needed protein and fresh vegetables, but Pedro would get his ice cream. Not today, but soon.

THE NEXT DAY Lisa was dragging folded tables around the dining room of the mission center, trying to arrange them for the best use of the small space, when a man walked in carrying a cardboard box of salt and pepper shakers.

"Sister Maria said to bring these," he told her, setting the box down on the floor with a thump and looking around curiously at the newly painted white walls and the calico curtains sewn by Lisa and Adele, her housemate.

"Thanks," Lisa said distractedly, pushing at one of the folded-up tables with all of her might and wishing that she were six foot two and lifted weights for a hobby. She had never dreamed that she'd need muscles for this job.

"Want some help?" he asked, and at the sound of his voice, she turned and looked at him for the first time. And then she looked again, because he was a man who deserved a second look.

She'd thought at first that he was the janitor from the school, but she saw now that she was mistaken. The school custodian was small and squat, with whiskers blue beneath the skin of his face, and he was over fifty years old. This man's frame was spare and supple, and although he wore a pair of well-faded, paint-spattered jeans, she could tell by his posture and bearing that he was no janitor.

He stood with his hands perched jauntily on his hipbones, his head cocked and every inch of him charged with energy. In that split second, Lisa decided that he was quite simply one of the most beautiful men she'd ever met. Beautiful, but definitely all male.

He wasn't one of those men who was blow-dried, perfumed and exercised to the artificial max. His hair was brown and straight, shading toward red; his brown eyes glimmered with amber depths; and he had a nose so perfectly straight that it might have been filched from a department-store mannequin. His lips were fine and full, and they were smiling in her direction.

Lisa smiled back. "Now that you mention it, yes, you could help me arrange the tables," she said, wishing she had worn something besides baggy overalls and a dirt-streaked T-shirt. She was pierced by a sudden desire for him to see something special in her, but at the same time she was acutely aware that there was nothing special to see. She felt colorless and, what was worse, shapeless inside the baggy overalls.

"Why isn't the lady in charge of this place doing this? They shouldn't let kids do this kind of hard work," he said, and she realized that he had mistaken her for a child, which was not so unusual. She was used to it.

At that point she could have pulled herself up to her full height, but on past occasions when she had done so, she'd always felt like a kid playing grown-up.

"I *am* 'the lady in charge,'" she said quietly. "I'm Lisa Sherrill, the dietitian. How do you do?" and she held out her hand, realizing with a sinking heart how dirty it was. Even so, she could hardly snatch it away again, so she brazened it out, looking him directly in the face. She prayed that he wouldn't dismiss her with his eyes before he even knew her.

He may have noticed the dirt, but he grasped her extended hand, anyway. His grip was strong, his forearm sinewy and yet graceful, and his smile was apologetic.

"I'm Jay Quillian," he said. "Sorry about my mistake. I was expecting someone—well, like Sister Maria.

The way she talked about you, I thought you'd be just like her."

"That's a compliment," she said, trying to recover her equilibrium. "You're the art instructor, right?"

"Part-time art instructor, gardener, and today it looks like I'm the deliveryman."

"Do you move furniture?" Lisa asked.

He grinned back. "It's one of my many talents," he said.

"Would you mind grabbing that end of the table and helping me swing it around?" she said.

"Why don't you relax and let me take care of this? These tables are too heavy for you," he said.

"I managed to set up all the other tables," she pointed out. She lifted her end of the table, leaving him no other choice but to pick up the end nearest him. She guided him to the place where the table would fit best, and they set it top down on the floor.

"Now we pull out the legs—that's right," she said, "and fix the supports so they won't collapse. There! Let's turn it over," she told him.

"How about the chairs?" he asked once they were finished with the table. Metal folding chairs lay in a heap on the floor in one corner.

"Eight chairs to a table," she said, going to get two of them. He followed her. When she drew herself up to her full height of five feet one inch, Lisa's eyes were at the level of the top of Jay's shoulder.

"If I'm keeping you from something—" she said.

At that moment a beautiful child with sawed-off black hair and flashing dark eyes erupted through the door.

"Jay, come quick!" she said. "Jean-Claude poked a stick down a gopher hole near the canal and we hear rattles in there! Maybe it's a rattlesnake!"

Jay dropped the chairs with a clatter. "I told Jean-Claude—" he said.

"You know how he is," the girl said.

"Let's go," Jay said. "Sorry, Lisa, it's an emergency," he said on his way out the door.

Lisa was right behind him, racing down the steps and toward the canal bank where a group of seven or eight kids were watching in rapt fascination while a small barefoot boy repeatedly jabbed a broomstick down a large hole in the ground.

Jay immediately grabbed the boy with the stick and swung him away from the hole. The boy appeared to be no more than six years old, and when Jay set him down on the ground beside Lisa, he started squalling.

Jay wrested the stick from the boy's chubby fingers. "Hold on to him, will you?" Jay said to Lisa. "Keep him out of the way." Lisa immediately knelt in the sand and wrapped her arms around the child, who continued to cry.

Jay pushed the rest of the children away from the hole and peered into it.

"We heard the rattles," said the boy, whom Lisa recognized as Pedro. "It's gotta be a rattlesnake. Shut up, Jean-Claude, we can't hear with you crying."

Lisa knew enough to realize that the children had been in real danger. This hole in the ground, which was about the size of a stovepipe, had been dug by a gopher turtle. In the winter months snakes often holed up in gopher holes to escape the cold. Gophers didn't seem to mind sharing their quarters, but snakes could get nasty when disturbed by humans, especially pint-size humans who jumped around excitedly and nudged them with sticks.

Now that Jean-Claude had stopped his wailing, they could hear the ominous sound of whirring rattles deep down in the hole.

"Hear it?" Jean-Claude asked. "Let me kill it, Jay! Sister Maria wants us to kill all rattlesnakes! She said so!"

"Sister Maria most definitely didn't say that it's okay for *you* to kill rattlesnakes," Jay said firmly. "I'll take care of the snake as soon as you kids clear out."

"We don't want to—"

"Aw, Jay, come on. I've never seen a real live rattlesnake."

"Let us stay, oh, please—"

Lisa had to speak loudly to be heard over the din of protest. "Let's all go eat ice cream. I've got some in the freezer in the kitchen," she said.

Jay shot her a grateful look. "Everybody go with Lisa, and I'll come over to fill you in later," he promised.

"With the dead snake?" Pedro asked hopefully.

"How are you going to kill it?" one of the girls wanted to know.

"Never mind about that, Serafina," Jay said, keeping an eye on the hole.

Lisa herded the children into a small group and urged them toward the dining hall. "Come along, boys and girls. There's vanilla, chocolate, and lime sherbet. Who likes chocolate?"

"I do!" said the girl named Serafina.

"I don't!"

"Well, I do!"

As she and the children rounded the corner of the dining hall, Lisa looked back toward the canal. Jay was bending over and studying the inside of the gopher hole.

In the dining hall, she sat the kids down at the table that she and Jay had set up earlier, handed out cups of ice cream and sherbet, and led a lively discussion on the subject of snake safety, on which she was something of an authority by virtue of living in a house on several country acres adjoining the Loxahatchee River in nearby Jupiter.

"And when you step over a log, never *never* step directly over it. Put your foot on top of the log, look down to make sure no snake is nestled up to the other side of the log and then put your other foot down on the other side," she told the children.

"I always do that," said the girl named Connie. "My daddy taught me about it."

"Huh, your dad couldn't have told you. He ain't been around for a couple of years," Pedro said.

"Before he and Mama left, you dummy," said Connie. She glared at him.

The first of the children had barely finished their ice cream when Jay came in through the kitchen.

"It was a rattlesnake, all right, and a long one, too," he said, stopping at their table. "I'd say it was a good four-footer."

"A snake with four feet," Pedro snickered.

"Four feet *long*, stupid," said one of the other boys as he dug his elbow into Pedro's ribs.

"I wanna see the rattlesnake," Jean-Claude demanded as he slid off his chair.

"Sorry, no one gets to see it. I chopped the snake's head off with a hoe and threw it in the canal," Jay told them.

"Both pieces? The head *and* the tail?" Serafina asked in an awed voice.

"All of it," Jay confirmed.

This statement was first greeted with silence and then expressions of dismay.

"We wanna see that snake," Pedro said indignantly.

"Yeah, I heard that they wiggle around after they're dead," Serafina said.

"They do," said Connie wisely. "But I don't want to see it. Yuck!" And she made a face.

"You could have drawn a picture of it," Pedro reminded her. "You're always drawing some kind of picture."

"I don't want to draw pictures of headless snakes," Connie said scornfully. "My pictures are for making people understand things. For making them see beautiful or sad things about something."

"The sad thing about a snake with no head is that it's got no head," Jean-Claude pointed out.

"So why should I draw it? Come on, let's go look for the gopher that belongs in that hole," Connie said, jumping up.

"You kids stay far away from that gopher hole. You never know when another snake might take up residence," Jay told them as they were on their way out the door.

"But Jay—"

"I mean it, kids. Go water those sunflower seeds we planted in the garden last week. The sprouts need some tender loving care. The gopher hole is forbidden, and if I find out any of you have been playing near there, I'll tell Sister Ursula."

"Sister Ursula! Oh, no!" said Pedro, and that was apparently enough warning to scare them away from gopher holes for the time being. The door slammed after them, and soon the group was running toward the fenced garden, the gopher hole apparently forgotten for the present.

"Sister Ursula must be a real deterrent," Lisa said.

"All she has to do is frown at them, and they back off. It makes her a great disciplinarian. Say, do I get any ice cream for my efforts?" He smiled down at her.

"You bet," she said. He followed her into the kitchen, where he looked around at the institution-size refrigerator, the big shiny range and the wide, stainless-steel sinks, all specially installed for the new nutrition program.

"Chocolate, vanilla, or lime sherbet?" she asked, bending over the deep freezer.

"Vanilla," he said, and she sensed that he was studying her as she reached deep inside the freezer to get the ice cream. He wasn't the type to strip her with his eyes, but she was pleased to see that he was regarding her with a certain speculation when she turned around, and she was amused at how quickly he masked it.

"Let's go into the dining hall," she said. "It's more pleasant in there."

They sat down across from each other at the table and he opened the ice-cream cup. "I like what you've done in here with the curtains and things," he said approvingly.

"It was pretty dismal in here when I checked it out last week," she agreed.

"Looks like you've done a lot of work," he told her.

"I'm proud of the dining hall," she said truthfully. "My housemate and I worked hard on the curtains. And this room will be my classroom when I teach nutrition classes, so I wanted it to be bright in the daytime—the curtains don't shut out the light. The one thing I still don't like is that the walls look so bare."

"How about some pictures to perk the place up? One of my students has already suggested painting pictures for this room on some large plywood panels that we had left over from building the garden shed." He regarded her quizzically, both eyebrows raised.

"What a good idea! Tell me more about it," she said.

"Connie Fernandez—that's the girl who came in to tell me about the snake—is the one with the ideas. She's made a few sketches. Would you like to see them tonight after dinner? Will you be here then?"

Lisa could hear a clatter in the kitchen, which meant that Sister Ursula and Sister Clementine had arrived to cook the evening meal, the first meal to be served in the new dining hall.

"I'll be here," she said.

He scraped the last bit of ice cream out of the cup. "I'd better get back to the garden," he said. "We're supposed to be painting designs on the fence today, and when I leave the kids alone for a minute or two, they always seem to get into mischief, like poking sticks down gopher holes. I'll see you later." He smiled at her again and she thought irrelevantly that he had a kind smile. He had a kind voice, too.

She headed toward the kitchen but turned to watch him as he walked out the dining hall door and down the steps. He called out a cheerful greeting to three or four children who hung around outside and then he was out of sight.

Lisa looked down at her overalls, wishing that she'd been more attractively dressed. Jay Quillian was definitely someone she'd like to impress, and she was afraid she hadn't.

"Lisa?" called Sister Ursula, banging the pots and pans around much more than necessary. "What in the world are we supposed to do with all this cornmeal?"

Lisa sighed. "Put it in the pantry for now," she called back, and she hurried to her small office off the kitchen to wash and change into a colorful blouse and a well-tailored but short skirt. If Jay came for dinner, she'd like to look decent. Not only decent, but grown-up.

SISTER MARIA WAS FIRST in line when they began serving the meal that evening. With her was Jay, whose hand rested benevolently on the head of one of the children. He still wore paint-splashed jeans, and Lisa still thought that he was one of the most beguiling men she had ever met. Certainly he was not the kind of guy she'd ever thought she'd find at the Faith Mission School; he looked as though he ought to be mingling with fashionably dressed women at cocktail parties, not leading a bunch of ragtag kids through a soup line.

Sister Maria waved at her and called, "Lisa! Over here!" Lisa hurried forward, glad that she'd at least brought along a skirt short enough to call attention to her legs.

"I get to sit next to Jay," said one child, a boy, as Lisa approached.

"No! I do!" argued another.

And Jay said, "Hey, kids, take it easy. I'll park myself at the head of the table and Sister Maria can take the foot, and the rest of you can spread out between us."

"Can we just get dessert?" asked Connie.

Jay shot Lisa a questioning look. "You'll have to ask Miss Sherrill," he said.

"Well," Lisa said, wondering if she should use the opportunity to launch into a speech about the value of good nutrition.

But Sister Maria, who noticed Lisa's hesitation, said, "Try the pasta, Connie. I bet you'll like it."

"I already ate," Connie said.

"That doesn't matter," Lisa said, taking her cue from Sister Maria. "You may certainly eat again." She guided Connie toward the food and supervised as Sister Clementine filled her plate.

Connie cast a dubious look at the food. "We never had this at home," she said, but the next time Lisa glanced at the table where she sat, Connie's plate was empty.

That night they served more than eighty people in the community center. There were kerchiefed mothers and patient fathers with small children clinging to their knees; there were teenagers carting babies, some of them their own; there were debilitated old people who looked as though they hadn't eaten a square meal in weeks.

After everyone had left, Lisa and Sister Ursula and Sister Clementine were cleaning up when Jay appeared at the kitchen door. Lisa hadn't expected him so soon, and she looked up with a surprised "Oh!" when Sister Ursula said, "Here's Jay!"

"If you're busy, I can come back another time," Jay said through the screen. He had changed clothes and no longer wore the old jeans he'd had on earlier; now he wore khaki trousers with soft pleats at the waist and a sport shirt in a bright plaid. He carried a portfolio under one arm.

"Right now is fine," Lisa said quickly. She hung up the dishcloth that she had been rinsing under the faucet and went to the door to open it for him.

Several large mosquitoes threatened to accompany him inside until he brushed them away, and as the door slammed after him, Lisa wished she had been doing something more glamorous; she probably smelled of onions and dirty dishwater. But she didn't want to postpone this meeting.

"You run along, Lisa," said Sister Ursula.

And Sister Clementine piped in, "Yes, do. We're almost finished in here."

"Let's drink a cup of coffee while we talk," Lisa suggested, pouring one for Jay and one for her from the coffeepot on the stove, and they carried the steaming cups into the dining area, where they found a table beside a window looking out over the small village where the migrant workers lived.

"I was thinking," Jay said, studying Lisa's face for a reaction, "that we could hang the children's paintings on that long wall over there." He gestured toward the unbroken white space where the kitchen was partitioned off from the dining area. "The pictures will need to be big and colorful. These people's lives inside those houses are so drab that they respond strongly to beauty and color."

"I saw the mural at the school," she said. "It's lovely."

"The kids had fun doing it. Well, so did I," he said with a boyish grin. His eyes glowed from deep within, and he focused them on her face. Being the object of his attention here, where they were all alone, warmed her so that she actually felt her face flush.

"You come to the mission every week?" she asked, the words fairly tumbling over themselves as she began to realize that she was actually nervous. She wanted him to like her. She wanted him to like her a lot.

"Twice a week—most weeks, anyway. I hate to cancel, but sometimes I have to. Whenever I do, the kids become indignant, which shows me how important art classes are to them. They swarm all over me the next time, demanding to know why I wasn't there. It's a sobering experience to realize that I'm that important to so many people."

"Sister Maria said you practice law."

"That's how I make a living, but sometimes I think my heart is here. Most of the kids are so needy. Like Pedro, for instance. And Connie. She's really special."

"In what way?" Lisa asked.

His expression softened. "Connie's talented. And determined. You don't find many kids like that out here," he said, and he gestured toward the dim shapes of the migrant houses outside the window.

Lisa especially remembered Connie's eyes, so bright and full of vitality; moreover, she was intense in a way that many of these children were not. Lisa hated to think of her becoming like any of the tired women they had served tonight, women who had grown old before their time by wearing themselves out with work and bearing too many children too soon.

"What are Connie's chances to escape this life-style?" she asked.

"She's highly intelligent and her grades are tops in her class. She has a dream—a wonderful dream—of finishing high school and going to college. Sister Maria is already trying to figure out a way to arrange for a scholarship when the time comes," he said. He pulled papers out of the portfolio and fanned them out in front of her. "Here are her sketches for the wall panels," he said in a tone of voice that reflected pride in his pupil.

"Very nice," Lisa said, forcing herself to concentrate on the panels and not on his hands. His left ring finger was bare. So was his right one. That could mean that he wasn't married, but it could also mean that he didn't like to wear jewelry.

"Each panel's a picture of one of the vegetables grown on the nearby farms," Jay explained, outlining in the air the shapes of the large, juicy, ripe tomatoes, the succulent green beans hanging from the vine, a large cucumber sliced on a plate.

"I see," she murmured. The possibility that he might be married filled her with instant dismay.

"Connie's thought was that the dining room should be decorated with pictures of the vegetables that provide the people's livelihood. Besides," Jay added with a little laugh, "she thinks they're beautiful, and she says she wishes that the other people here thought so, too. She says that they look at the vegetables with eyes that don't see."

Lisa swallowed and made herself speak in a normal voice. "And she wants to make them see?" she said.

"I believe that's her idca. It's surprising that Connie would think that way when you know more about her. She and her cousins were more or less abandoned by both sets of parents a couple of years ago, and Connie's been mother and father to her cousins ever since. She never lets things get her down—she's always cheerful and happy. I think it's because she expresses her pain through her art. That way her sadness doesn't ever spill over into her real life."

He was so earnest, and she sensed that he genuinely wanted her to appreciate Connie's work. How could she when she was mesmerized not by what he said but the way he said it? A sudden heat rose from her throat to her cheeks. She would assume for the time being that he was single. He didn't look married; over the years she had developed a kind of second sense about such things.

He shot her a keen look, but she didn't know if it was because he had noticed her high color or because he was assessing her interest. Maybe he was wondering if she was single, too.

"I have more of Connie's work in the trunk of my car," he said, watching her. "I could bring it in if you'd like."

It was almost nine o'clock, and Lisa knew that Adele would be expecting her and would worry about her driving home to Jupiter on the treacherous canal-banked road. Still, she didn't want to leave now.

"I'd like to see whatever," she said, zigging over to Plan B, which meant telephoning Adele to warn her that she'd be late if necessary, and she was glad when Jay looked relieved and said, "I'll only be a minute," before hurrying out to the parking lot, where Lisa saw him unlocking the trunk of a dark blue Honda Prelude.

Lisa paced back and forth in the dining hall while she waited for him. She felt breathless and crazy and her heart was beating a mile a minute, and at the same time she was aware that she could do nothing about it. It was as though Jay Quillian had cast some sort of benign spell on her.

When he came back he spread Connie's work on several tables, Lisa bent over it, enchanted in spite of herself by the simplicity of the drawings. He waited expectantly for her comments.

What to say? She was fearful of driving him away forever by saying something stupid. Finally she said, "Connie has a good feeling for color." They were looking at a picture of several children grouped around a storyteller.

"Her composition is excellent, too," Jay pointed out. From the way he said it, Lisa could tell that he wasn't at all bowled over by her the way she was about him. How could he sound so normal? How could he be so interested in these pictures when if they each moved two inches closer to each other, their hands would touch?

"Look at this watercolor of the fields outside Yahola. I like the way she's positioned the children so that we can see only their faces and none of the adults'," Jay said.

Lisa's attention really was captured by this one. Connie's painting portrayed children working beside their parents, picking vegetables among the rows. The parents looked very big, the children very small. What struck Lisa most was the expressions on the faces of the children. Without exception they were woebegone and forlorn.

"What a disturbing picture," she said under her breath. When she looked at Jay, she realized that he was moved by it, too.

"That picture always makes me sad," he said. "Children shouldn't work in the fields."

"How often does it happen?" Lisa asked. She noticed that one of the children in the painting resembled Connie. The girl had dark straight hair cut at chin length, and her eyes were big and dark.

"It's more common than you'd think. Child labor laws are inadequate, and where are the parents who work in the fields supposed to leave their children? Wait until you know the kids better. It's heartbreaking sometimes, the way they live, the way they never stay in one place for more than a few months."

"But the mission school is open for the children throughout the school year," Lisa said.

"Too few of them are here for the whole session. Connie and her cousins usually arrive in Yahola late in the fall when the harvest begins here. They're lucky if they can stay through April or May, when their grandmother packs them all up in that rattletrap she calls a car and hauls them to the next job." Jay straightened and began to slide some of the paintings back into the portfolio.

Lisa took a deep breath. She couldn't overcome her attraction to him, and it had been a long day; she was tired. But through it all, she felt an overwhelming compassion for these children. It bubbled up from some deep well within her, flooding her conscience and her emotions.

She had responded to one of those ads in a magazine once, a picture of a big-eyed orphan begging for a sponsor. Now she sent money every month to a boy in El Salvador who would graduate from high school soon. Lots of people sent money to children like that; how many of those same people realized that such children lived here, in the United States, and were perhaps as needy? She supposed she had been aware of it before, but now she felt overwhelmed.

She walked over to a window and toyed with a loose flap of the hem on one of the curtains. When she spoke it was from her heart. "I—I came to this job because I thought it would be different from my last job, where I worked in a tiny office all day. I thought it would be good to be directly involved with the people who needed what I have to offer, and yet—"

She felt Jay close behind her, so close that she thought she could feel his warm breath on her neck.

"And yet?" he said softly.

She dropped the curtain and turned to face him. "I didn't expect to be caught up in feelings," she said, the words tumbling out in a rush.

He looked puzzled. "You didn't think you'd feel anything?" he asked.

"I never thought about it. It was just an interesting job. And now the kids and the old people and the mothers and fathers who have to work so hard tear at my heart. This is different from any other job I've ever had." She lifted her shoulders and let them fall. She really should go home. She was exhausted. She hadn't meant to pour out her feelings to this man she hardly knew, this man to whom she was so attracted that she felt dizzy when he looked at her a certain way.

"Oh, Yahola can get to you, all right. I know. I know all about it. After a while you'll be proud to be part of the good the mission is doing. I can promise you that." He studied her quietly and seriously, and a current of recognition ran through her like a jolt of electricity. It shook her to her very soul, and she blinked her eyes in confusion.

In that brief moment, she was aware that they had each acknowledged like meeting like, and it was as though they had truly seen each other for the first time. Whole vistas opened up and spread out before her, her world expanded and contracted, and she wondered if he knew what was happening to her. Of course he knew. This man would know everything about her, just as she knew everything about him; everything important, anyway. She stared at him, stunned and unsure what to say or what to do.

But the flicker of recognition that had passed between them in that instant was over. He was moving away from her now, picking up the portfolio, turning toward the door.

"Thanks for the cup of coffee," Jay said on just the right note of politeness. He wasn't looking at her anymore; he was absorbed in wrapping the little piece of string around the cardboard circle on the flap of the portfolio.

"Anytime," she said as casually as she could.

She sensed that he was stalling, that he wasn't ready to leave. She felt a tug of impatience. Why didn't he ask for her phone number and be done with it? Next time she had to stand up to his scrutiny, she hoped it wouldn't be under these long fluorescent lights that made her naturally blond hair look green. She gave him plenty of time, but apparently she hadn't made an impression, after all, because he gave her no cause for thinking that he was eager to see her again.

"See you," he said, and then he turned and was walking away from her, his step almost jaunty, the portfolio tucked under one arm.

She felt a sharp hot prickle of tears behind her eyes as the door slammed after him; she watched through the window as he threw the portfolio into the trunk of his car. In a few seconds the car was kicking up a cloud of dust as it negotiated the sandy rutted road leading toward the highway. She must be out of her mind; a man hadn't asked for her phone number, and she felt on the verge of a crying jag? What was the matter with her?

Sister Clementine peeked around the door leading to the kitchen, her eyes twinkling beneath the graying ruffle of bangs escaping her short veil. "Jay likes you, Lisa, he really does! He's such a nice man—too nice to remain a bachelor."

"So what?" said Sister Ursula, who was right behind her. "You act like the man is God's gift to women."

"Sister Maria says that he's God's gift to the mission," Sister Clementine said calmly.

"I even doubt that," Sister Ursula retorted.

"Sisters, have you poured the cornmeal into those screw-top jars I brought? If you don't, we're going to be plagued with insects in the kitchen," Lisa said by way of diversion.

"Insects—that must be a nice way of saying 'roaches,'" Sister Ursula huffed.

"It's also a way of saying 'butterflies,'" Sister Clementine reminded her gently, but they retreated into the kitchen, leaving Lisa in peace.

If that was what you could call it. She didn't feel peaceful; instead she felt unnerved. The news that he was a bachelor was exhilarating, but it shouldn't make her heart pound wildly and her knees turn to jelly.

As Sister Ursula would say, "You must be sick."

And as Sister Clementine would say, "No, she's not sick. She's in love."

## Chapter Two

For his part, Jay Quillian was sure that he would never marry. As he drove back to his town house in Jupiter after showing Lisa the sketches, he congratulated himself for remaining free of entanglements until the ripe old age of twenty-eight.

So why was he thinking about this woman, this Lisa Sherrill? Somehow during one short afternoon and evening, she had invaded the space of his mind, convinced him that she shared his compassion for the people of Yahola and reminded him that his sex life was inadequate.

Loneliness. Maybe that was it. He didn't admit to being lonely often, and when he did it was usually in a fit of self-pity that he managed to overcome by immersing himself in work.

He could have understood his fascination with Lisa if she'd been a great beauty, but if he'd been pressed for a description of Lisa Sherrill, he would have described her as *cute*. How else would you describe a pixie kind of a person with wispy blond hair, eyes that sparkled even when she tried to appear dignified and a figure that was diminutive but very appealing to him?

Not that those eyes merely sparkled. He had seen for himself how they could glow with excitement, crinkle with humor and deepen with emotion. He could only imagine how they might darken with passion; why was he thinking about that?

He waved at the guard at the gatehouse to the development where he lived, decided that he should backtrack to his office and pick up a folder of work to bring home, and just as quickly changed his mind. He didn't want to face another evening spent with his nose buried in his work and his eyes burning from staying up so late.

He parked his car in its usual slot beside his town house and unlocked the gate to the cypress-fenced courtyard with his key; Hildy, his half mutt, half Old English sheepdog, ambled painfully out of her doghouse and nuzzled his knee.

He bent down to scratch her behind the ears. Poor old Hildy was getting along in years. He could remember the days when she used to come bounding out of her doghouse at the sound of his key in the lock and plant her big paws in the middle of his chest to welcome him. Often as not, her greeting would include a loud slurpy kiss, as well. Nowadays, she was hard of hearing and she barely managed to wag her tail when she saw him.

What would he do when she was gone, when there was no more Hildy to greet him at the gate? He didn't like to think about it. The truth was, he hated to be lonely, and his town house smelled of loneliness—a smell of too many store-bought frozen dinners and rooms left closed all day to incubate a faintly doggy smell.

"Hildy, old girl, how about some chow? How about it?" he said as he let them both in the front door, and she waited eagerly as he poured dry food into a dish beside the kitchen closet, where she slept when she stayed inside.

He wasn't hungry. The meal he'd eaten in the dining hall had been delicious, and it had seemed to be a hit with the people of Yahola, too. He was glad that the mission had decided to hire a dietitian and to start a meal program. Some of the kids in school had a hard time concentrating on their lessons, and he knew the reason was that they didn't get enough to eat at home.

He wondered about Lisa and how someone like her had ended up at Faith Mission. She didn't look like the type to isolate herself at a nowhere kind of place at the edge of the 'Glades where her coworkers would be nuns and where poor families predominated. She looked as if she'd be more comfortable in classier surroundings.

But perhaps she wasn't what she appeared to be. Some of the things she'd said tonight made him think that maybe she felt the same way about the mission as he did, which was probably impossible. He had begun his association with the mission out of atonement, but he continued it out of love. Lisa hadn't been there long enough to fall in love with the place yet.

The first time he'd ever driven to Yahola, he'd been overwhelmed. First of all, there was the wilderness surrounding the labor camp—a wilderness dominated by water. Silent water, slipping through the saw grass toward the sea; lazy water, green with algae, lapping at the sides of the canals on both sides of the road; water that weltered out of the sky in great thunderstorms, the likes of which he'd never experienced anywhere else in Florida or in Tennessee, the only other state where he'd ever lived.

Then there were the nuns at the mission, exceptional women all of them, who were devoted to the migrant children with a passion that burned so strong that he was in awe of it. And of course there were the children, who were the main reason for the mission's existence in the first place. He had grown to love the children, two hundred or more of them, whose lives and futures held little good fortune and even less promise.

Of course, Sister Maria disagreed. "Many of them will succeed in ways that their parents have not. If we enable just one to finish high school, to go to college, to find hope in the midst of despair—then we have succeeded," she had told him.

At first Jay didn't know if it was possible to change the courses of the migrant children's lives even with the single-minded devotion of the dedicated Sisters of Perpetual Faith. He only knew that art could make a difference, that self-expression could be an outlet for young people who had no other way of getting their feelings out in the open. In this he was no less dedicated than the good sisters.

He could have been a partner in a busy Palm Beach law firm after he graduated from the University of Tennessee law school, but he'd turned the offer down flat. Instead, he now shared a partnership and a cramped office with another up-and-coming young lawyer, and their office was by no means located in the best area of Jupiter, but it was sufficient. He made enough money to support himself rather well, and his practice was growing. The growth worried him. He didn't ever want to give up his work at Faith Mission School; he didn't ever want to renege on his commitment to Connie, his prize pupil.

The first time Jay had seen Connie Fernandez in class, she had gripped a blue crayon tightly and concentrated on a picture she was drawing. Her thick black hair curved over her cheekbones, and she had brushed it back behind her ears from time to time with a distinctive impatient flip of the wrist. She was a beautiful child with that brown skin, black eyes and slim legs, but that wasn't what had impressed him the most. It was Connie's sheer raw talent and her own placid acceptance of it that struck him on that first day. It was only later that he realized Connie's rare capacity for interpreting the human condition with her head as well as her heart.

Three years ago, when he had first remarked upon her, Sister Maria had told Jay that Connie was the brightest student in the third grade. Since then Connie had never earned less than an E for Excellent on any of her report cards.

Connie looked to him, her beloved art teacher, for guidance, and he'd done his best. One life, a twelve-year-old girl's life, hung in the balance. Art could be her salvation, so it was up to him to offer encouragement, to show her that there were better ways to live than the way she was living now.

After Hildy ate her dinner and had retired to her bed in the kitchen closet, Jay flipped on his stereo and flung himself down on the couch in the living room. He should throw in a load of laundry, clean up his studio, coax Hildy outside for a walk.

He should have, but he didn't do any of those things. Instead he pictured Lisa Sherrill, who looked like a child when she was wearing overalls, like a mother when she was taking care of children and like a temptress when she wore a short skirt. And who would have expected to find a temptress in the dining hall at the Faith Mission?

"SISTER MARIA, you can do me a favor," he said on the following Wednesday, his regular day at the mission.

"I'd give you the world if I could," she said, beaming up at him from the desk in her office. It was loaded with paperwork.

He sat down in the chair across from her.

"I don't need the whole world," he said. "Only a phone number."

"I'd give you the phone number to heaven itself if you asked," she said. "But, then, we have other channels to God, so perhaps it's one of his angels you'd prefer to speak with."

"Maybe she is at that," he said lightly. "It's Lisa Sherrill."

Sister Maria lifted an eyebrow. "Lisa Sherrill. Yes, she's delightful, isn't she?"

"Don't go getting any ideas," he warned.

"Ideas? Me? I'm sure you only want to discuss business with her, right?" Sister Maria blinked innocently at him from behind her bifocals.

"The children are going to paint panels for the dining hall. I need to discuss it with Lisa, and she's not in the kitchen this afternoon. Sister Clementine said that she's gone to West Palm Beach for a meeting," he said.

"Yes, a meeting of professional dietitians, I believe. Here it is in her personal folder—her telephone number at home." The nun scribbled Lisa's number on a scrap of paper and handed it across the desk to Jay.

"Thanks," he said.

"Jay," Sister Maria said when he turned to go.

He looked over his shoulder, saw that she looked unusually serious, and halted in the doorway. He turned around to face her.

"Jay, you really should have more of a social life. I worry about you," she said.

Sister Maria was the only person at Faith Mission who knew why he gave so much time to their work; the two of them had mined this conversational ground before.

"I'm fine, Sister," he said patiently.

"It isn't natural for a young man like you to—I believe the term is 'hang out with'—a bunch of children and nuns," she said.

"For me it is," he said quietly. "You know why."

"And I think it's not a good enough reason. You deserve a life, you know. And what you have isn't much of one by most people's standards."

"I don't live by most people's standards—not any more."

"I never want to lose you as a volunteer at the mission, but even I can see that it's not enough for you. And if you're thinking of becoming friends with a young lady, you couldn't find a nicer one than Lisa. By the way, the advice is free."

"The trouble with giving me advice is that someday I may want to repay you with the same currency." His voice rose on a teasing note, and he grinned at her.

She laughed. "Fortunately, your advice is always welcome. You don't know how happy we are to know a lawyer to call when we need one."

"Thanks for the help," he told her as he left, and she called out a *de nada,* Spanish for "you're welcome."

Once away from her office, Jay unfolded the piece of paper and read Lisa's phone number. The first three digits were exactly the same as those of his own phone number, and it was a relatively new exchange confined to Jupiter, which meant that she might live nearby. It was an encouraging thought, and that night, prepared with an excuse for calling, he dialed Lisa's number.

The phone rang for a long time, and when someone answered, it wasn't Lisa. When he asked to speak with her, the voice, which was female and for no reason that he could fathom distinctly hostile, said, "Lisa's not here."

"When do you expect her to come back?" he asked in his most businesslike tone of voice.

"I don't know," was the tart reply.

"I see," he said, halfway unwilling to leave a message with someone who sounded so angry.

"I'll tell her you called," said the woman on the other end of the line before she slammed the phone down in his ear.

Jay dropped the receiver back on its hook, thinking that he would have laughed if he hadn't been so disappointed. The woman couldn't very well inform Lisa that he had called when he hadn't even given her his name.

The best thing that he could say about his abortive effort to reach Lisa Sherrill was that it had produced some information about her. She lived with a woman, and from what he could gather from the sound of her voice, it was an older woman. And if Lisa lived with an older woman, she probably wasn't living with a man. Encouraging news, indeed.

LISA HAD EXPECTED Adele to be nodding in front of the television set when she arrived home that night, but the house was dark when she drove her car into the garage. As Lisa opened the door from the garage into the kitchen, Adele shuffled in wearing her bathrobe and old terry-cloth scuffs.

"A man called you," Adele said abruptly.

"A man? What man?" Lisa asked, suddenly alert.

"I don't know," Adele said. "He didn't give me his name."

"Great. I haven't been out with any decent guys in the past six months, and you didn't get his phone number," Lisa said with more than a little exasperation.

Adele ignored this. "Want to play a game of gin rummy?" she inquired hopefully.

Lisa fought an urge to pursue the discussion about the importance of taking telephone messages; it would do no good to argue. Instead she said, "I'd rather not. I'm so tired after a whole day of meetings."

"I remember when I taught you and Megan to play gin rummy," Adele said reminiscently as she sank down on one of the kitchen chairs. "I thought one of you would never catch on."

"I was the official gin rummy dummy, but we crowned Megan the gin rummy queen that summer," Lisa said with forbearance as she opened the refrigerator door and took out the orange juice. Sometimes Lisa thought that Adele's memories of Megan were the only vivid part of her life.

"You made a golden crown out of gilt paper from an old wallpaper sample book and I played a song I'd composed for her on the piano," Adele said.

"Why don't you ever play the piano anymore, Adele?" Lisa asked. She poured orange juice into a glass and sipped it.

"I've forgotten how. Anyway, it's out of tune. If you don't want to play cards, I'll go watch TV. Are you sure you don't want to watch television for a while?" Adele asked.

Lisa shook her head, avoiding Adele's reproachful eyes. "Thanks Adele, but I'm bushed," she said.

Lisa rinsed her glass under the kitchen faucet and made a graceful exit to her bedroom, where she tossed her briefcase in the closet and dumped her cardigan into a drawer. Adele had straightened her room for her; it was one of the kindnesses that she liked to perform for Lisa. Whenever Lisa protested, Adele said that she enjoyed doing it; it was something she would have done for a daughter if she'd had one, Adele said.

Lisa threw herself across the bed and stared at the telephone, willing it to reveal the name of her mysterious caller. It didn't ring again, and she finally fell asleep in her clothes. When she woke up it was one o'clock in the morning, and after she realized what time it was, she roused herself and stumbled into the bathroom, where she stared at her bleary-eyed reflection in the mirror.

It could have been Jay Quillian who had called, and now she would have to wait until Monday to see him again. If only Adele had asked the man his name, if only Adele would learn to take a message now and then. At this rate, Lisa thought irrationally, she'd never find a permanent relationship and she'd live here with Adele forever.

Which was probably exactly what Adele wanted, come to think of it.

LISA DIDN'T HAVE to wait until Monday to see Jay, after all.

On Saturday she was standing in line for the cashier at the drugstore on Jupiter's Indiantown Road, reflecting that there weren't that many eligible men left in the world and that few of them in her corner of it were particularly interesting. When she'd been twenty, she'd thought she had plenty of time to find the right man; then she'd turned thirty and they all seemed to have disappeared.

She wondered precisely when that realization had first come to her. Had it been five years ago? Four? Or was it a year ago when she turned thirty?

Somewhere along the line she'd begun to think of herself as a woman, not a girl, but it was hard to remember that she wasn't young anymore when she looked in the mirror and saw round cheeks and wispy blond hair.

As for men, she'd never found one who offered more than a passing attraction. Since her last failed serious romance a couple of years ago, she'd dated a real-estate broker who'd badgered her about giving him an exclusive listing on her property with her body thrown in for good measure, a yacht salesman who entertained her on a cabin cruiser anchored so far out in the river that she'd almost drowned when she'd tried to swim back to shore after his unwelcome advances and an automobile mechanic who'd wanted to tinker with more than her carburetor. Adele hadn't liked any of them, which was an aggravation at first, but Adele had been right in the end.

She was wondering idly what Adele would think of Jay Quillian, when she glanced over her shoulder to see how many other people were waiting. At the end of the line stood Jay, holding a tube of toothpaste. A pair of dark glasses swung from a cord around his neck; he wore jeans and a boat-necked white shirt and he looked uncommonly agitated.

*What a stroke of good luck,* Lisa thought, her eyes lighting up at the sight of him.

"Jay," she said, leaning around a woman behind her who carried a full basket. "If you'd like me to have your toothpaste rung up with my things, I'd be glad to."

His smile was wide with both recognition and relief. "Lisa! That would be great," he said, breaking out of line and handing the toothpaste over, despite an annoyed look from the woman behind Lisa as he attached himself unassumingly to Lisa's position in line.

"You look as though you're in a hurry," she said as they inched toward the cash register.

"I am, sort of. I promised Connie Fernandez that I'd take her to visit some horses at a ranch that belongs to a friend of mine, and I'm late. Not to mention that the friend doesn't answer his phone, so that I think he's forgotten we're coming."

"Will you go, anyway?" she asked.

"I don't know. There's a security gate with a combination at the entrance to his property and I can't get through if he's not there. Connie will be disappointed if she doesn't get to see the horses."

"Is she with you?"

"No, I'm going to ride out to Yahola to pick her up. I thought I'd take the toothpaste along because she mentioned that she ran out and her grandmother won't buy her any more."

"Won't buy it for her! Why not?"

Jay's shoulders rose in an expressive shrug of annoyance. "You'd have to know the woman. She's not the kind of grandmother who bakes cookies and heaps presents upon her darling grandchildren."

Before Lisa could reply to this, the cashier said, "Next?"

After Lisa had paid for her purchases, she and Jay walked out the door into a January morning bright with sunshine. It sparkled off the chrome bumpers and hubcaps and gleamed off the windshields of the cars, and it danced off the reddish highlights in Jay's hair.

"Here's the toothpaste," she said, handing it over, and he sifted a dollar and some change into her palm.

"Thanks a lot," he said. "I really appreciate this. Now my next problem is what to do with Connie for the afternoon if I can't get in touch with my friend."

"I have an idea," Lisa said suddenly. "If you'd like to hear about it, that is." For a moment she wondered if she was making a mistake. Maybe he wouldn't go for it.

"What's that?" he said. His eyes were deep brown and shiny, like cool polished stones, a welcome relief after looking at the hot bright parking lot. She thought for one disastrous moment that maybe he was only being polite; perhaps he wanted to be on his way. But then his pupils widened and she detected a flicker of something more than compliance with social convention, and she told herself to stop thinking like a teenager. She might look like one, but she didn't have to act it.

"I—I have a canoe," she said, watching carefully for his reaction. "I was going out in it this afternoon, and if you and Connie would like to join me—well, I hate to think of her being disappointed."

"Do you mean it? You wouldn't mind if we went along?"

"A canoe probably isn't as good as a horse, but it's all I've got," she said half-apologetically.

"My guess is that Connie has never been in a boat of any kind. That sounds wonderful, Lisa. Would you like to ride along with me to Yahola to pick her up?"

Lisa regretfully shook her head. "I have some errands to run for the mission—birthday candles for the cake we're going to bake for Pedro next week, that sort of thing."

"You're baking a cake for Pedro's birthday?"

"He told me he's never had one before. I want this to be a birthday he'll always remember. What flavor should we bake?" she asked.

"You can never go wrong with chocolate," he pointed out. He liked the way her brows drew together when she looked serious.

"Chocolate it is. I'll need another half an hour or so to do the things I need to do. Why don't you bring Connie to my house in about an hour?"

"Good enough," he said cheerfully. "You'd better give me directions to your place."

She told him how to turn onto the winding river road and how the road doubled back on itself before crossing the county line and fronting on the river again. He drew a map on a pad of paper from his glove compartment, and as she watched, Lisa had the absurd notion to reach out and touch the edge of his shirt where it was so white against his tan.

*It's starting again,* she thought helplessly, wondering how he could act so unaware of an attraction so strong.

She fluttered a hand at him out the window of her car on the way out of the parking lot. Jay was an unexpected treat on a day that had promised nothing special, only a blank space to be filled in. And now he was going to fill it, and she was glad.

FOR JAY IT WAS a Saturday morning that had so far been purely exasperating, which was why he couldn't believe his luck. Lisa Sherrill, in line ahead of him at the drugstore! Lisa Sherrill in the parking lot, her pale gleaming hair lifting like wings in the breeze as she asked him to go canoeing with her!

As his car rolled into the shell-rock parking area near the community center in Yahola, he looked for Connie. She was usually waiting for him in front of the community center, but this time she wasn't there.

He saw her running, her hair flying out behind her, as he braked to a stop. She wore a yellow shirt and blue denim shorts, and tears streamed down her face. Alarmed, he got out of the car and hurried to meet her, and she flung her arms around his waist.

"Oh, Jay, I didn't think I'd be able to meet you today. Nina threatened to make me stay home if I didn't clean the kitchen and I did, but she said the floor was dirty, so I swept it again and she yelled at me, but I told her I had to go and finally she said to get out," Connie said in a rush.

Jay handed her handkerchief. "She said you could go?"

"Y-yes," Connie said. She blotted her tears and managed to get control of herself before handing the handkerchief back to Jay.

He bit back his anger and swung the car door open. "Hop in, Connie. You'll forget all about the trouble at home when I tell you about the surprise."

"Surprise?" Connie said, clearly interested through her tears, but he didn't enlighten her until he was in the car and backing out of the parking space.

"Actually, there's bad news and there's good news. Which do you want first?" he asked her.

"The bad. So we can get it over with," Connie said.

"The man who owns the horse isn't home. I think he forgot about our visit."

"Oh," Connie said. Her face fell. "How about the good news?" She asked after a downcast moment.

"We're going out on the Loxahatchee River in a canoe."

"A canoe! Really?"

"Really," he said, accelerating past the last few buildings in Yahola and heading back toward Jupiter.

"Do you have a canoe? I didn't know you had a canoe!" Connie bounced excitedly in her seat.

"No, it's Lisa Sherrill's canoe. Remember her from the community center dining hall?"

"Yes. Do you know her?"

"I do now," he said with a grin.

"She's nice. And pretty. But how can I go canoeing? I don't know how to paddle."

"Lisa and I can take care of that—at least at first. Can you swim?"

"No, I never learned."

"You'll wear a life vest, so that's no problem. But you should learn to swim. Maybe I'll arrange for swimming lessons."

"I don't know if Nina would let me go. She's scared of the water."

"There's no need to be frightened of the water if you know how to swim. Perhaps Nina never learned."

"I guess not. Wow! We're going out in a canoe! Wait till I tell my cousins about this!" Connie said.

"Maybe you shouldn't," Jay suggested.

"Oh. You're right—it might only make trouble with Nina," Connie said in a subdued voice.

Jay could have bitten his tongue for dampening Connie's spirits, but he had learned that Nina had to be handled very carefully. He sometimes felt that he was walking a fine line; one slip, and his access to Connie would be denied forever.

He tried not to think about that. Instead he watched for the sign that would tell him where to turn onto the river road, and he thought about spending a pleasant uncomplicated afternoon on the river with Lisa.

"There's the sign," Connie pointed out, and as he turned onto the river road, he felt his spirits lift. So many times he'd met women who interested him initially, and so many times he'd been disillusioned. They didn't like to share him with the children; they didn't like it when he had to hurry to Yahola to help Sister Maria with some problem. They were, in a word, selfish, and he was tired of selfish women.

But this time, with this woman who on her day off shopped for birthday candles for a little boy who'd never had a birthday cake, perhaps he wouldn't be disappointed. After all, if Sister Maria was pushing her, Lisa Sherrill must be something special.

# Chapter Three

Jay had no trouble finding his way to Lisa's house after he saw the mailbox marked Sherrill—Finley. He swung his car into the driveway that wound lazily between clumps of pine and palmetto trees and immediately saw the house nestled amid an opulent fringe of greenery. Beyond the house the river, pale and sparkling golden in the sunlight, shimmered through a lacy cluster of Australian pine trees. A covey of quail scurried in the path of his car before he pulled to a stop behind Lisa's white Toyota, which was parked on one side of the house's big double garage.

He heard a shout and looked toward the river where Lisa was standing ankle-deep in the water, steadying an aluminum canoe with one hand.

He watched as she waded out of the water and walked carefully up the bank. The tiny seed cones from the Australian pines were scattered here and there on the bed of fallen pine needles, and she picked her way carefully through them so that their sharp teeth wouldn't prick her feet. Her hair was tied up in a ridiculous little ponytail that somehow suited her, and wisps of it hung down around her face. It looked like strands of spun sugar, Jay thought. He saw in that moment that he had been mistaken about her earlier; she wasn't merely cute and pretty. She was beautiful.

Connie, realizing that she was out of her element, hung back, suddenly bashful.

"Connie, I'm glad you could come," Lisa said. Her smile toward Connie was warm and welcoming, and Jay was grateful to her for that.

Connie ducked her head and looked at Lisa out of the corners of her eyes.

"Now," Lisa said briskly, seeming not to notice Connie's shyness, "Connie, you'd better put on this life vest." She tossed an orange collar in Connie's direction, and Jay caught it. He draped it around Connie's neck and showed her how to tie it while Lisa busied herself with loading the paddles.

"Connie, you'll need to take off your shoes. If you wear them, they'll only get wet," Lisa instructed.

Connie obediently removed her sneakers and cast a dubious glance toward the house. Someone was standing at one of the windows—a woman. Jay was looking, too, and he saw that the woman ducked behind a curtain when she saw Connie staring at her. So, that was the woman who had answered the phone. Who was she to Lisa—some weird, unpresentable relative?

He flicked his glance toward Lisa in time to see her frown and cast a quick look toward the house, where the curtain was still swaying behind the window. She didn't say anything, and when Connie asked him a question that he didn't hear, he transferred his attention to her.

Lisa was glad for the distraction of Connie's question; her heart sank when she realized that Adele was watching. She had told Adele that some friends would be coming over to go canoeing, and Adele, who had been out of sorts all morning because Lisa had gone out to run errands instead of listening to her account of the made-for-TV movie she'd watched on television last night, had mumbled something about taking a nap and had disappeared into her room. Considering Adele's morose frame of mind, Lisa had hoped that Connie and Jay would be able to avoid her.

"I don't know where you should put your shoes," Jay was saying. Connie was protectively cradling her sneakers close to her chest.

"Here, I'll set your shoes inside the garage for you," Lisa offered. She was startled when Connie backed away as though Lisa had suggested that she throw the shoes in the river.

"I can do it," Connie blurted, and leaving Lisa looking baffled, she marched across the narrow strip of grass to the garage, which was on the other side of the house from Adele's room.

Adele might be watching from her window, but she wouldn't walk all the way over to the other side of the house to confront Connie in the garage, so Lisa put Adele out of her mind and turned to Jay. "Did I say something wrong? Connie certainly didn't take to my suggestion that I put her shoes away for her."

Jay shrugged. "I don't know. Sometimes these kids from the mission operate on a different wavelength. Their frame of reference is so different from ours that it's hard to figure them out."

"What do you mean?"

"Well, an example would be the time I took Connie to my house to look at a piece of sculpture that I was working on, and I mentioned that I had to telephone my office before we left to take her back to Yahola. And Connie headed out the front door, and she stopped and looked over her shoulder and said, 'Aren't you coming?'

"I said, 'Sure, after I make that phone call,' and she said, 'Well, isn't the phone down at the store?' and I said, 'No, it's right here in the kitchen.' I showed her the phone on the wall, and her eyes grew round, and she said, 'It's a pretty color,' because it's burgundy, and she watched me with eyes as big as two moons while I made the phone call.

"Afterward she said in a small voice, 'I didn't know houses had telephones in them,' and I realized that Connie had been on the move all her life, a few months here and a few months there to pick the crops, and never has she lived in the kind of house that would have a telephone. My guess about her shoes is that they're precious to her and bought at some expense, so she wants to know they're safe."

"I can't imagine—" Lisa began.

But Jay held a finger over his lips. Connie was returning from the garage, and he turned his most reassuring smile on her. "Come on, doodlebug," he said, holding out his hand, and he helped her into the center of the canoe.

After making sure that Connie was securely in place, Lisa climbed into the bow, and Jay pushed off into the thin fringe of reeds on the bank. They glided smoothly into the middle of the river, disturbing a school of mullet as the canoe knifed its way toward the deeper water.

Lisa's paddle dipped and swung to and fro in the sunlight as she paddled. Behind her, Jay hummed under his breath, a song that Lisa didn't recognize. They passed a number of houses on the curving shore and then they entered a cove dominated by mangrove trees with their thin spidery roots arching over the tea-colored water.

Nearby a silvery fish flipped out of the river and slapped back into it, spreading a pattern of concentric circles on the surface.

"Having fun?" Lisa called over her shoulder to everyone in general.

And Connie said, "Yes!"

They passed a fisherman in a small boat with an outboard motor; he sat motionless, and after the canoe slowed to a stop, Lisa stilled her paddle in the water so that it wouldn't drip and scare away the fish. The canoe rocked to and fro on the gentle current, and the fisherman was intent on his slack line.

Suddenly something bit. Jay said, "Whoa!" when the pole bent under the weight of the strike, and he pushed the canoe forward with his paddle to provide a better view. The fisherman played the fish skillfully, letting out the line so that it could run, then reeling it in. The catch was a big, shiny snook, a good two feet long, and Jay whistled in admiration as the fisherman maneuvered his glistening trophy into the boat.

Now that the show was over, they left the cove, and presently, beyond the heavy domed spread of mangroves, they approached a shadowy bank where soft fragrant brown pine needles spread a thick carpet beneath the trees. Lisa and Jay paddled onto the narrow strip of white sand, and Jay held the canoe steady while Lisa and Connie stepped out.

"I'll bring the cooler," Jay said, and Lisa took the drinks out and popped the tops while Connie wriggled out of the life vest and proceeded to explore the bank.

Here scrub pines crowded against each other, sheltering deep vine-shrouded thickets and the spiky fronds of an occasional saw palmetto. Lisa sat down and settled her back more comfortably against the trunk of a pine tree.

The sun filtered through the pine needles overhead in gently moving patches. Somewhere behind them Connie flitted through the shadows, and the high fluting notes of a mockingbird trilled overhead.

"Connie seems a little overwhelmed," Lisa said when she was sure Connie was out of hearing range.

"Her grandmother almost didn't let her out of the house today," Jay said. He stretched his legs out full-length and swallowed a long draft of root beer, the muscles of his throat working rhythmically. When he was finished he cupped the can loosely in his hand and watched the rivulets of condensation run into the pine needles where it rested. His mood seemed thoughtful, contemplative.

"Why didn't Connie's grandmother want her to come?"

"I don't know. From what I can tell, her grandmother resents having to raise Connie and her four cousins, and she tries to make things hard for her."

"You'd think that a grandmother would have a child's best interests at heart," Lisa said.

"Nina—that's what Connie calls her—may not even be her grandmother, for all I know. Connie's parents and aunt and uncle rode away one day, leaving Nina to care for their children while they harvested crops up in Apopka. They left a twenty-dollar bill and three cans of chili, and they never came back. That was two years ago, and Connie and her cousins have been living with Nina ever since. If it weren't for the nuns at the school, I don't know how Connie would have survived."

"Isn't Connie in contact with her parents?" Lisa asked. She remembered how Connie had said that her father had taught her how to step over logs in order to watch out for snakes, and she thought that Connie had spoken of her father with pride and love.

"Her mother called the school about a year ago and told Sister Maria that she had left Connie's father in Texas and that she had a new husband. She wasn't eager to see Connie. Connie's father can't read or write, but somebody wrote her a letter from him about six months ago. He said he wants to get the two of them back together soon. Connie treasures that scrap of paper beyond anything she owns," Jay said.

"Poor Connie," Lisa said.

"Her story gets worse. When they first arrived here, and Connie enrolled at the mission school, she told me that Nina, the woman with whom she lives and whom she regards as her grandmother, insisted on turning off the lights in their house at eight o'clock every night. Connie was upset because she couldn't study. I bought Connie a little battery-powered lamp, the kind campers use, and she was thrilled, but one of the other kids in the house broke it before long."

"So Connie still can't study at night?" Lisa asked.

Jay shook his head. "After that, Connie found a neighbor who would let her curl up in a bright corner of her house with her schoolbooks after dark, but that lasted only until Nina stormed into the house and demanded that Connie come home. 'You got no business over here,' she told Connie. Now Connie hauls herself out of bed earlier in the morning than anyone else and hurries to the church, where Sister Maria lets her study before Mass and school."

"Maybe Nina thinks Connie spends the time praying," Lisa said dryly.

"Exactly. And Sister Maria wisely says nothing to enlighten her," Jay replied with a chuckle.

"How about the other kids in the house? Is Nina cruel to them?"

"They're boys, and she seems to have a soft spot in her heart for them. Connie rubs her the wrong way for some reason."

Lisa's eyes were soft and brown now, reflecting the color of the bark on the tree trunk behind her. "How did you get involved with Connie, anyway?" she asked.

"I went to work at Faith Mission School, and Connie was a standout," he said.

"Did you know some of the nuns? Is that how you became a volunteer teacher there?" Lisa asked.

He shook his head. "I'd been a volunteer art teacher at a West Palm Beach home for unwed mothers that closed, and the housemother suggested that I call Sister Maria Francisco, who desperately needed an art teacher at Faith Mission School but couldn't afford to pay anyone. I thought at the time that it was an ordinary school, but a trip out there showed me that it was like no other place I'd ever seen. I fell in love with the kids, and I admired the nuns. So—" and he shrugged his shoulders and laughed as if to say that he'd had no choice but to help.

"Most people wouldn't have cared," Lisa said softly in a way that told him that she admired him, which only embarrassed him. He didn't want admiration; he didn't think he deserved it. The way he saw it, he could never give too much. Never.

"I don't do enough," he said tersely.

"You feel as if you should be doing more?" she asked. Her eyes met his, and she looked incredulous. He didn't want that, either.

"I don't have as much time to devote to the mission as I would like. Or to Connie."

At that moment, Connie crashed through the clearing. "I saw a deer! It ran away when it saw me! I know it was a deer!" she cried.

"I'm sure it was," Lisa said, collecting herself quickly. "Sometimes I see them tiptoeing out of the woods near my house before it gets dark at night."

"I never saw a deer before," Connie said, settling herself comfortably between Jay and Lisa and accepting the can of strawberry soda that Jay dug out of the cooler.

"Not even at the zoo?" Lisa asked.

"I've never been to a zoo," Connie said.

"Not been to a zoo!" Lisa said in surprise.

"Once we passed a sign on the highway that had an arrow pointing in the direction of a zoo, but Daddy said we had to keep going because the boss man at the farm up the road wouldn't wait and the crop wouldn't, either, so we never went," Connie said.

"How about it, Lisa? Would you like to go to the zoo with Connie and me sometime?" Jay asked.

A quick look at him told her that he was serious.

She drew a deep breath. "That sounds like fun," she said, hoping she sounded casual.

"Good," he said with more enthusiasm than she had expected. "I think we should go to the zoo in Miami and make a whole day of it."

"When will we go? I can't wait," Connie said. She looked as though she could barely contain herself.

"Well, doodlebug, I'll have to look at my schedule and see if next weekend is free. That is, if Lisa can go then."

"Next weekend would be fine," Lisa said.

"Yay!" Connie said, hopping up and running down to the water, where she splashed for a while in the shadows and soon interested herself in the fiddler crabs that scurried in the sand.

"Now," Jay said to Lisa as he sprawled out more comfortably so that his face was fully in sunlight, "tell me more about yourself. Do you go canoeing often?" He was regarding her with an intriguing mixture of interest and pleasure.

"I head for the canoe whenever I want to get away from the house," Lisa admitted before she could stop herself.

"Your housemate—is she the one I talked with on the phone?"

She stared at him. "Are *you* the one who called?" she asked.

"I'm afraid so. She didn't give me a chance to mention my name before she hung up." He smiled at her, and she could only return his smile with embarrassment.

"You'd have to understand Adele," she said. "Adele is—well, different," she said.

"Maybe you should find another housemate," Jay pointed out.

"I couldn't do that," Lisa said quickly.

"Why not? Who is she—your aunt? Mother? Grandmother?"

Lisa gazed across the river, a host of visible emotions playing over her face.

"Adele isn't my mother, although she's more or less taken the role of one since my mother died. And she lives with me because she doesn't have anywhere else to go. I really do like her. She's had a lot of difficulties, that's all."

A quick glance at Lisa's expression told Jay that she was sincere. Sincere—and something else. Worried? Guilty? He wondered why.

"What's her story?" he asked gently.

"Do you want the long version or the short?" she asked.

"Short," he said. "Unless you prefer the long, of course."

Lisa took a swig of root beer; it wasn't easy to swallow it. She still found it hard to talk about Megan's death.

"Adele was the mother of my best friend when I was growing up. My friend died years ago, and Adele's marriage fell apart when her husband left her for his secretary in the aftermath of the tragedy. Adele remarried happily, but that husband died. She had to sell her house to pay his medical expenses, so I invited her to live with me. At first we both thought that it was going to be a temporary arrangement, but as time passed, we both realized that it was impractical for either of us to consider anything else. Fortunately I remember Adele from the days when her disposition was unfailingly sweet. Everyone loved her then. Now maybe I'm the only one in the world who does," Lisa said wistfully.

"Both your parents are dead?"

She nodded. "That's how I ended up with this house. Dad built it, and it was supposed to be a retirement home for him and Mother, but shortly after they moved in, he had a heart attack and was dead on arrival at the hospital. Mother died a few months later. My sister and I will always believe that she died of a broken heart."

"I didn't know you had a sister," he said.

"She's six years my senior. Her name is Heather, and she lives with her husband and three children in Rochester, New York. I don't see her often."

"That makes it even sadder that your parents died. I'm sorry," he said.

"When Dad had his heart attack, he was in his boat, fishing with a group of his friends, when he felt a pain in his chest. The last thing he saw was the sunlight on the rippling water and the blue sky above the mangrove trees. That's not so bad when you think about it."

"You must miss them terribly," he said. At least he still had his mother and stepfather, although they lived on the other side of the country.

"I do, but I like living in the house. It's a lovely house, and the view of the river is beautiful. The problem was that I didn't feel comfortable living there alone. I couldn't get over the feeling that Dad would walk in with a basket of fish that he'd just caught or that Mother would be standing at the kitchen counter squeezing fresh oranges when I got up in the morning. Also, I didn't think it was safe to live in such an isolated place with so many people fishing on the river late at night. My arrangement with Adele works out well in many ways. I don't mean to give the impression that she's impossible. In fact, I think if she had some interests that took her out of the house, that drew her out of herself, she'd be okay."

"Doesn't she work?" he asked.

"She works three days a week at a gift shop only a couple of miles from the house. She hardly ever goes anywhere else, and when she's at home, she's often depressed. I've tried to get her to see a counselor, but she won't hear of it."

"That's too bad. It might help her," he said, gazing off into the distance. He'd had a lot of counseling himself a long time ago. It had helped him to become a different person, a better person.

"Adele says anyone would be depressed if they were in her place, and perhaps she's right. At least she's got me. That's what she always says, anyway."

"She's lucky," he said, and he meant it.

Lisa was sitting with her legs crossed, leaning back slightly; she was a small-breasted but well-proportioned woman, with a tiny waist and ankles. Her legs were tanned honey-gold and were slim and shapely. He noticed for the first time that her eyes were a changeable hazel, the outer rims of the irises dark, almost black, and the inner part pale and shaded a soft brown like the bark of the tree trunk behind her. Tendrils of yellow hair trailing around her face wafted slightly in the breeze from the river, and again he thought she was beautiful. He sensed that she had the potential to become someone important to him, someone whose eyes would glow when he walked into a room, whose hand would seek his at quiet times.

The idea, cropping up unexpectedly as it did, pleased him. He focused on her lips, which were full and expressive. Her teeth were small and white. Suddenly everything, absolutely everything, about her seemed important, and he was seized with a desire to know her, the deep recesses of her mind, the depths of her emotion and the geography of her body. Unexpectedly, his throat contracted with the pain of wanting her.

At that moment Connie bounded up, and he was forced to abandon his thoughts. Lisa reluctantly cast an eye toward the sun, which was falling lower in the western sky. "We'd better go," she said. "The trip back always seems longer than the trip out."

The three of them loaded the canoe and pushed off from the clearing. As they were paddling home, Connie said suddenly, "Lisa, do you think I could ever learn to paddle?"

Lisa looked over one shoulder at Jay. He nodded almost imperceptibly.

"Of course you can," she said warmly to Connie. "I'll teach you next time, when Jay brings you."

"Is there really going to be a next time?" Connie asked, her eyes wide.

"Yes," Jay said, his eyes warm with pleasure. "Yes, there really is."

## Chapter Four

Wednesday was cloyingly hot and humid, a real tropical day in South Florida. Flies hummed in the community center's kitchen windows, and when Lisa glanced out and saw Jay and some of the children working in the school garden that afternoon, she took pity on them because of the heat and carried a pitcher of fresh lemonade outside.

In the garden, just as in the surrounding farm fields, beans and tomatoes grew in lush profusion. The children were pulling weeds and toting buckets of water, and one boy was trundling a wheelbarrow to and fro. When the children saw Lisa approaching with the lemonade, they dropped whatever they were doing and ran to greet her.

"Lisa, Lisa, we're growing radishes and scallions for you to use in the kitchen," Connie said as she threw her arms around Lisa's waist.

"Somebody hold the cups while I pour," Lisa instructed, and Connie did the honors.

"I like this lemonade," Pedro said, smacking his lips.

"Me, too," said Serafina, who gulped hers down in a hurry and, like the others, presented her paper cup for seconds.

"That's enough, kids," Jay called when he saw the admiring group circling Lisa. "Get back to work before Sister Maria comes out and sees you slacking off. She'll drag you into her after-school study hall."

After the children scampered away, Lisa leaned on the fence, grateful for the chance to have a few minutes' private conversation with Jay.

"If you've got one more glass of that lemonade left, I'll take seconds," he told her.

Jay was wresting a huge encroaching vine from the thick black muck, but he dropped it and wiped his hands on a rag while Lisa poured the lemonade into a cup. As she handed it to him, she watched a small trickle of sweat slide down his chest; she could feel her own thin blouse beginning to stick to her back. It must be miserable working out here in this heat.

"Connie's grandmother won't let her go to the zoo," Jay said abruptly.

"Won't let her go? But why?" Lisa asked.

Jay drank deeply before crushing the paper cup in his fist and dropping it into the bag she held out. He reached down and ripped the vine out of the soil by its roots as though he were grappling with Nina herself. After he'd tossed it aside, he stopped and leaned on his hoe, his eyes smoldering with a barely concealed anger.

"I don't know why she won't give her permission. The conversation didn't get that far. When Connie told me about it, I went to talk with Nina, but before I'd managed to get ten words out, the woman slammed the door in my face. She could use a charm-school course, that's for sure," he said.

"Connie must be so disappointed," Lisa replied in dismay.

Jay shrugged and wiped his forehead. He picked up the hoe and returned to his task. "She—certainly—is," he said, timing his words to fall between vigorous chops. He stopped again. "So am I for that matter," he said, managing a smile at last. His hair had fallen across his forehead and glistened with sweat; a gnat hovered around his right eyelid.

Lisa stared off into the distance again, an expanse of the Everglades that glimmered wide and green and boundless like the future, or at least the way the future could be if Jay were a part of it.

"Maybe I should speak with Nina," she said slowly.

"You can try it, but I can't offer any hope," Jay said. "The woman seems suspicious of everyone who tries to talk to her about Connie."

Jay had said nothing about their going to the zoo together if Connie couldn't go; perhaps he wouldn't want to.

"I'll go talk to her," Lisa said, hoisting the sack of used paper cups in one hand.

"Don't," Jay said. "You'll be wasting your time."

"Maybe not," Lisa replied. "Where do Nina and Connie live?"

"Three doors down from the community center, number one eighty-six," Jay said.

"At least I can try," Lisa said.

"Let me know how it turns out," Jay called after her as she turned to go. The overtone of disgust in his voice warned her that he saw no point in approaching Connie's grandmother.

Feeling defeated before she'd even begun, Lisa climbed into her car and sat behind the wheel for a moment, watching the man and the children working together.

*If you don't tend the garden, nothing will grow,* Lisa thought fiercely. The same thing applied to relationships, and now that the seed had been planted, she was not about to let her budding relationship with Jay Quillian wither and die.

She threw the car into gear and backed out onto the road. It was late afternoon, and Nina should have returned from her work in the fields by this time.

A PAIR OF small scrappy boys in dirty blue jeans stared curiously as Lisa stepped out of her car in front of the small drab house.

"I'm looking for Nina," she told the boys. "Is she around?"

"Inside," one of the boys said. The other one gaped at her openmouthed.

"Thanks," Lisa replied, and mounted the sagging steps. The boys stopped jabbing each other and watched silently as she knocked.

A woman whose face was baked hard by the sun opened the door slightly. She eyed Lisa suspiciously through the tiny chink between the warped door and its frame.

"Hi," Lisa said, offering a smile. "I'm Lisa Sherrill, a friend of Connie's from the mission. May I come in?"

The woman—Lisa was sure that this must be the woman called Nina—silently and reluctantly widened the crack to a space barely large enough for Lisa to slip through. Inside, a piece of linoleum was laid upon the bare concrete floor, and a lumpy couch of indeterminate color faced a blaring TV set. Limp curtains were drawn across the windows, and through the dimness, Lisa could make out piles of things in the corners—clothes, cooking utensils, wadded-up pieces of paper. Lisa stood awkwardly, uninvited and too fastidious to sit.

"Is Connie in trouble?" Nina asked abruptly. One of her front teeth was missing.

"No, everything is fine. I'm hoping that I can set your mind at ease about our invitation to Connie—Jay Quillian's and mine—to go the zoo on Saturday," Lisa said.

"It's only a matter of time before that girl gets in trouble," muttered Nina with great certainty.

Lisa refused to be thrown off balance by this remark, which as far as she could tell was completely unwarranted. By all accounts, Connie was a well-adjusted child who gave no one cause for worry.

"Jay would pick Connie up in the morning around eight o'clock, and we'd bring her home by nine or ten o'clock that evening," she said.

"Connie has to take care of the younger children on Saturdays till I get back from working in the fields. Anyway, I can't let Connie run off on pleasure trips when her cousins never get to do nothing," Nina replied.

Lisa gathered her thoughts for a moment. There *was* a way to overcome this objection. She hesitated for only an instant before plunging ahead.

"Nina, we'd be happy to take the other children with us if that means that Connie can go," she said.

Too late she saw the crafty glint in the woman's eyes; too late she realized that she'd been had. Nina clearly relished the idea of getting all the children off her hands for the entire day. Lisa stifled a feeling of revulsion and tried to keep her expression neutral.

"If you mean they can all go, sure, but Connie has to wash the clothes in the morning first." Nine fairly spat out the words.

Lisa heaved a sigh of relief. She couldn't believe how edgy and anxious this woman made her feel. Now that her purpose had been accomplished, she could hardly wait to leave.

She backed up until her hand found the doorknob. "Thank you," she said. "We'll pick up the children at ten on Saturday."

Nina dismissed her with a triumphant little jerk of her chin, and Lisa nudged the door open. On her way out, she almost tripped over the two small boys who had apparently overheard every word through the screen.

They dogged her footsteps as she descended the steps. "We're going to the zoom? We're really going to the zoom?" asked the littlest one. He plucked at Lisa's jacket.

"*Zoo,* stupid—it's called a *zoo,*" the older boy said gruffly. He shoved the smaller boy behind him and gazed up at Lisa with liquid brown eyes. "*Are* we going?"

"Yes, we are," Lisa said, smiling down at them. They might be grubby, but they were certainly cute with those floppy home haircuts and round rosy cheeks. "Since we're going to spend all day Saturday together, you'd better tell me your names."

"I'm Miguel, and that's Alejandro," the older one said.

"Connie's name is Consuela, but she doesn't like it," Alejandro volunteered.

"I like to be called Mike," Miguel told her.

"I'm Alejandro, and I'm the only one in the whole school. There's a lot of Mikes," Alejandro said with an air of self-importance.

"Well, Mike and Alejandro, I'll see you on Saturday. Tell the other boys I'm looking forward to meeting them."

"Looking what?" Mike said in a tone of puzzlement.

"That I'll enjoy meeting them," Lisa substituted.

"Okay," Mike said. They stood and watched silently as she walked to her car.

When Lisa drove away, Mike and Alejandro were tumbling over and over in the dust like two frisky puppies, and she had to smile. She didn't smile for long, however. She realized belatedly that it was up to her to inform Jay that she had just agreed to take not only Connie, but four small and very active boys to the Miami Zoo on Saturday.

"WHY YOU WANT to get personally involved with those children at the mission school is beyond me," Adele said that night, regarding Lisa through her thick pebble glasses. Her knitting needles clicked at breakneck speed, which was always the case when she was being emphatic.

"Connie is special," Lisa said. She flipped through a Miami guidebook looking for information about the zoo. Here it was—a map showing how to get there from the interstate highway, as well as a blurb telling the hours that the zoo was open.

"Special? A lot of kids are special. This Connie is going to pick up and leave as soon as the crops are in and then you'll be attached to her, which will make you feel sad after she's gone. Keep your emotional distance if you know what's good for you."

"I can't do that," Lisa said firmly, for once wishing that Adele had managed to keep emotional distance from her, Lisa.

"At least you don't have to drive all the way to Miami," Adele said, keeping her eyes on her knitting. Adele always worried when Lisa drove anywhere, even to the supermarket.

"Mmm," Lisa said in a noncommittal tone. She stood up and tossed the guidebook onto the coffee table. "I'd better call Jay," she said, escaping into the kitchen.

She punched out Jay's phone number as Adele paused in her knitting and peered over the top of her glasses at Lisa, who stood just inside the open door.

"Who is this Jay, anyway?" Adele asked in a slightly elevated tone of voice.

"Oh, just a volunteer at the school," Lisa said, glad that the ringing of the telephone on the other end of the line stopped her from having to elaborate.

Jay answered his phone on the third ring.

"Jay, it's Lisa," she said.

"Lisa. It's good to hear from you. How did it go with Nina today?" His voice was warm, and she took heart from it.

"Nina agreed that Connie could go to the zoo," Lisa said.

"She did? Why, that's wonderful! And I must say that it's a complete surprise. What did you do—twist her arm?"

"Not that it would have done any good. No, I did worse than that. I'm not sure I even want to tell you."

"It can't be that bad. Come on, what gives?"

"I told her that we'd take Connie's cousins with us," she said, prepared to be chastised.

Instead, Jay laughed, a long drawn-out and delighted laugh.

"You don't mind?" Lisa asked quickly.

"Not a bit, although I'm beginning to doubt your sanity. You haven't decided to back out, I hope. I'm going to need all the help I can get to keep up with Mike and Alejandro, Ruy and Felipe."

"Don't worry, I'm looking forward to it. I've met Mike and Alejandro. What are Ruy and Felipe like?"

"Ruy and Felipe are even more so, if you get my drift. More noisy, more nosy and more trouble."

"More cute?"

"Did you think Mike and Alejandro were *cute?*" Jay asked incredulously.

"In their scruffy little way," Lisa said with a laugh.

"All four boys are bright and active and loud, and our day at the zoo will probably be as much fun as a barrel of monkeys. It's just that I didn't anticipate *bringing* the monkeys," Jay said.

"I told Nina that we wouldn't pick the kids up until ten on Saturday morning so that Connie will have time to get her chores done before we go. That seemed to be a big problem as far as Nina was concerned," Lisa said.

"She makes Connie work too hard," Jay said darkly. "Scrubbing floors, cooking, taking care of the boys. Connie never gets a chance to be a kid."

"From what I can tell, not many of the children at the mission do, but at least this Saturday five of them will have a vacation from the hopelessness they see all around them."

Jay's voice softened. "Thanks to you. I'm glad you invited the boys." He paused, and, assuming that the conversation was over, she tried to think of a graceful exit line.

"Am I going to see you before then?" he asked unexpectedly and much to her surprise.

"I'll be at the mission all day tomorrow and Friday," Lisa told him.

"I'm not due there until Monday. Why don't we go out tomorrow night? I think we should fortify ourselves against Saturday's ordeal, don't you?"

Lisa smiled into the phone. "And how would you suggest that we 'fortify ourselves'?"

"Dinner? A movie? A moonlight walk along the ocean?"

"Any of the above," she said.

"A walk, then. Want me to drive over and pick you up?"

"How about if I meet you at your place?"

"If you don't mind, I'd like that. I'll treat you to one of my famous smoked-turkey sandwiches afterward," he said.

"It's a deal for a meal. What time?"

"Seven o'clock? That gives me a chance to clear things up at my office."

"Seven o'clock it is. I'll see you tomorrow," Lisa said. She was still smiling when she hung up and walked slowly into the living room.

"It sounds as though you like the guy," Adele said, rolling up her knitting in preparation for getting up to change the television channel.

"Oh, I like him, all right," Lisa said, unable to keep the telltale lilt out of her voice. "And I'm pretty sure he likes me, too. Want me to change the channel for you?"

"Sure, if you don't mind." Adele consulted the TV schedule that she saved from the paper every Sunday. "Switch to channel twelve, please, Lisa. There's a movie we'll both enjoy, Bette Davis and Paul Henreid, or is it Conreid? Well, whatever. It got three stars in the movie guide."

Lisa turned the channel obediently, fighting the smothered feeling that swept over her at the idea of yet another night of companionable television watching with Adele.

"That man who called—what's his name again?" Adele wanted to know as the movie's theme music swelled.

"Jay Quillian," Lisa said.

"Jay Quillian—no, I don't know anyone by that name. There are so many new people moving into the area all the time—it's hard to keep track of who's who. I remember when I used to recognize every name from here to Delray, not to mention Fort Pierce and Stuart. Now I never know anyone and they're building big ugly condoms everywhere for those people to live in. Why, Florida must be the fastest growing state in the whole U.S."

"'Condos,' Adele. The abbreviation for *condominium* is 'condo,'" Lisa said.

"Condo, condom, whatever you call it, we never heard anything about them before and now they're all over the place," Adele replied.

Hiding her amusement, Lisa settled deep into the cushions of the couch and counted on the program to silence Adele. It did, but instead of watching Bette Davis artfully exhaling curls of cigarette smoke, Lisa lapsed into thoughts about tomorrow night, which were far more interesting. She pictured herself walking beside Jay, the wind whipping their hair around their faces and with the ocean stretched out like infinity beside them.

JAY'S METICULOUSLY landscaped two-story town-house villa was located in a large development about a block from the ocean. Lisa recognized his car parked outside the cypress-fenced courtyard, its open gate illuminated by soft lights.

She walked inside the courtyard, rang the front door bell and waited, and when no one appeared, she rang it again. When Jay finally threw the door open, he wore a slightly abashed look and a head of tousled hair. He had obviously been toweling it dry.

"I'm too early," she said when she saw him.

"No, you're exactly on time, and promptness is a quality that I admire in a woman, except when it catches me like this." He ushered her inside, ran a careless hand through his damp hair and laughed. "Make yourself comfortable—walk around, read a magazine, get yourself something to drink from the refrigerator in the kitchen. Excuse me for a minute, I'll be right out," he said before disappearing through a door off the living room.

When she heard the hum of a hair dryer, she looked around curiously. Her first impression was of neatness, of everything in its place. The living-room furniture was modern, all black and white and chrome, unlike her own mixture of older pieces inherited from her parents and supplemented by Adele. She walked around the room, evaluating the bright colors and clean lines of the paintings adorning the walls.

She walked into the kitchen, which turned out to be spare but well equipped and she looked around in surprise as a closet door creaked open and a big, furry and very perplexed dog peered out. The dog blinked at her from behind a curtain of shaggy hair, and Lisa almost laughed at its baffled expression. The dog, which overcame its amazement at finding her there in only a few moments, rolled over on its back and presented its stomach. Lisa regarded this as a request for a stomach rub, and so she complied, tentatively at first, then with more enthusiasm. It was a cute dog, if something that big *could* be cute.

When the dog began to fidget, Lisa stood up and wandered into the living room, the dog padding companionably along behind. On the marble-topped coffee table, a bedraggled copy of *The Florida Bar Journal* peeked out from a slightly more respectable-looking *Time* magazine, and the room, with its leather couch, entertainment wall with large-screen TV and dhurrie rugs over a cool tile floor, was inviting.

She sat down on the couch and picked up the *Time*. The dog collapsed softly at her feet and watched her with its tongue lolling out.

In a minute or two, Jay appeared in the doorway. "I should have warned you about Hildy," he said. "She's part Old English sheepdog and I don't know what else. She's thirteen years old, has a heart ailment and is hard of hearing, but she's my best girl—has been ever since she was a pup."

"She's beautiful," Lisa said. The dog stretched blissfully, exposing her stomach again. Lisa good-naturedly took the hint and bent over to scratch it.

"I got Hildy when I was fifteen," Jay explained. "She more or less runs things around here."

"Let's take her along on our walk," Lisa suggested.

"She might like it, but this time she's staying home. She hasn't been eating normally for the past day or so, and I'm worried about her." Jay ordered Hildy back into the kitchen and paused for a few moments to murmur a reassurance to the dog.

The kitchen telephone rang, and he answered it. Lisa was curious about the conversation, which proceeded in fits and starts and ended abruptly.

When Jay came out of the kitchen, he looked agitated.

"Let's go," he said, and she wondered if the phone call had been bad news.

"Is anything wrong?" she asked as they strolled through the courtyard and out the gate.

"Not for me," he said ruefully.

"For someone else?"

"A client of mine. My partner just called with some new information about a divorce case I'm handling," he said.

"I'm sorry. Maybe I shouldn't have asked," she said.

"I'd never violate the lawyer-client privilege, but I don't mind telling you that my work can be nerve-racking sometimes. People expect me to solve their problems, and I can't always provide a Band-Aid solution," he said.

They were walking along the dark street, passing in and out of the circles of light cast by streetlights on the corners. Around the corner, Lisa glimpsed the aquamarine glimmer of the development's swimming pool.

"Tell me about your work," she said. "What kind of practice do you have?"

"A little of this, a little of that," he said, looking more comfortable now. "I handle a few traffic cases, some divorces, real-estate closings—whatever comes my way."

"Did you always know that you wanted to be a lawyer?"

"I didn't decide to go to law school until it was almost too late in my last year of college to apply," he said. "I must admit that I've always been glad I did. The law profession is definitely not dull."

"Do you handle a lot of divorces?" she asked.

Jay waited until they had passed the security guard at the entrance of the development before he answered. "More than I'd like," he said with feeling.

"It sounds like you're not happy about that," she observed. It was easy to match her gait to his; unlike most tall people, he walked slowly to accommodate her shorter stride.

"I'm not. Divorce shouldn't be necessary. How do you feel about it, anyway?" he asked.

"The same way you do, I suppose. It must be awful to go through one," she said.

"You don't sound like one of the previously married," he noted.

"No, I've never taken the plunge," she said, looking both ways as they crossed the road to the oceanside path.

"Any particular reason?"

"I never found anyone I liked well enough to marry. How about you?"

"Same here," he said.

It was a warm January night in South Florida, and at that moment the sky seemed alive with stars and possibilities. To their left the ocean curled upon the sand; the waves foaming milky white in the pale light. To their right an occasional car whizzed past, stirring up eddies of sand. They passed two teenagers on skateboards and one elderly couple strolling hand in hand.

"Thank goodness for the ocean," Jay said. "I like to take a walk almost every night. It helps get the kinks out of my system after a tiresome day in court or maybe a long day at the mission."

"I thought you liked your work at the mission," Lisa said, glancing over at him.

"I do, but sometimes it wears me out. Dealing with Connie's grandmother, for instance," he said.

"I know what you mean. Has Nina always been so difficult?"

"As long as I've known Connie, Nina has acted like a witch. You'd think she'd be pleased that people are tak-

ing an interest in the girl, but even the nuns have a hard
time getting around Nina.''

"How does Connie get along with Nina?" Lisa asked.

"Not so well from what I can tell. Connie seems afraid
of her," Jay said.

Lisa recalled the woman's implacability and the craft-
iness of her expression. To Connie, the woman must
seem formidable.

Jay took her hand and squeezed it. "There are stairs
down to the beach up ahead," he said. "Do you feel like
getting your feet sandy?"

She smiled up at him. "Sure," she said.

The breeze was soft beneath her hair, and the ocean
rolled in lazy billows toward the shore, the surf spending
itself upon the sand. At the bottom of the steps Lisa
slipped her shoes off. She nudged them with her toe until they were hidden beneath the bottom step. Jay did the
same.

"Which way—north or south?" she asked when they
reached the line of dry matted seaweed above the high
tide line.

"You call it," he said.

"North, then," she said.

Their feet punched deep holes in the crusty sand as
they walked.

"Tell me something about yourself that no one
knows," she said suddenly.

Was she imagining it, or did he draw away slightly? She
had used this opening gambit as an invitation to conversation many times before when she wanted to get to know
someone better, and it usually elicited a self-conscious
laugh and then a minor revelation, such as the confes-
sion of a silly habit or a memory of a childhood folly.

"There's not much," Jay said after a long moment, and she stared at him, wondering what nerve she had hit. He looked pained and was trying to cover it up, which surprised her. He'd always seemed so candid about everything.

"Actually," he said, recovering smoothly, "I'd rather know something about you. How did you become a dietitian, anyway?"

If that was the way he wanted it, she could oblige. Not too many people ever asked.

"In college," she said, "I watched as my girlfriends took up one fad diet after another. I didn't approve of what they were doing to themselves. Later I realized that the whole point of eating is to provide ourselves with good nutrition, and it was a revelation. I like providing a healthful diet for people. I like it even better when I can teach them to provide a healthful diet for themselves," she said.

"Will you do that at the mission?"

"It's part of my job. I'll begin nutrition classes as soon as possible," she told him.

"I suppose the migrant families have a lot to learn," he said.

"So do most people. Sometimes I sit down in a restaurant and watch people gobbling down fat-filled hamburgers and French fries dripping grease, and I want to shake some sense into them."

"Uh-oh," he said warily. "Now I'm worried about what you'll think of my famous smoked-turkey sandwich."

She wanted to laugh at the expression of consternation on his face.

"Don't worry, I've been known to wolf down a few French fries from time to time," she said reassuringly.

"And speaking of food, let's head back. I'm definitely getting hungry."

They turned back toward the stairs to the path and Jay pointed toward the horizon. "Look," he said, "there's a ship out there." They stopped and looked out to sea, where a light bobbed gently on the faint gray line between starlit sea and blue velvet sky.

"I wonder what kind of ship it is and where it's going," Lisa said.

"Sister Clementine would think it's a cruise ship full of happy people, and Sister Ursula would say it's a freighter crammed to the gunwales with illegal drugs," Jay said in a wry tone.

"Ah, Sister Clementine and Sister Ursula—how well they balance each other out," Lisa said.

He looked down at her, enchanted with the way her eyelashes curled against her cheek. It was a relief to find a woman who was waif-haired and looked vulnerable. She caught him staring at her and looked away.

He recognized the way she refused to meet his eyes as her admission of their mutual attraction. He slowed his steps and willed her to look up at him again, but she kept her eyes focused straight ahead on the waves unfurling on the sand. When he slid his arm around her shoulders, her bones felt small and delicate, and a wave of unexpected desire swept over him. She glanced up at him, a longer look this time, her wide eyes silvery with starlight. He would have had to be blind not to see that she was powerfully attracted to him.

He had intended to wait until after dinner, when things were cozy at his town house, when they had established a base of rapport and communication and when kissing her wouldn't seem like such a big step.

Suddenly he knew that he didn't want to wait. He wanted to feel the lightness of her in his arms. He wanted to bend his head protectively over hers, and he wanted to test the softness of her lips. He wanted to wind his hands through her hair and to feel for himself the silkiness of it, to inhale the fresh scent of it, of her.

If only she would turn to look at him again, but she didn't. Finally he stopped walking altogether, and he turned her to face him. She lifted her eyes, those incredible eyes that outshone the stars, and he knew that there was nothing he could say to explain what he was about to do because he wasn't sure he understood it himself.

"Lisa," he said, the syllables of her name blending with the sound of the surf, and then he folded her in his arms and felt the straining of her head lifting to reach his, and his arms raised her slightly off the sand so that their lips would meet, and he kissed her.

## Chapter Five

Lisa had been aware of the electricity between them even before he was, she was sure of that. It was something she had felt from the first time she'd seen him, and it was what had fueled her imagination.

But this—this supercharged jolt of energy surging through her veins—was totally unexpected. He relaxed his grip so that her feet again stood solidly on the sand, his head bent over her upturned face to extract every last bit of pleasure. Their lips fused, blended, explored the limits of sweet sensation, almost parted and then came together again in the swift realization that they couldn't stop now, not yet.

After the first shock of sensation passed, she was aware—but only barely—of her hands pressing against the front of his shirt, then sliding upward and unclenching against the corded muscles of his neck; then, as she felt herself melting inside, her hands met at his nape and her fingers twisted through his hair, pulling his head down even farther. When she sensed a lessening of intensity, she made a soft sound somewhere in her throat and realigned her head to make it more comfortable for him, and his lips renewed their quest, his tongue seeking more, more, until she opened her mouth and clung to him in unabashed passion.

He was the one who ended it, pulling away and staring at her in the moonlight, his breathing rough. She closed her eyes, willing her heart to stop leaping about inside her rib cage.

"I didn't know anyone could kiss like that," he said in clear bewilderment, which helped bring her back down to earth.

"I didn't, either," she whispered.

"That was—"

"Was what?" she asked.

"Wonderful," he said, his hands on her shoulders positioning her so that her face rested against his chest. He hadn't expected it to feel so right. He'd thought that given the unexpectedness of this, the lack of planning, the utter spontaneity, they would bump noses or scrape chins or something equally as awkward, but aside from the fact that she had to bend her head so far back to kiss him, it seemed perfect, and he'd decided long ago that there was no such thing as a perfect first kiss.

"Are you cold?" he asked when he felt a little tremor run through her.

"Warmer now," she murmured, her voice muffled by his shirt.

He pulled away. "We should have brought jackets. And, maybe, a blanket."

"I'm comfortable," she said.

"I feel like a kid, kissing you on the beach out here in front of strolling senior citizens and tourists and skateboarders," he said. He had to fight to control his voice so that it wouldn't tremble.

"I feel like—" she said, but she stopped.

"Feel like what?" he asked.

"Like doing it again," she said, sounding more helpless than he felt, and he laughed and pulled her close.

"In that case, we will," he said, and this time he spent more time at it, reveling in the softness of her lips, the sweetness of her breath, the delight he felt at indulging himself in something that was pure perfection.

Up on the bike path the teenage skateboarders whooped as they rolled past, their wheels noisy on the asphalt path, and Lisa reluctantly pulled her lips away to see whether the skateboarders were stopping to come down the steps to the sand.

"Are you ready to go?" Jay said after a few moments. The skateboarders and the accompanying noise had receded into the distance, and the path above them was now deserted.

"Perhaps we should," she said, not sure if she meant it. If they left, he wouldn't kiss her anymore, at least not now.

"One thing I know for sure, and that is that we don't need to leave right this minute," Jay replied, and he led her up the beach to a spot where he bent to touch his hand to the sand. He straightened and sifted a few grains through his fingers. "It's not too damp," he said. "Do you want to sit here and decompress for a few minutes? I feel like I'll get the bends if I come up for air too fast."

Lisa smiled, happy that he could joke about it. She sat down and settled into the curve of his arm, leaned her head against his shoulder and inhaled the pungent scent of sea air. He could make jokes, but she hadn't reached that point. She was still overwhelmed.

"I, um," he said, but he didn't finish.

"Mmm," she said, moving even closer. She liked the way her shoulder fit exactly under his arm. He rubbed her upper arm slowly and gently, and she swallowed. She very much wanted to kiss him again.

"I don't usually make a habit of necking on the beach," he said after a while.

"Where *do* you neck, then?" she said, sliding an impish glance up at him.

"What I mean is that this seems extraordinary to me. I've always been able to wait until I managed to find a private place. With you, it was kind of an urge. An imperative. A necessity," he said.

"A *necessity,*" she said, and she started to giggle; she couldn't help it.

"You *would* laugh. Lisa, I'm being serious," he said.

"It's funny, what you said. A necessity is something that you *need,*" she pointed out.

"Who says I didn't need to kiss you? Like now. I think I need to kiss you again."

"By all means, do it," she urged, and he cupped her cheek in his hand and kissed her gently on her forehead, her nose and finally her lips. One kiss, then another; soon he was leaning over her and she was trying to keep her balance, which deserted her so suddenly that she fell backward in the sand with him on top of her.

He righted himself and pulled her up after him. Sand clung to her hair, stuck to her eyelashes and slid scratchily down the front of her shirt.

"Did you need *this,* too?" she asked slyly.

"I must have," he said, and she tried to brush the sand off his face, whereupon he captured her hand in one of his and said "Don't," and when she saw the seriousness of his expression, she forgot about everything else.

"You've got sand in your eyebrows," he pointed out after a few minutes.

She brushed at it. "I really think we should leave before there's something else you need," she said. Her eyes sparkled up at him.

He stood up and reached a hand down to pull her up beside him. "What I need is you—just you. Your smile, your warmth, your companionship," he said.

*Don't analyze this too much,* Lisa warned herself. Even though she knew that he now realized the impact of the attraction between them, he might not feel any real emotion for her. It might only be fascination of a sort. She couldn't dare to hope for love, didn't dare even to think the word, even though she had known in her heart from that first day that she could easily love this man and perhaps already did.

They made their way slowly up the wooden stairs, only to realize that they had forgotten their shoes, and they bumped into each other all the way down the creaking wooden steps again, put on their shoes and, laughing, ran back up.

At Jay's place, Hildy greeted them with a couple of enthusiastic barks and Lisa followed Jay into the kitchen and sat on a stool to watch as Jay piled turkey on thick slabs of pumpernickel bread.

"Did you roast the turkey yourself?" she asked.

"Yes. It's one of the few things that I eat that doesn't come already cooked out of a zip-open bag at the supermarket," he admitted. "Mustard or mayonnaise?"

"Mayonnaise, please," she said.

"Mustard for me," he said, applying it with a heavy hand.

The sandwich was good, but it was Jay who was the real treat. She liked sitting across from him, liked the way he seemed to enjoy watching her. She found herself growing more animated as they sat and talked. It was a heady feeling, a powerful feeling, to find herself the focus of attention of one very handsome and charming man. Sometimes his eyes flickered with appreciation at something she said, and she fought the impulse to become reckless with wit, to laugh louder, to toss her head, bat her eyelashes—anything to impress him.

But that would be a mistake. He *was* impressed; she knew it. She was flattered. And the attraction between them was magnetic. He must feel it as strongly as she did.

After dinner, when Hildy had retreated happily to her bed in the closet, Jay turned out the overhead light, leaving their faces illuminated only by the hood light over the stove. She held her breath and felt her heart fluttering in her chest. Almost ceremoniously he put his arms around her and kissed her.

"You're a girl who really knows how to kiss," he said after a few minutes.

"Only when I'm kissing the right person," she said.

"You must have had lots of practice."

"Not with the right person."

"What makes me so right?" he asked, his mouth close to her ear.

How could she explain that she'd wanted him to want her from the moment she'd seen him standing in the community center at the mission in his paint-splashed blue jeans? That his caring and compassion for the children stirred her more than even his physical presence, which was at this very moment making her think erotic thoughts that would embarrass her in the extreme if he were to guess them?

"Oh," she said, striving for but not attaining a lightness of tone, "it's some kind of special undefinable something, I guess."

"A good way of putting it," he agreed, and he drew her into the living room and turned out one of the lights, the brightest one, leaving only the glow of recessed indirect lighting above the paintings on the wall.

Jay drew her down beside him on the couch and reached out with both hands, tunneling them under the feathery hair at her nape and rubbing gently. Her skull seemed so small and delicate, as fragile as a bird's. He wanted to kiss her again; in fact, he wanted to do more than that.

"Do you like this, or shall I stop?" he asked.

"I like it," she said, and her lips remained parted in open invitation.

He kissed her, fascinated with the way she sank beneath him with submission yet rose to meet him in ardor, and the somewhat contradictory tenderness of her lips measured against the urgency of her kisses. She was so tiny, and yet her kisses packed a wallop that left him gasping for breath. Lisa didn't look like a femme fatale, but he was rapidly beginning to think that she was more *fatale* than any other *femme* he had ever known.

What could have happened didn't. He had no idea whether she would have shown restraint or not, but summoning what he thought were remarkable scruples, he managed to pull himself up short. He kissed her for as long as he could stand it without going any further, pleaded an early court appearance, which happened to be true, and saw her to her car. Then he kissed her chastely on the cheek, slammed the car door after her and watched her as she drove away.

LISA THOUGHT ADELE was asleep when she let herself quietly into the house, but before she had tiptoed past the kitchen, she realized that Adele sat in her usual chair, the blue images reflected from the television screen flickering across her face.

"Did you remember to pick up the bread?" Adele called out in a querulous tone.

Lisa paused in mid-tiptoe. "I'm sorry, Adele," she said. "I completely forgot about it, but I'll get it on my way home from work tomorrow," Lisa told her.

Adele's reply was lost in a burst of gunfire from the program on TV, and Lisa fled to her room.

Tonight of all nights Lisa was in no mood to deal with Adele. Tonight she wanted to mull over in exquisite privacy everything she and Jay had said to each other, to explore every nuance, to hug her happiness close.

Soon she would ask Jay over so he could see how she lived, to show off the house with its bright sun-splashed rooms, its vivid colors, the Spanish-tile floors cool to the feet even on the hottest days of summer, the shadowy alcoves in the den lined with books jam-packed into bookshelves. She hoped he would love as she did the incomparable view of the Loxahatchee.

But that would mean that Jay would have to meet Adele, and she wasn't ready for them to meet yet. Adele always made it clear that she considered Lisa's friends a threat.

Lisa pulled off her clothes and got into bed, blocking out the chatter of the television set in the living room by recreating in her mind Jay's eyes alight with happiness as he bent to kiss her. But tonight she couldn't create a fantasy; it was lost in the realities, in the very real memory of his kisses.

EARLY ON SATURDAY morning, zoo day, when Jay stopped by Lisa's house to pick her up, he was driving a faded red station wagon of ancient vintage. It sported a conspicuous patch of rust below the back bumper and a dent in the right front fender.

"Where did you find such a vehicle?" Lisa asked when she stepped outside her front door and saw it.

"It belongs to my law partner's wife," Jay said, opening the station wagon's door for her. "We exchanged cars for the day."

"So he's off with his wife in your Prelude?" she asked.

"Yes, and he thinks I should have my head examined for trading," Jay said, but he laughed and started the car, which coughed and trembled its way up the driveway. Lisa settled back on the worn upholstery and grinned back at him, and the station wagon settled down by the time they were on the highway heading toward Yahola. The sun was bright, the air fairly shone with the blue brilliance of the sky and the water in the canals on both sides of the highway glistened between tall spears of saw grass. Altogether it was a wonderful day to be feeling expansive and eager and on the brink of a new adventure.

They talked of nothing, they talked of everything, and when their eyes met, they acknowledged their new relationship with a glance. Once Jay reached across the seat of his car and took Lisa's hand; she liked feeling connected to him and was sorry when he dropped her hand to steady the steering wheel at a particularly sinuous curve in the road.

They arrived at Nina's house precisely at ten o'clock, and they waited patiently for fifteen minutes or so after the bleat of the car horn until the four boys erupted from the front door amid a maelstrom of churning knees and elbows. The boys were slicked up and attired in painstakingly ironed shirts and pants, and Connie wore a red dress and carried her constant companion, a sketchbook.

Jay settled the three older boys in the back seat of the station wagon, and Connie and Alejandro, the youngest, clambered into the middle seat.

"We're going to the zoo, we're going to the zoo," sang Ruy, but his brother shushed him and Alejandro began a warbling rendition of "Binkle, Binkle Little Star," until one of the older boys, Lisa wasn't sure which, leaned over the seat, punched him in the shoulder, and informed him that it wasn't "binkle," it was "twinkle," and anyway, if he didn't stop singing it, he'd feed him a knuckle sandwich.

"If you boys don't behave yourselves, I'll tell Jay to put you out of the car right here," warned Connie in a surprisingly grown-up voice, which must have struck fear into their hearts, because the horseplay stopped immediately.

They had reached "forty-eight bottles of beer on the wall, forty-eight bottles of beer" by the time the car left the concrete-lined expressway in Miami. Lisa and Jay had joined in heartily, with Lisa vainly trying to speed up the song's dragging tempo. Occasionally Jay glanced over at Lisa, surprised that she actually seemed to be enjoying this. When she sang, she threw her head back, exposing the white skin of her throat where it was shaded by her chin, and the sight made him catch his breath and stop singing for a verse or two until Connie complained that she couldn't hear him.

Jay wondered how it was that Lisa had never married. Someone like Lisa should have been snapped up long ago. While he was having this thought, she smiled at him—not her usual impish smile but one of incomparable sweetness. It left him feeling slightly undone.

Behind the zoo was a park with a picnic area, and when Jay drove through the entrance, the boys began to ply them with questions.

"What are we doing here?"

"Where are the animals?"

"Why are you stopping?"

"We'll eat our lunch before we go into the zoo," Jay said, and two of the boys groaned, until Connie said, "Listen, you guys, we're doing what Jay *says*." After they got out of the station wagon, the boys were oddly quiet and watched goggle-eyed as Lisa produced bowl after bowl of picnic fare and spread them on the table in the sun-stippled shadows under the trees.

"Don't you like picnics?" Jay asked when he saw the dubious expression on Ruy's face as Lisa unwrapped the carrot and celery sticks.

"I don't know. I never been on one before," Ruy said in a low voice.

It wasn't long before Ruy and Mike were flipping chick-peas from the cold chick-pea salad across the table at each other. Alejandro loved the celery sticks but managed to nearly choke on one, and Felipe refused to eat any grapes but wolfed huge mouthfuls of the potato salad. Ruy ate grapes, but only if someone else, usually Lisa, peeled them first. Connie sat through all their antics with an expression of forbearance on her face, daintily eating in her most ladylike way and ignoring the boys as much as possible.

"The granola brownies are delicious," Jay told her after he had polished off three of them.

"Mmm," Alejandro agreed, and Lisa had to laugh because he wore not only a beard of brownie crumbs but a white mustache of milk.

After they had eaten, the boys were especially impatient to get to the zoo, and when they finally stood in line at the entrance, waiting for Jay to pay the admission price, Lisa hung back to observe Jay with the children. He was so tender with them, so caring, wiping their faces with his handkerchief, resting his hand on the sun-warmed top of one small head as they walked through the gate to the zoo. Jay was the kind of guy who had every right to swagger but was instead content to saunter, matching his gait to the kids'.

The boys were in awe of the monorail, but Connie wanted to attend the elephant show, which was about to begin. Afterward, all the children rode on the elephant. Then they visited the zoo's amphitheater to see a wildlife show, where they had to wait in line again, but Lisa didn't mind. Every moment of this day seemed permeated with happiness; she felt lighthearted and happy. She'd never realized before how burdened she'd become with the responsibilities of her house, Adele, and her job.

As she watched the children clinging to Jay's arm, climbing up his leg, being hefted in his arms to see over a particularly tall fence, she realized that he was a fill-in father for them. These kids had very little male influence in their lives, and now they were basking in Jay's attention. She realized that none of that attention could be hers at the moment, but she didn't care in the least. What mattered now was that for one day she and Jay had created the semblance of a normal family outing for these kids.

As they made their way through the zoo exhibits, the children were never still, and Lisa had to look in all directions at once in order to keep them in her field of vision. Alejandro loved the koalas, Ruy was enchanted by the white Bengal tigers and Felipe's eyes grew wide at the sight of the two-level river-otter exhibit.

During a quiet moment in the free-flight aviary, Lisa made a point of sitting down on a bench beside Connie, who was swiftly finishing one of her sketches.

Connie greeted her with a smile. "That Ruy," she said as her pencil flew across the paper, "you just have to grab him by the shirttail and pull him along with us no matter how much he hollers. And Alejandro, he's not going to stop talking about koalas for another month, so don't let him blackmail us into going back and watching them or we won't get to see anything else. Mike's the easiest one. Felipe, well, you're on your own with him."

Lisa stifled a smile. "You sound like their mother," she said.

Connie looked up briefly to study the movements of a kingfisher through narrowed eyes. "I have to take care of the boys a lot," she said matter-of-factly as she began to sketch again. "Nina works, and sometimes she's not at home. They take a lot of worrying. Mike is real good with them, though. He can cook almost as good as me." Jay walked up and sat beside Lisa; he took advantage of the lull to crook his arm around Lisa's shoulders.

"Are you having a good time?" he asked.

"Very," she said, smiling up at him.

"So am I," he said, but he took his arm away before the children could crowd around. He would have liked to keep his arm around her, to run his fingers over the sun-warmed skin just above the top of her scoop-necked blouse, but he knew he had to observe proprieties. Even though he felt a great compulsion to touch her, he didn't want any of their little charges running to Sister Maria and telling her that he couldn't keep his hands to himself.

He was watching tourists taking snapshots of the birds, keeping an eye on Felipe so that he didn't fall into the waterfall and imagining Lisa lying naked on a moonlit beach, when Ruy yelled, "Alejandro's gone! I can't find him!"

## Chapter Six

If Jay had thought things were lively before, this was sheer panic. After Ruy's shout, Lisa turned pale and Connie shook Ruy by the shoulders until his teeth chattered.

"I told you to watch Alejandro," she said fiercely, whereupon Ruy began to wail, long keening notes that would do justice to a fire engine's siren. A frantic search of the aviary produced no small stray boy, so Jay and Lisa hurried the children out to the distracting accompaniment of Ruy's crying.

An older woman in baggy Bermuda shorts stopped and said in a tone of concern, "Is something wrong? Can I help?" while at the same time her husband urged, "Come along, Gladys, it's none of our business."

Felipe said, "Alejandro could have left the bird exhibit as soon as we got there. He *could* have," but Mike said, "No, no, he wouldn't do that. I saw him trying to frighten the flamingos." The two boys began to argue loudly in Spanish.

A uniformed security officer driving a golf cart rolled to a stop beside them. "Is there some problem?" he asked.

"Yes, a missing child," Jay said hurriedly, as Lisa and Connie began searching the nearby bushes for some sign of Alejandro.

"You'll have to come to the administration building and file a missing-child report," the man told Jay.

"We've just discovered he's gone," Jay said. "We're looking for him right now."

"Nevertheless, the best thing would be to file the report. What does he look like? What's his name? His age?"

"The boy's name is Alejandro, and he's, uh—Mike, how old is Alejandro?"

"He's five," Mike said. He had sent Ruy and Felipe to help Connie and Lisa search, and he stood quietly beside Jay.

"The boy has short black hair, dark skin and eyes, and he's about this tall," Jay said, measuring out Alejandro's height as well as he could. "And he's wearing a red shirt."

"Come with me, sir, and we'll file that report," the security officer said.

Felipe bounded over and tugged at Jay's hand. "All we have to do is go back to the koalas. Alejandro probably went there," he said.

Lisa appeared at Jay's side. "Felipe's right, Jay," she said. "Alejandro was crazy about the koalas. We had to drag him away from them."

"Okay," Jay said. "Lisa, you take Connie and Ruy and Felipe and make sure they stay with you. Look for Alejandro with the koalas and Mike and I will go with the security officer to file the missing-child report. How about meeting me at the zoo office after you check the koala exhibit?"

He and Mike joined the security guard in the golf cart, much to Ruy's disgust. "*He* gets to ride. *We* have to walk," he said indignantly.

"Come on, Ruy, don't waste time," Connie scolded as she tugged him along, but Ruy kept turning and watching the golf cart until it disappeared into the throng of people.

"Don't worry," Lisa said to the children, "we'll find Alejandro," but she was more worried than she sounded. The zoo presented all kinds of dangers for a lost little boy, particularly one who was as fearless as Alejandro.

"He's all right—I know he is," Connie said, trying to soothe everyone's spirits.

"Look! Is *that* Alejandro?" Lisa asked, spotting the red shirt on a little boy ahead of them on the path, and they all ran ahead, only to startle a child who was clearly with his parents and was definitely not Alejandro.

"We have to go to the *koalas,*" Felipe said patiently.

And indeed they did find Alejandro, his red shirt hanging out of his pants and one shoe untied, blissfully standing motionless and staring openmouthed at the koala exhibit, where one adorable baby koala stared back.

"Alejandro!" Connie said sharply. Alejandro turned around and blinked at them.

"Alejandro, you shouldn't have left the group. We were so worried," Lisa lectured, kneeling until she was on his eye level.

"I don't like birds. I only like koalas," Alejandro said stubbornly.

"You hold fast to my hand, Alejandro Fernandez, and don't give us any more trouble," Connie said sternly.

Alejandro sighed. "Okay," he said, surrendering his hand to his cousin, and the five of them straggled out of the exhibit and toward the zoo administration building.

Jay had barely finished filling out the missing-child report, when they arrived. He broke into a broad smile and tore up the report when he saw their little group trooping into the cubicle where he sat.

"I don't know about anyone else," he said when they were outside again, "but I'm ready to call it a day."

Lisa, who was leery of letting Alejandro put a distance of more than two feet between them, rolled her eyes and said, "I'm with you."

The afternoon sun had dipped down behind the trees and the crowd at the zoo had thinned out. Jay and Lisa patiently guided their little group back to the parking lot. Alejandro looked so tired that he could barely plant one foot in front of another, and finally Jay picked him up and carried him. Lisa led Ruy and Felipe by their hands, her own footsteps lagging. When they reached the station wagon, everyone silently piled in.

"I sketched a lot of animals," Connie said as they backed out of the parking space. She was the only one who still had enough energy to talk.

"What will you do with your sketches?" Jay wanted to know as soon as they had left the parking lot behind.

"Make some paintings. I want to see if I can mix the beautiful pink color of the flamingos, and maybe I can remember the exact way the elephants looked so happy with each other when they touched trunks, but I don't know about painting them. Their color wasn't so beautiful, and anyway, I can't paint as good as Jay," Connie said.

"Remember what I always tell you?" Jay said.

"That I can do whatever I set my mind to," she said.

"Right. You're a better artist than I was at your age."

"I don't think so. Anyway, I can only draw and paint. I can't sculpt," Connie said.

"You will someday. I promise," Jay said.

"Everything Jay promises really happens," Connie said to Lisa. "Absolutely everything."

Jay laughed. "My clients wish that were true, I'm sure," he said.

"I've never seen any of your sculpture," Lisa said.

"Lucky you," Jay replied.

"No, I'd like to see your work," Lisa insisted.

"I'll show you something I've been working on for years if you're free tomorrow," he said.

A pregnant silence, and then Lisa said, "I'd like that," and she smiled at him.

"Are we ever going to eat?" demanded a sleepy voice from the back.

"Ruy! Be polite! You shouldn't ask questions like that," Connie said, turning around and glaring at her cousin.

Jay said, "Of course we're going to eat. We'll stop in a few minutes, so hold your horses."

"Hold your horses," Ruy said with a snicker.

"Hold your anteaters," added Felipe.

"Hold your hippopotallus," said Alejandro, laughing so hard that he couldn't stop.

Soon they stopped at a shopping mall and filed into a cafeteria, where Alejandro refused to wash his hands before eating and where Ruy and Felipe wanted to push an empty high chair through the serving line. Lisa tried to close her eyes to Mike's chosen meal of Boston cream pie, cherry cobbler, onion rings and a soft drink and busied herself with trying to keep Alejandro from keeling over with exhaustion into his plate of mashed potatoes and gravy.

At last the seven of them were in the car again and headed toward home. It was about a two-hour drive, and

Alejandro insisted on lying full length on the middle seat of the station wagon, so Connie sat in front between Lisa and Jay.

"I think I'm as tired as the kids are," Jay said quietly to Lisa.

"I *know* I am," Lisa whispered back as she shifted slightly to accommodate Connie's head, which had settled on her shoulder as Connie fell asleep.

Jay's eyes met hers for a moment in the greenish glare from the dash lights, sharing a look, sharing the moment. With the children quiet, with no one talking or laughing or demanding, peace seemed to have settled over them.

*Happiness,* Lisa thought involuntarily. *I don't know what that word means to other people, but this is what it is for me—the kids lulled to sleep by food and fun and someone to understand how special this day has been.* She faced front again, shaken that she had settled into this easy domestic feeling with a man she barely knew. She would have given almost anything to know what he was thinking about it, but Jay concentrated on his driving, and neither one of them spoke.

After they left the interstate highway, the road to Yahola seemed dark and eerie. Connie stirred and mumbled something querulous in her sleep, then slumped even closer to Lisa. The boys in the back remained quiet, soothed by the hum of the tires as the car swallowed up the road on the way to Yahola.

A glow seemed to light up the sky as they approached the labor camp.

"What's that?" Lisa asked, knowing that the small store at the camp's entrance would be closed this late at night.

"The Club Two Spot," Jay said quietly. "You've noticed it before, haven't you?"

In fact, Lisa had passed the place every day that she went to the mission, but it had never been open. Tonight, Saturday night, the joint was jumping. From a quarter of a mile away they heard the blare of music, and as Jay slowed their speed to a crawl in order to accommodate the cars that were both leaving and entering the highway, Lisa turned her head for a closer look.

The Club Two Spot was a low white building with its name scrawled on one wall with an uninhibited swoosh of aerosol paint, and people inside were laughing and dancing. Two women staggered out the front door as they passed, and a man hollered a suggestive remark at them from the back fender of his car, where he sat nursing a bottle in a brown paper bag.

"Some people from Yahola head straight for the Two Spot after they get paid on Friday night, and the party lasts all weekend," Jay said in a low tone to Lisa.

Connie stirred sleepily and lifted her head. "Do you see Nina there?" she asked when she saw where they were.

"No, I didn't," Jay said. They had passed the Club Two Spot now and were rounding the corner into the camp.

At the sound of the others' voices, the boys woke up grumpily and pressed their faces against the windows. There were no streetlights in the labor camp, and the house where the children lived with Nina looked closed and dark. A bedraggled cat ran across the bright wedge of the car's headlights and slunk into a dusty patch of weeds. As the car slid to a stop, Connie silently groped on the floor of the station wagon for her sketch pad.

"Thanks, Jay and Lisa," she said through a yawn. "We all had a real good time."

"So did we," Lisa said, putting an arm around Connie.

"I'll carry Alejandro," Jay offered, but Alejandro would have none of it. "I can walk," he said loudly, climbing out of the station wagon and heading unsteadily through the murky darkness in the direction of the front door.

Lisa hugged Connie close for a moment, surprised that Connie hugged back so intensely.

"I love you, Lisa," Connie said.

Lisa hadn't expected this, but she was moved by the declaration. "Why, I love you too, Connie," she managed to say.

"Nobody ever tells me that," Connie said, sounding perilously near tears before she ran toward the door of the house.

Lisa waited beside the station wagon as Jay walked the other children to the house. She saw the front door open, watched the children go inside, and still there was no sign of Nina. After Jay disappeared for a moment, lights sprang to life behind the window of the front room. Not knowing what else to do, Lisa got back in the station wagon and waited, expecting Jay to emerge any minute.

It was a good ten minutes before he came outside, and he looked exasperated as he walked to the station wagon. He bent over and rested his forearms on the edge of the open car window to talk to Lisa.

"Nina's not here," he said. "The kids don't know where she is."

"I'll help put them to bed," Lisa offered, moving to open the car door, but Jay rested a restraining hand on her shoulder.

"Connie's taking care of them. She'd said she'd be embarrassed if you saw how they live," he said gently.

Lisa fell back against the seat. "Oh," she said. She looked up at Jay. "Are you going back inside?" she asked.

"I told Connie I'd check out the Club Two Spot and see if Nina's there. You could sit right here until I get back—I'll only be gone for a few minutes."

She looked up at him and saw from the lines between his eyes how concerned he was. "Okay," she said, trying to smile. "I'll wait on the front steps so you can take the car."

He rested his hand against her cheek for a moment. It felt warm. "Thanks, Lisa, but I think you should stay in the station wagon. I'll walk because I'll be less conspicuous that way."

"Be careful," she called unnecessarily out the window, and he waved as he retreated down the street.

Lisa stretched her legs out full length and yawned. She looked at the house, then at the entire row of houses. Some were dark, some dimly lighted. She could see shapes moving in the house across the street, and she heard a peal of bright laughter. At least someone around here was having a good time tonight; Yahola wasn't all misery and squalor. A young couple sauntered past the station wagon, their arms looped around each other's waists, and there was something very sweet in the way they inclined their heads toward each other.

In the house where Connie and the boys lived with Nina, all the lights went out, and through the gloom Lisa thought she saw a small shape stand at the door for a fleeting moment before disappearing. *Connie,* she thought. *Connie's wondering if I'm still out here.* She could understand why Connie would be embarrassed for her to come inside, but she wished she had. Lisa would have liked to tuck the boys into their cots, would have liked to smooth Connie's unruly black bangs back from her forehead. Lisa was aware that she had well developed maternal instincts; the problem was that she seldom had a chance to act upon them.

After about fifteen minutes she turned and looked out the back window of the station wagon, and she saw Jay walking toward her through the inky darkness. He was alone. Slowly, she got out of the car, stretched and waited for him. "You didn't find Nina?" she asked.

"Nope," he said. He stood there for a moment, considering, and she waited to hear what he was going to say.

"The way it looks to me, we have three options," he said finally. "We could take the kids home with us, which isn't a good idea. We don't have Nina's permission, and she might try to blow it all out of proportion. We could wait here until Nina or some other responsible adult comes along to take care of them. Or we could leave." He studied Lisa's face for a long moment, as though judging her reaction. "What do you want to do?" he asked.

Lisa thought about Alejandro disappearing at the zoo and how frantic she'd been. If they left the children alone here in this darkened house, she'd worry all night. Connie was capable of supervising the boys over short periods of time, she knew that, but at the moment her mind was ranging over all the possibilities—fires, poison, illness, you name it.

"I can't leave them here," she said.

Jay nodded as though this proved something in his own mind. "I knew you'd feel that way. And I don't think we should take them home with us. So that leaves staying. Do you mind?"

She shook her head. "No, but don't you think we should go inside with them?" she asked with a glance toward the silent house.

"I promised Connie I wouldn't bring you in. I don't want to go back on my word. Let's sit on the porch. The windows are open, so we'll hear if there's any problem."

"Okay," Lisa said. She shivered. "I didn't bring a jacket, and it's turning chilly," she said.

"You can wrap up in the tablecloth," Jay said, and he got it from the back of the station wagon and shook it out, wrapping it loosely around Lisa's shoulders like a shawl.

"That's better," she said, and he rested his hands upon her shoulders for a moment before releasing her.

Slowly, hand in hand, they went up on the front porch, but there were no chairs, so they sat on a lower step, using the next highest one for a backrest. Lisa huddled in the tablecloth, continuing to shiver until Jay turned half-sideways to protect her from the wind. He slid his arm around her and she moved closer.

There was no sound from inside the house, and Lisa knew that as tired as the kids were, they must have gone to sleep immediately.

Jay could tell when Lisa felt warmer; she stopped trembling against his chest.

"Does Nina spend much time at the Club Two Spot, do you think?" Lisa asked, lowering her voice so that Jay had to dip his head to hear her. Her bangs brushed his cheek, so soft, so gentle. He resisted the urge to touch them.

"Probably," Jay said. He shifted his position, unable to get comfortable. He looked off into the distance, trying to be fair. It wasn't easy.

"I suppose we should look at this from Nina's point of view, too," he said. "She works hard doing stoop labor in the fields all day, and she's the only support of these kids. When she gets home, she's supposed to take care of them. She has a hard life."

Lisa shot him a surprised look. "I'm surprised to hear you defend her," she said.

"A successful lawyer should be able to argue both sides of a case. I'm not defending Nina, not by any means, but when you live the way she does, you learn to take pleasure where you find it. If the only happiness for miles around happens to be at the Club Two Spot, well, that's where you go," he said.

"Happiness for me today was being with those kids," Lisa said.

"I'm glad to hear you say that," Jay replied. She was the only woman he knew whom he could imagine taking on an outing like today's, and when he thought about her kindness to Connie and her expert handling of the boys, he wondered again why she had never married. He could imagine Lisa as a young suburban matron with a flock of children in tow; he liked thinking of her that way.

A car slowed as it went past, and they hoped it was Nina, but it was only the next-door neighbors returning home.

"Guess I'd better go talk to them," Jay said, removing his arm from around her shoulders and slowly unbending. He stood up, hurried across the front yard and carried on a quick, low conversation with the neighbors before hurrying back.

"They're the Martins, the parents of two of my art students, and they say that the Fernandez kids can come and stay with them, but they know from past experience that Nina gets angry if the children go over there. I'm afraid it will only make trouble for everyone if we insist," he said. He sat down again and drew in a long breath, which he exhaled slowly. He looked over at Lisa. "You didn't ask for all this, I know. You're being a good sport about it," he said.

She worked her arm out of the folds of the tablecloth and slid it through his. "It happens that I agree with you one hundred percent about Nina's neglect of the children," she said.

He studied her reflectively, his perception of who she was expanding. "When you look at me like that—" he said, and stopped. There were so many things he wanted to say to her, and this wasn't really the place to say them. If they were making love he could tell her everything, could feel as close to her in the physical sense as he did in his mind; he was only beginning to sense how rewarding the physical expression of their closeness could be.

"When I look at you like this, what?" she said, and he thought he saw a hint of amusement in the quirk of her smile.

"I think you're the most wonderful woman in the world," he said with great finality, and he kissed her.

Lisa didn't care if everyone in Yahola was watching or even everyone in the whole world. She shifted her weight until he had no choice but to take her in his arms. Slowly he enfolded her and pressed her close; after he released her lips he rubbed his cheek slowly against hers. She felt the faint stubble of his beard.

"You're so soft," he murmured. "So soft and sweet, and it's been torture to be with you all day, being able to look and not touch." His hands moved under the tablecloth, resting lightly against the indentation at her waist, seeming to count her ribs one by one, brushing over her breasts and coming to rest on her shoulders. He twisted her toward him and she accommodated herself willingly, eagerly, and that was when the car lights swung across the front of the house and pinned them in their glare.

They sprang apart guiltily and leaped to their feet. As they watched, Nina jumped from the car and slammed the door behind her without bothering to say goodbye to the driver, who backed away in a spurt of dust and exhaust fumes before roaring back toward the highway.

"You was looking for me?" Nina said. She stood below them with her hands on her hips, her pocketbook swinging from one wrist.

"I didn't want to leave the children alone, so—" Jay said.

Nina pushed past both of them on her way up the steps. "You could have. I do it all the time. Connie is old enough to take care of them."

"Nevertheless, it didn't seem like a good idea. Connie is too young for such responsibility. If you're going to be gone this late at night, you should hire a baby-sitter or let them stay with the neighbors until you come back," Jay said heatedly.

"I don't need you to tell me how to take care of them kids," Nina said. With that she opened the door and went inside, letting it slam behind her. The conversation was clearly over.

"Well, that's that, but at least I managed to get my licks in," Jay said ruefully. He rubbed the back of his neck. "Now I suppose we might as well go home."

Lisa moved closer and slid her arm around his waist. "You did the best you could," she murmured.

He lifted his eyes heavenward, and with a rueful smile he reached toward her and pulled her close. Together they walked to the station wagon. He opened the door for her and hurried around to the driver's side. Tonight he couldn't wait to leave the migrant village behind.

When they were on the outskirts of Yahola, he said, "It was quite a day, wasn't it?"

"Quite," Lisa said as she swallowed a yawn. Jay switched the radio to a station playing smoky jazz music, and she slid closer to him, her head resting on the back of the seat. After a while she let her head drop so that it nestled against his shoulder, and he looked down at her and smiled.

They spoke very little on the long dark ride to her house. When they arrived, no lights showed through the curtains.

"Adele must be asleep," Lisa said. Jay had turned off the engine at the head of the driveway so that the old station wagon glided soundlessly up to the house, and the only noise to break the silence other than her own voice was the racket of the crickets and the shrill of the tree frogs. She looked at Jay, wondering if he was in a hurry to go home. "Would you like to come in for a while?" she asked tentatively.

She couldn't read the expression in his eyes, even though he turned in her direction. She didn't know what he thought she was offering, and she wasn't sure herself. She only knew that she wanted to be with him. He picked up her hand and grazed the back of it with his lips. They felt gentle, like the brush of a butterfly's wing.

"If you'd like me to," he said.

"I would," she answered, feeling a certain solemnity about the moment.

As they got out of the car, Lisa warned in a whisper, "Careful, don't slam the car door—it will wake Adele," and Jay latched the door of the station wagon behind him so carefully that the click of it blended with the night sounds from the river. He caught Lisa's hand in his and, fingers linked, they made their way carefully to the front door, where Lisa inserted her key and swung it open.

She held a cautionary finger over her lips and oriented Jay toward the kitchen, which was closer to her room than to Adele's. Adele's room had a private entrance in the wing of the house closest to the road; it had been meant for Lisa when she'd lived here with her parents, but now Lisa occupied the master bedroom on the river side of the house, and unfortunately, there was no entrance to that wing other than the door they had just used.

Lisa had not yet reached for the light switch that would flood the kitchen with light, when they heard a cough from the direction of Adele's room. Lisa hoped that Adele was in bed. She was sure that even if Adele was awake, she wouldn't come out to meet anyone in her old chenille bathrobe. They heard another cough and then a light popped on behind Adele's closed door.

Lisa pressed close to Jay, cautioning him to keep quiet and trying to figure out if she should go speak to Adele and reassure her or if she should encourage Adele to think that she was alone and going directly to bed. Once in the kitchen, she and Jay could close the door to the rest of the house and put the coffeepot on. They would be able to talk undisturbed, or, if they wanted to, they could even—

"Lisa?" Adele called.

"I just came in," Lisa called back. To her ear, her words sounded fast-spoken, nervous.

"Are you going to bed?"

In the darkness, Lisa could feel Jay's questioning eyes upon her.

"In a little while," she said as normally as possible. "I thought I'd eat something first."

"If you're going to eat some of those granola brownies you made, I'd like one, too," Adele said.

"Look, if this is difficult for you, I'll go." Jay's whisper was urgent in her ear.

Lisa shook her head. "It's my house, after all. I'm allowed to have guests," she whispered back.

"I can see that it's awkward for you," he said.

She gazed up at him. Her eyes had adjusted to the darkness now, and she could see that he looked resigned. He also looked very tired.

"I apologize," she said in a low tone. "I thought Adele was asleep. I'd like you to meet her, but not tonight."

"I do understand. I'll call you tomorrow, okay?"

She could taste her disappointment in the back of her throat. "I'm sorry," she said.

"So am I." He was smiling at her.

She nodded, not trusting herself to speak.

His eyes held a warm glow as he pulled her close. Her arms started to go around him, but he caught one of her hands and lifted it to his face, where he cupped it against his skin for a moment, then let it go and touched his hand to her cheek. Slowly he brought her face within kissing range, adjusting it just so, and she tasted his breath upon her lips before she felt his kiss.

One kiss, and it wasn't enough; they lingered over it and tended it and then let it subside bit by bit until they stood breathing so heavily in each other's arms that it seemed that Adele would surely hear.

"Tomorrow," he murmured, and she had the idea that he'd meant to say it lightly but failed. He hesitated as if there was something else he would have liked to say, but he didn't. Then, leaving her trembling and feeling as though she should be able to control her own response to him, he melted soundlessly into the darkness. In a moment she heard his light retreating footsteps on the flagstones outside.

"Lisa?" said Adele, sounding querulous. "Are all those brownies gone?"

"I'll see," Lisa said shakily; it had been only one kiss and her senses were still swimming. She groped her way toward the light switch and flicked it in time to cast a bright path on the grass outside the kitchen window. She looked out barely in time to see the station wagon spinning up the driveway.

She stood for a few moments getting her bearings. Then she located the brownies in a plastic container in the cupboard and put one on a plate for Adele. She'd plead exhaustion when she delivered the brownie and then she'd go directly to bed.

Which is exactly what she did. Once she was lying in her own comfortable bed with the river flowing past, with the crickets singing their usual songs outside her window, with the wind sighing in the Australian pines, she'd thought she'd be caught up in her imaginings about Jay. As she lay there she had a brief vision of the two of them feeding on each other's hungry mouths, their hearts shuddering in their chests; she even thought beyond that to the possibility of swirling over and over through tumbling sheets with him, their flesh welded together.

But it didn't last long. After a few moments the pictures faded and for some reason she could only think about those five children alone in that dark dirty house with Nina, and of the way Connie had told Lisa she loved her and had hugged her so desperately when she'd said good-night.

## Chapter Seven

"You've never invited a man to Sunday brunch before," Adele pointed out the next morning as she measured out flour for crepe batter.

Lisa considered how to reply as she wiped a few spots of tarnish off the best silver, which she'd dug out of the silver chest after Jay's phone call earlier.

"I've never known a man I wanted around in the morning before," she answered at last.

Adele shot her a keen look. "You've mentioned this one's name quite a few times," she observed.

"Jay and I work together at the mission," Lisa replied curtly. "By the way, Adele, do we have any bananas? I could make fruit salad."

"'Yes, we have no bananas,'" Adele said. It was her idea of a joke, and Lisa took heart from it. At least Adele appeared to be in a cheerful mood.

Lisa was mixing the fruit salad in a large crystal bowl when she saw Jay's car pulling into the driveway.

"Oh, my goodness, here he is," she said, suddenly nervous. She dodged Adele's stately bulk to check her own muted reflection in the black plastic door of the microwave oven. "My hair looks limp," she said in distraction. It was important that everything be perfect, and her hair was no exception.

"Your hair looks all right," Adele said stolidly, and Lisa decided that Adele was to be believed but that hair that looked all right was not as desirable as hair that looked terrific.

When Jay rang the bell, Lisa hurried to open the door. When she saw him standing on her doorstep, one hand resting on the door frame, the other behind his back, all her misgivings faded. He was smiling at her in quiet good humor, and once again she was overwhelmed with the potent charm of the man. It had been roughly twelve hours since they'd parted, but it seemed like forever.

He swept one hand from behind his back with a flourish. It held a single, perfect pink rosebud. "For you," he said.

"I didn't expect—" Lisa began.

"That's why I'm giving it to you. Surprises are supposed to be unexpected, and besides, I feel guilty for phoning and waking you up so early in the morning."

"Not that I minded. Anyway, come in," she urged, ushering him inside. She slid her arm through his and, after a quick look toward the kitchen, pecked him on one cheek.

"Hi," he said under his breath. She saw that with any encouragement he would sweep her into his arms, and she tried to keep her heart from speeding up, but it was no use.

"Come on, I'll show you around the house," she said.

She showed him the guest room and Adele's room at the end of that hall; she showed him her mother's collection of antique wooden toys in the living room and the marlin that her father had caught, now mounted over the fireplace in the den.

They sat down on one of the window seats in the den and looked out at the Loxahatchee. A sailboat went by, its sails billowing in the breeze.

"I see why you love this house," he said. "It has a lot of charm." Suddenly his own bachelor digs with their chrome-and-Formica furniture seemed to cry out for a woman's touch. Here, with the sun-spangled river flowing past the windows, with sweet-smelling potpourri filling the air with fragrance and with soft stools on which to rest tired feet, life seemed peaceful and calm.

"Adele likes it here, too," Lisa said. "And by the way, she's eager to meet you." He raised his eyebrows in a silent, skeptical question. "Yes, really she is," Lisa assured him, a statement that was greeted with an elaborate shrug.

Adele looked around briefly as the two of them came into the kitchen, but she covered the plate of hot crepes with aluminum foil and wiped her hands on her apron before turning to meet Jay.

"Jay Quillian, this is Adele Finley," Lisa said, but her formal tone evaporated when she turned to Jay. "Adele makes the best crepes in the world," she told him.

"Oh, I don't know about that," Adele said tartly. She inspected Jay at close range, hardly making a secret of her interest. He withstood her scrutiny well, although Lisa thought it bordered on the rude.

To distract Jay, Lisa said, "I'd better find a vase for this rosebud. Come help me look for one," and she led him through the door to the garage, shutting it firmly behind her.

"One thing I don't understand," Jay murmured, close behind her as she balanced on tiptoe to survey the crowded shelves until she saw the bud vase half-hidden behind the aerosol rug cleaner and a partly used bottle of laundry detergent. "Why does it matter so much about Adele? Here, I can reach that," he said, edging her out of the way.

"I'm all Adele has," Lisa said, standing aside. "I'm like a daughter to her."

"But you're not her daughter," Jay said patiently.

"Her daughter was my best friend," Lisa reminded him, keeping her voice low so that Adele wouldn't hear.

Jay bit his lower lip. "Okay. So you're all she has, and the lady has been depressed for—how many years?"

"Megan died in 1979," Lisa said. "Before that, Adele was always cheerful and happy. She had a sense of humor. Why, I remember her singing to us, wonderful old songs like 'When Irish Eyes Are Smiling,' things like that. In those days, she was a different person from the sad, lonely and defeated woman that she is now."

"It isn't your job to make everything up to her, Lisa," Jay said soberly.

"I know, but I can't help wanting to. It's like you and Connie, Jay. You know you can't make the circumstances of her life a whole lot better, but you want to brighten it as much as you can."

He smiled at her. "Well, let's go in and brighten Adele's Sunday, shall we? We're just little rays of sunshine, you and me."

They were both laughing when they went back in the kitchen, and Adele looked at them strangely. "Lisa, why don't you put that flower on the table?" she said, and Lisa, feeling reassured that things were going well, filled the vase with water and left the two of them alone together while she went into the dining room.

Jay leaned against the counter and watched Adele pouring batter into the crepe pan. To make a crepe, she swirled the batter around the pan until it completely covered the bottom. In less than a minute, she expertly flipped the crepe over.

"I've always wondered how people do that," Jay said musingly.

"Oh, it takes practice to do it properly," Adele said. She turned the finished crepe out onto the plate and poured more batter.

"I'll bet it's all in the wrist," he said.

"What?"

"The way you flip the crepe. It probably has to do with the way you move your wrist."

"No, I think it's more in knowing the surface of the pan. You know, some pans just aren't slick enough and require more of a toss. This one, now, it's perfect." To demonstrate, she flipped the crepe, and Jay saw that her wrist didn't have that much to do with it. Timing did.

She finished cooking that crepe and poured another. "Would you like to try it?" she asked, surprising him.

"I might ruin it," he warned.

"A ruined crepe isn't such a big deal," she said. He thought that if she'd smile, her face would be almost pretty.

"Okay, I'll give it a try," he said, moving over to take her place.

"It's almost done now, so get ready," she cautioned.

Jay jiggled the crepe from side to side. "Are you sure?" he said nervously.

"Don't waste time talking—just do it!" Adele said.

Awkwardly he whipped the pan up and the crepe slid crazily out of it and onto the floor. He stood looking down at it with a mortified expression.

Lisa walked in and saw them staring at the crepe, which had puddled into a gluey mess.

"What in the world—" she said, her eyes darting from Adele to Jay and back again to Adele.

"Jay is learning to cook crepes. Remember when I tried to teach you?"

"I was fourteen," Lisa said.

"And you didn't do much better than this. Pour another one, Jay. About two tablespoons of batter will do the job."

"I'll clean up the mess," Lisa said, reaching for a paper towel. She was secretly pleased that Jay and Adele were hitting it off so well.

After the ruined crepe had been consigned to the garbage can, Jay resumed his position at the stove. He waited until Adele said, "Now," and tried flipping again. This time he caught the crepe, although he didn't exactly catch it dead center. Batter oozed down the size of the pan, but he was heartened when Adele said, "Good! The next one will be perfect."

The next one was perfect, and the next, and the next, until Adele said, "Jay, you don't need any help from me. I'll start putting the filling in," and after that the two of them worked together while Lisa watched.

"What a great view of the river you have from this window," Jay said when the crepes were arranged on a platter and they moved into the dining room. Outside a powerboat cut through the rippling blue water, laying down a curling white wake. Across the river two boys fished from a white dock, their hair ruffling gently in the breeze.

"You two really should go out in Lisa's canoe this afternoon," Adele suggested.

"Jay has asked me to his town house to see some of his artwork," Lisa supplied.

"Oh? What kind of art do you do?" Adele said with interest, and the conversation was off and running again, much to Lisa's relief. She watched Jay as he charmed Adele, noting the way he asked perceptive questions at exactly the right places and admiring his ability to listen instead of talk. Her heart warmed to him for caring about Adele. So few people did.

After brunch, Lisa and Jay escorted Adele into the living room and insisted that she settle down with the newspaper while the two of them performed the necessary cleanup chores.

"But—" objected Adele.

"No buts," Jay told her firmly, and he brought a footstool from across the room so that she'd be more comfortable.

"Shall I invite Adele to go with us to my place this afternoon? Out of politeness, I mean?" Jay whispered when he and Lisa were alone in the kitchen.

"Nice of you, but she'll be perfectly happy to sit all afternoon looking out at the river and knitting as she watches television," Lisa told him. She gave the counter top one last swipe. "Besides," she said, tossing the towel over the rod, "after yesterday when we were so well chaperoned, I'm looking forward to being with you and only you."

He slid his arms around her from behind and kissed the top of her head. "My sentiments exactly," he murmured.

Adele bade them a cheerful goodbye when they left, and Lisa slid her hand into Jay's as they walked to his car.

"You've opened the sunroof," she said, delighted.

"I wanted to see you with the wind in your hair," he told her.

"You want me to look like one of those shampoo commercials on TV," she accused.

"No, actually I'd prefer another kind of commercial—you know, those late-night nine-hundred-number commercials that show the woman lying on a couch wearing one of those lacy things? You know what kind of thing I mean—I think it's called a tommy," he said. He started the engine and turned the car around toward the road.

"A *tommy?* What in the world is—oh, you mean a *teddy!*" and she dissolved into gales of laughter.

"Have I said something funny?" he asked in bewilderment.

"No, I suppose if you don't know what it's called, you haven't been seeing many of them lately," she said.

"If you want to know if there are any other women in my life, the answer is no," he said firmly. Then he chuckled. "Unless you count Connie and a bunch of nuns," he added. He turned suddenly serious. "How about you, Lisa? Any other suitors?"

She looked at him. "Not one," she told him, and she was glad when he looked pleased.

At the guardhouse at the entrance to the development where he lived, Jay spoke to the security guard.

"This is Lisa Sherrill," he said. "Put her on my list of visitors."

After they were inside, Lisa said, "What was that all about?"

"He'll let you in whenever you come to see me without calling me to find out if it's all right," he said, smiling at her.

"I'm invited to visit when I'm not invited?" she asked.

"Anytime," he said. "Especially if you're wearing a teddy."

She had to laugh. "The only teddy I own, unfortunately, has one eye and stuffing falling out of his side," she said. "And his last name is *B-e-a-r*."

"You know what I like about you?" he asked suddenly.

"Something, I hope," she responded.

"Oh, a lot of things, but this thing in particular. You don't wear huge shoulder pads. So many small women try to make themselves look bigger by making their shoulders so enormous that they could play linebacker for the Green Bay Packers," he said. He stopped the car in front of his town house and got out.

She got out, too. "What brought that on?" she asked.

"Thinking about what you wear," he said, opening the gate to the courtyard and ushering her in, and she laughed again. It was fun to be with him, bantering back and forth, and it was good to know that he'd been thinking about her enough to notice what she wore.

Amused, she followed him to the front door and waited as he unlocked it. Inside, Hildy recognized Lisa immediately, and Lisa greeted Hildy like an old friend.

"She likes you," he said.

"The feeling is mutual," Lisa said as Hildy delivered a long sloppy kiss. "I haven't had a dog since my parents gave Peanut to me after we moved to Stuart from West Palm Beach. She was supposed to make up for moving away from my best friend, and she did, in a way."

"You should get another dog," he said. "Then you wouldn't be lonely."

"I will someday," she said, stroking Hildy's silky ears and thinking that a dog around the house might be a good idea, something to make Adele's life more interesting and to get her more involved with practicalities.

"Have you ever seen a dog who could count?" Jay asked with mischief in his eyes.

"I can't say that I have," Lisa said.

"Watch this," Jay told her. He went into the kitchen and returned with a handful of dog biscuits, one of which he held up in front of Hildy.

"How much is one and one, Hildy?" he asked. Hildy barked twice.

As he fed her a biscuit as a reward, Lisa asked skeptically, "What's the secret?"

"A dog with a brilliant mathematical mind," Jay said. He held up another biscuit. "Hildy, how much is three plus four?"

Hildy barked seven times and held her mouth open for the biscuit.

Lisa was mystified; there had to be a trick to it, but she couldn't figure it out.

"How do you do it?" she asked.

Jay laughed. "I'm not telling, and Hildy won't, either," he said.

"Let me try," Lisa demanded, but when she commanded Hildy to add two and two, the dog only whined and lay down with her head between her paws.

"I give up," Lisa said finally, surrendering the last of the biscuits to the dog.

"Hildy does, too," he said. "Back to the kitchen, Hildy."

Hildy stood up and, biscuit in mouth, trotted obediently back to the kitchen and her bed.

After a few minutes, Jay took Lisa's hand and led her upstairs to the room he used for a studio.

"This is it," he said, opening the door. "It's supposed to be a den, and the washer and dryer are in the closet, which is why there's a pile of clothes on the futon. It's not ideal for a studio to share quarters with a laundry, but, well, it works—more or less.''

He walked to the table in the middle of the room and threw the cover off his work. It was a sculpture in the making, a small, asymmetrical but definitely anthropomorphic figure. The form was fluid, rhythmic and full of strength.

''This piece is something that I started when I was in law school in Tennessee,'' he explained. ''I knew some stonecutters, who let me work in the back of their shop, and I discovered this slab of coral rouge marble in the storeroom. I knew that this stone was fragile and wasn't quarried anymore, and I saw the shape in it almost immediately. I put it aside from time to time, but I always go back to it. Someday I'll finish it,'' he said, and he ran his hand over its finish.

''How much is left to do?'' she asked.

''I'm at the polishing stage,'' he said. ''Go ahead—you can touch it.''

She ran her fingertips across the dramatic high contrast coloration. ''I had no idea you were so talented,'' she said, turning wondering eyes upon him.

He shrugged. ''I find sculpture the most satisfying medium. There's something about the physical demands of sculpture—it requires more strength than other media. I like chipping away the stone to find the shape within. And I like knowing that what I create has permanence.''

''What will you do with this when you finish it?'' she asked.

He laughed. ''Set it on a pedestal and enjoy looking at it, I suppose.'' He turned to her and circled his arms around her waist. ''Which is what I would like to do with you, Lisa Sherrill. Had any experience with sitting on pedestals lately?''

She smiled up at him, entranced by the good humor in his eyes.

''Not much, but I'm willing to give it a try.''

''Adventurous woman.'' Sounds of a warm lazy Sunday afternoon floated through the window—car doors slamming, people calling to one another, a revolving sprinkler slapping water against the fence. His face relaxed into a more serious expression.

''Exactly how adventurous are you today, anyway?'' he asked. He slid a line of kisses from her temple to her ear and skimmed his lips along the sweet-smelling curve of her neck. She felt the first sensations of desire deep in her stomach; she closed her eyes. She'd have been a fool not to know what he meant.

''Well?'' he said, his breath feathering across her cheek.

''If you mean,'' she said, and swallowed. His hands were under her shirt now, caressing the skin at the small of her back. ''If you mean will I have sex with you, I—''

''Don't say, 'have sex,''' he interrupted softly. ''Say, 'make love.' I think I'm falling in love with you, Lisa.''

She reared back to look at him, unable to trust what she had just heard him say, and he laughed softly deep in his throat. ''Don't look so amazed,'' he said. ''Don't you feel it, too? Don't the two of us seem right?''

''I feel—something,'' she whispered, closing her eyes, because then, just at that moment, she felt it so strongly. She had never thought to want someone so much that her mouth felt dry, that her legs wouldn't hold her up, that her insides felt as though they were melting from the heat of her emotion.

He cupped her face between both his palms and stared down at her for a moment.

"Why should it surprise you that I think about you all the time? That I daydream about kissing you, holding you and, yes, making love with you? That I think about your face, your lovely face, all of my waking hours?"

She started to demur, but his voice went on weaving its spell.

"If I'd sculpted a face like yours, I might have made your cheeks thinner, like so," he said, demonstrating with his thumbs to press hollows beneath her cheekbones. "And I might not have thought to make the eyes so wide, or the brows so feathery," he said. He studied her, taking in every detail as though he was memorizing the way she looked. "No, I would not have created you this way, and yet your face seems like perfection to me." He shook his head slightly and smiled. "Pure perfection," he whispered before kissing her again.

She remained motionless as his tongue explored textures of lips and teeth and skin. They stood in the square of sunshine from the uncurtained window, his face above hers cast in bright light—when she opened her eyes, she saw in clear detail the fanned-out creases at the edges of his eyes, the short spiky hairs of his eyelashes, the mole slightly in front of and below his left ear. She didn't find him lacking even under this intense scrutiny. No, he was still as handsome as ever, and he was still as exciting, probably more so.

The sun felt warm upon her back, and his hands moved to the buttons of her shirt. She trailed a string of kisses down the side of his neck, aware of his breathing and her own coming into rhythm; her skin seemed to be drawing in the heat of his. She welcomed the cool air upon her skin where he had parted the fabric of her shirt, and as he eased it off her shoulders, she lifted one shoulder and let it fall so that the delicate strap holding her brassiere slid away. He peeled away the sheer fabric, his breath coming faster now, and when she stood before him bare to the waist he stood as if transfixed, unable to tear his eyes away from the two fragile buds, small and pink tipped and exquisitely sensitive.

She moved toward him, suddenly shy, wishing that the sunshine were not so bright, wishing her breasts were bigger. His hands on her shoulders halted her movement.

"Beautiful," he said, and then, "I had no idea."

Before she could say anything he had dropped to one knee before her and touched his lips to her breast, gently, so gently, kissing the nipple where it rose against the creamy skin. She closed her eyes and wound her fingers in his hair, willing him not to stop, wanting to press him closer and closer, his face against her breast, her stomach, the secret flesh below.

At last, when his kisses had made her wild, he looked up at her. Slowly he drew her down to him until she was kneeling, too. He took off his shirt, his eyes never leaving her face. Lisa thought she had never felt such an emotional connection with another person. The light in his eyes was so passionate, so vivid and strong, that it seemed to draw her deep inside of him. She knew that what she felt was what he felt, too, and what's more she recognized her feelings as the natural culmination of the highly electrical fascination she had felt for him the first time she'd ever laid eyes on him.

He touched the fastening of her jeans, a question. She slowly reached her hands around and unsnapped them— her answer.

"Lisa," he said. "This doesn't have to happen today. Not if you don't want it."

She swallowed. Her mouth was dry, and her eyelids felt heavy. "I want to," she whispered.

He slid his hands slowly down her sides, following the lines of her figure in at the waist, out at the hips. His hands, his strong hands, rested there for a moment, then reached around her to urge her closer. She felt the springy hair on his chest brush her nipples, tried to swallow and couldn't. Then she was falling sideways with him, and the clean laundry that had been piled so neatly on the futon was tumbling about their shoulders, and it smelled of wind and salt and sun, and it billowed around them like clouds. He was cradling her close, saying her name into her hair, and she was smiling, yes, smiling, so happy to be making love with him.

He kissed her—he kissed her many times, kisses blurring into kisses, kisses wafting into sighs, sighs deepening into moans, moans flowing into motion so that she didn't now where she ended and Jay began. The boundaries were no longer there; they were no longer two bodies and two spirits, just one body driving toward the same goal, harder and harder until, until, and it was enough, yet not enough, would never be enough as long as they lived. He cried out, then clasped her to him as though he would never let her go. She could hear his heart beating in her ears.

She spiraled back into the world and sank down into a welter of sweet-smelling clothes, Jay on top of her, Jay around her, Jay beside her, drifting gentle fingers along the curve of her spine.

"Lisa," he whispered in her ear. "Lisa?"

She opened her eyes to look up at him, his eyes bright in his face. He wrapped his arms around her and rocked her to some soundless tune, but it was a song she already knew, even though she had never heard it before.

How could she tell him what was in her heart? Was it too soon? But how could it be too soon if she knew he felt it, too? If their two hearts were now one heart and would stay that way forever?

A voice inside her head—a very small voice—warned her not to think in terms of forever. How well did she really know this man, after all? Who was she to say what was in his mind and in his heart?

She had only to look at him, at his eyes reflecting his total absorption in her, at his mouth smiling before seeking hers again, at his strong fingers splayed across the white skin of her breast; she had only to take in all these things to know.

"We're perfect together," he said, pulling her into the curve of his arms and easing his body along hers, until they were so close that they might have been fused.

"I know—I know—I know," she said in time with the beating of her heart, her heart brimming over with happiness.

And just like in the old movies that Adele loved to watch on TV, that was when the telephone rang.

## Chapter Eight

"It's about Connie," Sister Maria said without preamble as soon as Jay picked up the phone.

Connie was the last thing Jay wanted to think of at the moment. He rolled over; the taste of Lisa's kisses lingered in his mouth. Her hair looked like doll's hair, fine and shiny in the slit of sunshine that fell across the pillow. She was so beautiful, especially now.

He forced himself to turn his attention to Sister Maria. "What's wrong?" he asked, although the world of Yahola seemed very far away and he didn't want to know. What he really wanted to do was to slide his body against Lisa's and bury his face between her breasts.

"Nina has thrown Connie out of the house," Sister Maria said. She sounded indignant.

Jay pulled himself to a sitting position. "Why?" he asked.

"I don't know. You know the woman—she's never cared anything about Connie. It seems they had some argument, and this morning Connie came to church crying her heart out. I immediately bundled her over to my office, where she poured out the story. Can Nina legally do this?"

"I'll find out," Jay said. Behind him Lisa stirred, and he turned around to reassure her. She lifted his hand and touched her lips to the tips of his fingers. She looked sleepy and satisfied, and his first thought was *I can't leave her now,* but he said into the telephone, "I'll come to Yahola right away."

"I'm sorry to bother you on a Sunday, but I didn't know what else to do," Sister Maria said.

"You did the right thing. Connie may need a place to stay, so I suggest that you call Mrs. Daniels, the housemother at a group home for girls in Stuart—it's called Pelican House, and it's listed in the phone book. Find out if she has any vacancies. Can you do that before I get there?"

"Yes, Sister Clementine has taken Connie under her wing and is feeding her something left over from lunch, so I'll call Mrs. Daniels right away. Thank you, Jay. I'll be in my office when you get here."

"Right," Jay said, swinging his feet to the floor.

When he replaced the phone, he answered the question in Lisa's eyes.

"I'm sorry," he said. "I wouldn't leave for any other reason, but it's Connie," and he quickly explained.

"I'll go to Yahola with you," Lisa said.

"You don't have to. I'll drive you home."

"I want to be with you, and I want to help if I can. You don't mind, do you?" Her eyes searched his, and she looked so concerned that he pushed Sister Maria's tale of woe out of his mind for a moment, combed his fingers through her hair and, his hand pressed to the back of her head, pulled her lips to his.

"It feels so good to kiss you," he said. "This should be one of those lazy Sundays where all we have to do is stay in bed and touch each other, learn about each other, find out what works and what doesn't—"

"Nothing doesn't," Lisa said, her face against his shoulder. The small puffs of her breath ruffled the hair on his chest.

"You're probably right, but I assure you that soon we're going to find out for sure. I'm sorry, Lisa." He kissed her once more, slowly and regretfully, before standing up and pulling on his clothes. She watched him, entranced by the way the slanting sunlight rippled over his ribs and feeling possessive of him: now he belonged to her.

He leaned over her and planted his hands on either side of her shoulders. "Would you like something to eat before we go? Getting Connie squared away may take a while."

"First I need to get dressed. And I'm not hungry," she said.

He straightened and stood over her, and she made herself memorize the way he looked now, at that very moment. She wanted to remember this day for the rest of her life.

She reached for her clothes. "Give me some time to repair the damage, and I'll be right downstairs," she said.

"Okay," he said. He smiled over his shoulder as he left the room.

Lisa looked around her at the sculpture on the work table, at the white walls reflecting bright sunshine, at the clean clothes scattered over the floor. She stretched luxuriously, glorying in the pleasure of being here in this sun-filled workroom, awash in the blue-sky smell of clean laundry and replete with love. She felt fragrant with the scent of their lovemaking, and she didn't think she had ever felt so happy.

She was thirty-one years old, and she had just made love with the man she was going to marry. There was absolutely no doubt in her mind that they were meant for each other.

She knew exactly what she wanted from the relationship.

*But what does he want?* she asked herself, and she found no answer.

CONNIE AND Sister Clementine were walking along one of the echoing concrete breezeways of the school when Connie spied Jay and Lisa getting out of Jay's car.

"Jay!" Connie cried, running to him and flinging her arms around his waist. She sobbed against his chest, and Lisa stood helplessly to one side, unsure what she should do.

"Shh, doodlebug, it's all right," Jay said soothingly, stroking Connie's wild hair.

"Nina—she said I can't live with her anymore," Connie said brokenly when she had stopped crying. Jay handed her a handkerchief and Connie mopped her eyes, only then noticing Lisa.

"Lisa," she said, managing a smile. "I'm glad you came too."

Lisa pulled Connie close for a brief hug.

"Come along, Sister Maria is waiting for us in her office," Sister Clementine said, and the three of them followed her into the school.

When they were all seated on the hard plastic chairs in her office, a harried Sister Maria asked Connie to recount exactly what had happened that morning.

Connie hesitated, drew a deep breath and plunged ahead. She shredded a tissue with her fingers as she spoke.

"It started when I woke up around six o'clock. I was pouring milk for the boys in a hurry because I wanted to go to early Mass, and I spilled some on the table. I started to clean it up, but Nina came into the kitchen and started yelling at me. At first I thought she was only mad about the milk I spilled, but then she kept saying how I must have made Jay and Lisa stay outside and wait for her last night, and how I shouldn't have told them that she was gone when we came home, and lots of other things. And she said, she said—" Connie lifted tear-filled eyes to Sister Maria.

"Go on," Sister Maria said softly.

"She said I was a troublemaker, and she said I was big enough to take care of myself. She said she was on her own by the time she was twelve years old, and that I don't need to go to school because all I'm good for is picking vegetables like everyone else."

"But—" Lisa said.

"Shh," cautioned Sister Maria. "Go on, Connie."

"Nina said that I shouldn't think I'm any better than the rest of them, and that I don't need a good education because all I'm going to do is be a field worker, anyway. And I should stop living in a dream world because it's stupid. She said—" Connie wiped away the tears with the back of her hand. Jay reached over and slid an arm around Connie's shoulders, and she seemed to take encouragement from it.

"She said I should take my things and get out. She said if I think the future is going to be so great I might as well start living it and find out what it's really going to be like. And I put all my clothes in a shopping bag and I went to the church." Connie's head drooped and the tears slid off her cheeks to her lap, where they left wet stains on her skirt.

"Don't worry, Connie, everything is going to be okay," Jay said.

"I don't know how," Connie said. Her face was tear-streaked and completely devoid of hope.

"Leave everything to me. Remember, everything I say will happen will come true," Jay said with a reassuring grin.

Connie's expression brightened, and when a solicitous Sister Clementine offered splashes of cold water from the sink in the teachers' lounge, Connie willingly followed her. When they had gone, Sister Maria looked at Jay and Lisa and shook her head.

"You see the problem? Can you imagine saying such things to a child? I shudder to think of what could happen to Connie. If she hadn't felt comfortable coming to us, she would have ended up on the street," said Sister Maria.

"I should go talk to Nina. Immediately," Jay said through tight lips. The expression in his eyes was steely.

"Don't bother, Jay. I went directly to her house after Connie came here, and the other children said that Nina wasn't home. In any case, the immediate problem is that Connie can't go back there tonight," Sister Maria said with great finality.

"You're absolutely right," Jay said. "We can deal with the legal aspects later, but right now our job is to find someplace for Connie to go."

"I called Pelican House, the place that you recommended," Sister Maria said. "Mrs. Daniels claims that they are already filled to capacity."

Jay thought for a moment. "Can Connie stay with you in the convent until we can find a place for her?" he asked.

"According to our regulation, we are not allowed to house children in our convent," Sister Maria said. "Connie truly has no place to go."

"She can come to my house," Lisa said.

Two pairs of eyes blinked at her in surprise.

"I mean it. Connie can stay there tonight and as long as she needs a place to live."

"But you already have Adele," Jay said.

"I know, but it's my house. We have an extra bedroom. Why shouldn't Connie have it?" Lisa began to warm to the idea. She had made her offer impulsively, but she began to see how it would work. She leaned forward in her chair and began to explain.

"I come to the mission every day," Lisa said. "Connie could ride to school with me in the morning. After school she could work in the school art room on the panels for the dining hall and go home with me when it's time to leave. And—and I'd like to have her. I like her," Lisa said, looking from Jay to Sister Maria.

She watched Sister Maria make a steeple of her fingers while she considered Lisa's offer. "Well," Sister Maria said, sounding nonplussed. "It would certainly solve the problem. Of course, we should ask Connie how she feels about living with you, Lisa, and we may have to make some provision for Connie to visit her cousins occasionally."

"Do you really want to do it, Lisa?" Jay asked. He had known that Lisa was kindhearted, but what single woman would want to take on a child, a child whom she barely knew and a child who would need, at the very least, a lot of love in order to overcome the trauma of being thrown away like a piece of garbage?

Lisa smiled at him, a supremely confident smile. "I really want to do it," she assured him. "It'll work out fine. You'll see."

Jay considered Lisa's proposal for a moment, then nodded decisively. "All right, it's settled. Shall we talk to Connie?" he said.

"I'll get her," Sister Maria replied. She stood up and started toward the door but halted for a moment in front of Lisa.

"You see, I *was* right about you. God bless you, Lisa," she said. She smiled and continued out the door, and Jay leaned over and kissed Lisa's cheek.

It wasn't what he'd wanted to do. He'd wanted to thank her for cherishing someone who was precious to him. He'd wanted to sweep her into his arms and tell her how her compassion and kindness had touched him.

He'd wanted to tell her he loved her.

WHEN THE TIRED little group comprised of Jay, Lisa and Connie arrived at Lisa's house that night, all the windows except the one in the living room were dark. Connie hung back when they reached Lisa's front door, but Lisa put her arm around her and urged her forward.

"Come on in," she said. "I'll introduce you to Adele and show you your room."

Jay held the door open for them. Adele was sitting in front of the television set, but she didn't look around. "Did you have a good time?" she asked.

"Yes," Lisa said smoothly, drawing Connie into the circle of light from the table lamp opposite Adele. "I'd like you to meet Connie," she continued. "She's going to live with us for a while." Connie blinked in the bright light.

"Live with us?" Adele said blankly, looking Connie up and down in disbelief.

Lisa telegraphed silently with her eyes, hoping Adele would get the message. *Don't make a big deal out of this,* she pleaded.

Jay stepped neatly into the breach. "Connie's here for a visit, Adele. I'll explain while Lisa shows Connie her room," he said. He planted himself on the couch across from Adele, making it clear that he wasn't going away.

"This way, Connie," Lisa said briskly, throwing Jay a grateful glance as she led Connie into Adele's wing of the house. As she swung the door open to the guest room, she heard Jay say to Adele, "Mind if I turn the TV sound off for a minute?"

"This is where you'll sleep while you're here," Lisa said to Connie. She walked into the room and turned on the lamp beside the bed.

Connie drew in her breath and looked uncertainly up at Lisa. "Come on in," Lisa urged.

Connie's shoes left imprints in the thick rose-colored carpet. Her eyes were wide as she took in the flowered chintz bedspread and matching dust ruffle, the quilted cornice with the sheer white draperies below and the skirted dressing table.

"*My* room?" she asked unbelievingly.

"For as long as you live here," Lisa assured her. She pulled down the shade at the window before opening the closet door and tossing a few hangers on the bed.

"You may hang your clothes in the closet, and you may put your things in any of the dresser drawers. If you want to use the bathroom, it's in there," she told Connie, nodding toward a door.

"A bathroom just for me?" Connie asked, her voice trembling.

"You'll share it with Adele. The bathroom joins her room with yours. Here, I'll show you," she said, swinging the door open and turning on the light.

"Oh," Connie said. "A mirror with lights all around it. And a pretty shower curtain. Ohhh."

"I'd better go see how Adele and Jay are getting along. Come out when you've put your clothes away and we'll see if there's something good to eat in the kitchen." She smiled at Connie and left to rejoin Adele and Jay.

Adele still looked stunned. "What in the world are we going to do with a child?" she asked when Lisa sat down beside Jay on the couch.

"Love her," Lisa said firmly.

Adele's lower lip quivered, and she looked as though she were holding back tears. "A child makes a lot of work. There will be clothes to wash, and she'll make noise, and she won't like to eat the things we eat. Lisa, you have no idea how this is going to change our lives."

"Adele," Lisa said patiently, "I wish it had been possible to discuss this with you before Connie arrived, but there was no time. Sister Maria is going to talk to Connie's father as soon as possible, so this arrangement isn't permanent. Certainly you can adjust to Connie's being here for a short period of time. She truly has no other place to go. And besides," she added as convincingly as she could, "Connie's adorable. You'll like her."

"I'm not so sure of that," Adele said gruffly. She stuffed her knitting into its bag. "I'm going to bed. That child had better not rattle around in the bathroom too early in the morning. You know how I hate to be awakened before seven." She stood up and stalked down the hall. In a moment they heard her bedroom door close sharply.

Lisa sank back against the pillows of the couch. She looked at Jay. "I did my best," she said.

"So did I. It's hard to get through to her, isn't it? All the time I was talking I could tell that she was only thinking of herself and how she was going to be affected. I don't think she even once thought about how tough it would be to be Connie."

"Maybe Adele will loosen up," Lisa said without much hope.

"I can flatter and wheedle and use my charm to get around her, but apparently not when Adele sees herself as the victim of some plot to take away her privacy, wake her up too early in the morning and—what was it?—oh, rattle around in the bathroom," Jay said.

Lisa relaxed, and he took her hand. "I was going to ask you out tonight, but I guess there's not much chance of that, huh?" he said.

"I have to baby-sit," Lisa said primly.

"You know, when I was in high school I used to walk over to the house where my girlfriend baby-sat, and after the babies were in bed we used to smooch on the couch. Like this," he said, and he bent his head to nuzzle the hollow of her throat.

She pulled back, but she had to smother a laugh. "I'm afraid it's against the rules here," she said.

Jay looked downcast for a moment. "Whose rules are these? Adele's? Yours?"

"Mine, mostly. I don't want Connie or Adele to know that we're—we're—" She searched for the right expression, couldn't find it and settled for a helpless little shrug. At the same time she edged over the space of one couch cushion and pulled a throw pillow into her lap for a barricade.

"That we're—um, *involved,*" Jay supplied. He pulled the cushion out of her lap and lobbed it across the room. It was round, and it rolled to a stop in a corner. Then he captured one of her hands in his and leaned across her lap for a long kiss.

"You shouldn't have done that," Lisa said afterward, but she was smiling when she said it.

"I happen to like kissing you," Jay said in a stage whisper.

"Oh," she replied, darting a cagey look at him from under her eyelashes, "I didn't mean that you shouldn't have kissed me. I meant that you shouldn't have thrown the cushion across the room."

"Isn't it called a throw pillow? Isn't that what they're for?" he asked innocently.

"You're impossible," she told him. She was still smiling at him when Connie appeared.

"I love my room, Lisa," Connie said. "It's beautiful. I never had a room all to myself before."

"I'm glad you like it," Lisa told her. She stood up. "I think I recall some frozen yogurt bars hiding deep in the freezer. Let's go into the kitchen and I'll see if I can rustle them up."

"Am I invited, too?" Jay asked.

"Of course," she told him, reaching down and pulling him up from the couch.

They sat around the small kitchen table and ate the yogurt bars. When Connie began to yawn, Jay stood up and tossed their napkins and paper wrappers into the garbage.

"Time for me to be going home," he said. "I can measure time by the size of the yawns."

"Oh, don't go," Connie said, clinging to his hand.

"Sorry, doodlebug, I have to," he said.

Lisa and Connie walked him to the front door, where he placed both hands on Connie's slim shoulders and said, "Don't worry about anything, Connie. Lisa will take good care of you, and I'll see you tomorrow at school."

"Okay," Connie said. She managed a smile and then yawned another enormous yawn, affording them a wide-angle view of her tonsils.

"Would you mind if I said goodbye to Lisa outside?" Jay asked Connie.

"Oh, you can kiss each other if you want. I've seen people kiss each other before," Connie said cheerfully.

Lisa and Jay exchanged startled glances.

"Just to make it easier for you, I'll go get ready for bed," Connie told them.

"I'll come in to say good-night in a few minutes," Lisa called after her as she'd disappeared down the hall. She could have sworn that Connie had winked at her.

"Take your time. I know how to get ready for bed by myself. I'm twelve years old now," Connie called back.

"Thank goodness we've finally gotten permission," Jay said, taking Lisa's hand.

She laughed and leaned her head briefly on his shoulder. After they'd stepped outside, the door swung closed behind them, and hand in hand they walked slowly toward Jay's car. When they were a decent distance from the house Jay pulled her away from the streamers of light from the windows and into the shadows of the surrounding trees, gathering her hungrily into his arms.

"I can't think of any way to tell you how terrific I think you are," he said, keeping his voice low. "What you did today was so kind." The shrubbery sang in his ears; the air was filled with the sound of the ever-present crickets, the chirping of the tree frogs, the hoot of an owl.

"I—"

"Don't say anything," he said. "Just kiss me."

She murmured, "I can't reach," and he lowered his head. Her hands fluttered briefly against his chest, then curved around his shoulders. An ache rose from somewhere deep inside him, a longing to be with her as he had been earlier.

She felt so soft against him, and yet he knew how strong she was inside. Strong enough to take responsibility for a child who wasn't hers and soft enough to melt in his arms when he kissed her. Or was she kissing him? Her tongue found his and her lips were sweet yet greedy, pliant yet insatiable. Quite simply, he could never get enough of them.

His self-control stretched to the limit. He pulled her hips against him, wanting her and knowing that there was no way, not here, not now. He forced himself to deliberately place distance between them and stepped backward, catching her by the hands.

"The way you kiss isn't the only reason I think you're wonderful," he told her shakily, "but it sure helps."

He was on the verge of kissing her again, when suddenly they were startled by a clatter from the direction of the garage. He jumped away, and Lisa dissolved in giggles. Over her shoulder he saw that the garbage can alongside the garage lay on its side and a furry gray shape was scuttling away into the woods.

"What's *that?*" he asked.

"It's only Pudge," she said. She was still giggling, but not so hard.

"Pudge?"

"Pudge the possum," she said. "Adele would like to get rid of him once and for all, but I won't let her."

Jay saw that bits and pieces of garbage were strewn on the grass—a bread wrapper, a tuna-fish can, an empty orange-juice carton.

"What is he, a pet?"

Lisa shook her head. "Not quite. He's wild and I've often put food out for him, but when I don't, he considers our garbage can his own personal cafeteria."

"I think I agree with Adele," Jay said with conviction.

"Why shouldn't Pudge have what we don't want? It can't be easy to scrounge a living from these woods, especially now that so many people have moved in along the river."

She was serious; he couldn't believe it.

He gestured at the garbage. "He makes a mess, that's why."

"Not so much of a mess. Anyway, I'm the one who cleans it up, and I don't mind," Lisa said. "I'd better go. It looks like I'm on call for tucking-in duty. Good night, Jay."

"Not so fast," he said, drawing her close so that he could claim the kiss that had been foiled by the possum, but she soon disengaged herself.

"See you tomorrow," she whispered. As she was hurrying away, he called after her, "Hey, what about the garbage can?"

"I'll pick everything up in a few minutes," she called back, and then she went in the house and closed the door.

He stood for a few moments thinking things over. Then, shaking his head in amazement, he slowly gathered the scattered garbage, put it securely in the garbage can and went and got in his car. He sat there staring at her house; he couldn't believe that anyone would cheerfully and willingly pick up garbage so that a wild possum could cadge a meal.

As he drove back toward town, he reflected that for the first time in his life, he had found a woman to whom he felt like committing himself heart, soul, mind and body. How was he going to get through the whole week without making love to her?

INSIDE LISA PAUSED for a moment to collect herself, then went to Connie's room. Connie was lying on her side in bed, her head pillowed on her hands.

"Just wanted to wish you sweet dreams," Lisa said.

"Thank you, Lisa," Connie said sleepily. "And thanks for letting me come here." She looked so small in the big double bed that Lisa couldn't help tenderly smoothing Connie's hair back from her face.

"I'm glad you're here. Tomorrow there's school, so we'll leave for Yahola at eight o'clock in the morning. Do you want me to set the alarm clock for you?" she offered.

Connie nodded, her eyelids heavy.

"Here, I'll show you how it works so you can do it tomorrow night," Lisa said, sitting down on the edge of the bed. She demonstrated how to set the alarm and how to pull out the button on the back.

After Lisa put the clock back on the table, Connie said, "You know, I don't think I'm as bad as Nina said I am." Her eyes implored Lisa with heartbreaking intensity.

"You're a sweet girl, and we're going to have a lot of fun together," Lisa said encouragingly. "You can teach me how to cook rice and beans the way you like it. And I can show you how to bake granola brownies."

"Mmm," Connie said, thinking it over. "That sounds like fun. Can we go out in the canoe sometime? And maybe I could learn to swim in the river?'' She looked hopeful.

"Of course you can. Now why don't you go to sleep, and I'll see you in the morning."

"Would you—would you mind if I hugged you, Lisa? My mother always used to hug me. I never had a hug at bedtime after she left me with Nina."

Lisa put her arms around Connie and held her close. Her heart ached for the child.

"At my house you can have a hug whenever you need one," she assured Connie as she stood up and turned out the light.

"I'm glad," Connie said in a small voice, and Lisa went out and softly shut the door behind her.

For a moment Lisa stood in front of Adele's closed door, wondering if she should knock. Maybe she could explain further to Adele; maybe she could make her feel better about Connie's presence in their home.

But if Adele was already asleep, she would only be stirring up a hornet's nest, and Lisa already felt emotionally strung out after the unsettling events of the day.

Slowly she turned away. She moved quietly around the house, folding the Sunday newspaper, turning off the muted television set and retrieving the round pillow from the corner where Jay had thrown it. She went out through the door into the kitchen and on into the garage. To her surprise, the garbage can was in its place, its lid was on tight and the garbage had been picked up.

*Jay,* she thought in surprise. *Jay did that for me.*

She went back inside, where Jay's rosebud stood in its vase on the kitchen counter. She touched a fingertip to one pink rose petal. Tomorrow the petals would begin to unfold, and soon the flower would be full-blown. Jay had only given it to her this morning, and yet it seemed like such a long time ago.

Her life had changed so much in the past few weeks; today everything had seemed to be on fast-forward. But she felt optimistic about the future, which seemed about to unfold like the petals of a flower.

## Chapter Nine

As he drove home that night, Jay Quillian, the confirmed bachelor, decided that the impossible had happened. He had begun to imagine being with Lisa for the rest of his life.

He could see it all in his mind. They could live in his town house, go to the beach on weekends, make love every night and most mornings, as well, and they could have children. They were both so comfortable with kids.

What a dream! He could play it out in all its enthralling detail in his head; he could *see* it. And as soon as it became real to him, he began to wonder if it was really possible. With other women, he'd never been able to get past the insurmountable problems.

Jay would never give up his work at the mission, not for any relationship, and most women couldn't comprehend that kind of dedication. But now he was sure that Lisa in all her benevolence could accept his commitment to the mission, and that in itself made her special.

Any woman who could provide a home for an older woman who had no home of her own, who didn't mind possums tipping over her garbage can because they were hungry and who could open her house to a kid with no place to go was the kind of woman he'd been looking for all of his life. But it was the way she had taken Connie to her heart that had been the deciding factor, because Jay knew more about being a throwaway kid than he let on.

When he thought back to his early years of growing up in West Palm Beach, the days seemed awash in sunshine; his life had been happy. Then one day when he was ten his parents had suddenly announced that they were getting a divorce, and his father had moved immediately to Baltimore. His mother found a boyfriend right away.

That year Jay had begun to make the rounds of his relatives' houses, staying with them for nights at a time when his mother was out of town. She liked to accompany her male friends when they traveled on business, and she liked to go to parties.

Sometimes the welcome wore out at his aunts' houses or at his mother's friends' places, and he'd sneak back into the closed-up house where he and his mother lived when she was in town and eat whatever he could scrounge, fending for himself as best he could. Sometimes there wasn't much food, and often he didn't have money to buy more.

After he became a teenager, life was easier. By that time his mother thought it was safe to leave him at home by himself when she left town. Most of the time he had enough food, especially after he got a part-time job washing cars at a car lot up the street. Later he bought a fast car with his earnings, and after that he was mobile.

He was a popular kid, a football player and an honor student. Girls liked him, and the guys enjoyed hanging out at his house. There they found the freedom that they didn't have at their own houses, and it was easy to pick up a few six-packs of beer as they passed an obliging convenience store on the way over.

Jay and his buddies spent a lot of hours whiling away their time, playing poker, experimenting with drinking games that they learned from a friend's older brother who was a junior in college, and anticipating what fun it was going to be when they all got to the University of Florida themselves.

Jay, who was known as Jamie at the time, almost didn't make it.

He could hardly remember the details of that day when his life had crashed down around him; it was all a blur. He and his football buddies had been drinking all day in celebration of their graduation from high school, and late in the afternoon his friends had accepted his high-spirited offer to go buy more beer when they ran out. He barely remembered the slick pavement, the yellow caution light switching to red, the squeal of brakes and then the rain on his face after they pulled him out of his smashed car. He never even saw the girl.

While he was sitting on a gurney in the hospital emergency room, holding a gauze pad to the little nick above one eye that was his sole injury, a somber policeman walked up and told him the girl in the other car was in critical condition and not expected to make it. Later she died.

Jay couldn't believe it. How could she be seriously injured? He was barely scratched. And he was only out to have a good time. He hadn't meant to hurt her.

While he was waiting to find out the girl's fate, he unexpectedly encountered her boyfriend in the rest room; the guy had been throwing up in the sink. He never found out if the other fellow had known who he was.

When the girl died, Jay had been duly charged with manslaughter and had pleaded guilty. After the sentencing, both Jay and his mother had gone for counseling and she had subsequently married a nice man who, in spite of everything, had loved Jay and had adopted him, Jay's birth father having died in the meantime. His mother sobered up and settled down. After she and Fred had two children, a boy and a girl, they had moved to Albuquerque, which was about as far away from West Palm Beach as you could get and still stay in the continental U.S.

Jay didn't blame them for moving so far away. People had talked after the accident, and he could understand why his mother wanted a fresh start for her new family, a family that she was rearing under a completely different philosophy from the way she had brought up Jay.

Some people would think that Jay had paid his debt to society; maybe he had. But Jay didn't think so. He had never forgotten the bleak anguish in the eyes of that man he had seen in the rest room at the hospital. Jay had not only killed someone, but he had stolen that man's life away by killing the girl he loved. He would be atoning for that forever.

He tried. He really did. He gave money to charities and he taught art to kids; he had so little personal life that his law partner kidded him about it.

If he had told people why he was making a gift of his life to others, maybe they would have understood. Then again, maybe they wouldn't. He couldn't take the chance. He didn't want anyone to know that he was the kid who had killed a girl and had gotten off almost scot-free. He was grateful to his stepfather for giving him a new last name, and he himself had changed his first name.

It was, after all, not such a big deal to become Jay instead of Jamie, to become Quillian instead of Watkins, and James Watkins, as far as most people were concerned, had disappeared from the face of the earth almost as completely as that girl he'd killed when he was only seventeen years old.

"I'VE LOCATED Connie's father," Sister Maria told Jay and Lisa when they met her in her office the next afternoon. "He's taken a steady job at a furniture factory in North Carolina."

"How did you manage to find him so fast?" Jay asked in surprise.

Sister Maria walked behind her desk and sat down. "I have to admit that I've been working on this case for a long time. I've always been concerned about those children living with Nina. Last week I talked with someone who had recently seen Carlos—that's the father's name. I telephoned the furniture factory where he works this morning, and he called me back on his lunch break. He's very concerned about Connie," she said.

"Will he send for her?" Lisa asked.

"He says he's living in a crowded house with another family, and there's no room for anyone else, but he's already rented a place that will be available this summer so that he can provide a home for Connie. Life has apparently been hard for him since Connie's mother left."

"You mean her mother isn't coming back?" Jay said.

"It looks like she's decided to stay in California with another man. This family has had a lot of hardship, but Carlos thinks it's all behind them now. Until June or July, when he is sure he can send for her, he wants Connie to stay with Nina. Or Lisa," Sister Maria said.

"Connie is welcome at my house as long as necessary," Lisa said firmly.

"I went out to the fields to talk with Nina this morning," Jay said. "She finally admitted that she doesn't have legal custody of Connie. Just as I suspected, she's not Connie's grandmother, only a distant relative. I told her that we'd see that Connie was taken care of, but she got on her high horse and said that Connie has to spend some time with her cousins once in a while, and that she should be allowed to visit.''

"Why didn't Nina think of that before she threw Connie out of the house?" Lisa asked skeptically.

"My guess is that the boys raised the roof when they found out that Connie was gone for good, and in order to shut them up, Nina told them that Connie would come back occasionally. I thought that Connie would miss the boys, so I agreed that she could visit Nina every other Sunday evening. If there's any sign of mistreatment, of course, we'll stop it. After all, Nina has no legal hold on Connie," he said.

"Did Nina say anything else?" Sister Maria asked.

"One other thing," Jay said, his voice tinged with irony. "She said she didn't want to see Connie hanging around the house uninvited."

"How could she say that? I'm so sick of her treating Connie like a disposable kid!" Lisa said, her eyes flashing.

Jay shrugged elaborately. "At least Connie's out of there," he said. "I still worry about the boys, though. I wonder if Nina's treating them well."

Sister Maria sighed. "Well enough, I think," she said. "Some of the other sisters and I have talked with the boys individually, and they seem to have a strong affection for each other. Also, Miguel, the oldest, is quite strong and capable. I can assure you that we're going to keep a close watch on the situation and will be in touch with the social-welfare department at the first sign of any problem."

Jay turned to Lisa. "How is Adele doing?" he asked.

"We didn't see her this morning before we left," Lisa told him. "I don't know what kind of mood she'll be in when we get home, but Connie and I are planning to eat dinner in the community-center dining hall, anyway. I intend to have a serious talk with Adele tonight."

Sister Maria walked them to the door. "Don't worry too much about all of this," she said encouragingly. "Migrant children are like little chameleons. They learn to adapt to different places over and over all their lives, but if you have any problems with Connie, Lisa, let me know."

After saying goodbye to Sister Maria, Jay and Lisa walked slowly back to the community center.

"Have you seen Connie since this morning?" Jay asked.

Lisa shook her head. "I've been in Sister Maria's office all day. She was filling me in on Connie's family problems. I wonder how Connie has been able to cope so far—her parents abandoning her, and Nina's coldness toward her and now the uncertainty of her future. It's a wonder she's not an emotional basket case."

"She's stronger than you think," Jay said. He sensed that Lisa was troubled, and he slid an arm around her shoulders. "How are you feeling?" he asked.

"Apprehensive," she admitted. "Maybe I've bitten off more than I can chew."

He felt a sudden sympathy for her. "I'll help all I can, you know," he said reassuringly.

"I'm counting on it," she told him. "To me, loving is giving. It sounds so easy, and I feel so glib when I say the words. At the same time I realize that I've never had the responsibility of taking care of a child before, and with the magnitude of Connie's problems—well, it's scary. I hope I'm equal to the task."

Listening to her speak, Jay felt deeply moved. At the same time he admired Lisa for voicing her fears. Yesterday she had jumped in with both feet; today she was having second thoughts. He was glad that she felt comfortable admitting them to him.

"Tell you what," he said as they approached the kitchen. "I'll pay special attention to Connie this afternoon. Occasionally she opens up to me, and I'll report to you if anything seems unusual."

"Thanks," she said, gazing up at him. Somehow she managed to look beatific as well as concerned; whenever he'd decided that her face had a finite number of expressions, he was treated to a new one.

He wanted to kiss away the worried line between her eyebrows, but he couldn't, not here. Instead he walked her as far as the kitchen door. "I hear the clarion tones of Sister Clementine singing at the sink, and behind her Sister Ursula is slamming pots and pans around," he said, trying to lighten the mood.

"In other words, everything is normal in the kitchen," Lisa said, and much to his relief, she laughed and went inside.

Sister Clementine greeted Lisa happily. "Connie stopped by the kitchen a little while ago. She's so excited about starting to work on the panels for the dining hall today," she said.

"I'm sorry I missed her," Lisa said, making herself think about work. She'd spent the whole day away from the kitchen, and there were things she needed to do.

She checked the pantry. "By the way," she said, "have either of you found that big can of cashews yet?"

"Cashew—it sounds like a sneeze," Sister Clementine mused.

"Sounds more like a curse," Sister Ursula said.

"Sister!" exclaimed Sister Clementine.

"Well, it does." Sister Ursula wiped her hands on her apron and folded her arms across her chest. "Lisa, are we going to have to put up with Connie bothering us in the kitchen every day after school now that she's going to be waiting around for you to take her home?" she asked.

"Connie will be working in the art room after school every day, but I'll speak to her if it's necessary," Lisa assured her through gritted teeth.

"Speaking of Connie," Sister Ursula continued, "Sister Catalina says that the girl wasn't concentrating in class today. Sounds like she's going all to pieces over this thing."

"She's more likely to be picking *up* the pieces," chided Sister Clementine. "Wouldn't you say that's it, Lisa?"

But Lisa had tired of their constant needling back and forth. She pretended she hadn't heard and closeted herself in her office.

Later, when she had developed a crick in her neck from bending over her paperwork, she took a break. Avoiding Sisters Ursula and Clementine, she walked outside and headed across the sandy field toward the school.

Most of the children had gone home for the day. The others had stayed behind to work in the garden, the art room or to attend Sister Maria's special study hall. In the art room, Connie, working with Pedro, was sketching a huge pencil outline on one of the plywood panels when Lisa arrived. Upon closer inspection, the drawing proved to be an immense tomato sliced in two.

"What do you think so far?" Connie asked.

"Seedy," Lisa said as Connie concentrated on making little circles.

Connie wrinkled her nose. "I mean really—does it look like a tomato?"

"Looks more like the attack of the killer tomatoes," Jay said, coming up behind Lisa and surreptitiously kissing the side of her neck when Connie and Pedro weren't looking.

"What can we do for you?" he asked Lisa, his smile starting in his eyes and working its way downward.

"I was just—checking on the progress of the panels," she said.

"And on Connie?" Jay asked in a low tone.

Lisa nodded.

"Everything is fine," he assured her.

"Lisa, what will we have for dinner tonight in the dining hall?" Pedro asked. He was mixing red-orange paint with total disregard for the walls, the floor and his clothes.

"Fish stew and rice," Lisa told him. "And I hope I'll meet your mother in my nutrition class tomorrow afternoon."

"Mama can't come, but my older sister will be there," Pedro said. He stopped churning paint and stepped back to assess Connie's tomato. It apparently met with his approval, because he picked up the paint stirrer and began to stir vigorously. "Did Connie tell you that we're going to draw the green peppers next?" he asked.

"Which reminds me—I'd better make sure that Sister Clementine doesn't add a whole bucketful of green peppers to the fish stew the way she did with the meat loaf the other night," Lisa said, moving toward the door.

Jay caught up with her in the hall. "I've been thinking," he said with an abashed grin. "How long do we have to wait until we get together?"

"Quite a while, unless we rendezvous in the pantry under the watchful eyes of Sisters Ursula and Clementine," Lisa said ruefully.

"No one's around. Don't you know what I want? Don't you know—"

*"Yes,"* she hissed, and then she fled.

"I'll phone you tonight," he called after her, and she knew he was laughing.

When she suddenly arrived back in the kitchen, her cheeks still pink, Sister Clementine spared a sharp glance in Lisa's direction.

"Lisa, do you think it's too hot in here? I could turn on the fan if you'd like," she offered.

"If you turn on the fan, you'll have to clean up the mess when this flour flies all over the place," Sister Ursula warned.

"I think the temperature is perfect," Lisa told them before disappearing into the pantry, where she peered anxiously at her reflection in the bottom of a stainless-steel mixing bowl until her color returned to normal.

JAY TELEPHONED Lisa early that evening.

"How's Adele?" he asked.

Lisa paused. "She wasn't around when we came in at seven-thirty, but her car's in the garage. I think she's barricaded in her room, sulking."

"How's Connie?"

"Okay," Lisa said cautiously.

"Want me to come over? I could bring my checkerboard and play checkers with Connie while you try to open a discussion with Adele. Or vice versa, whichever you think would work best."

Lisa didn't know how she was going to deal with her housemate, but she definitely wanted to see Jay.

"When can you get here?" she asked, smiling into the phone.

He could hear the smile in her voice. "Half an hour. Is that too soon?" Now that he knew he was going to see her tonight, he felt exhilarated beyond belief.

"Fifteen minutes would be better," she told him, and he laughed.

"I'll hurry," he told her.

After Lisa hung up, Connie pushed her math homework aside. "Is Jay going to be here soon?" she asked.

"Before you know it," Lisa said happily.

"I think I'll go fix my hair," Connie said, slipping off the chair and heading toward her room.

Lisa was sweeping the floor when Connie returned.

"Somebody cleaned my hairbrush," Connie announced.

"'Twasn't I," Lisa told her abstractedly.

"I think it was the other lady."

"Adele? Hmm. It could have been, I suppose," Lisa said in surprise.

"I left my brush next to the sink this morning and when I came back it was all clean and nice and it smelled good. And you know, when I left my shoes in the garage that day we went out in the canoe? They were clean, too, when I got them back."

"Adele is a very nice person," Lisa said carefully as she put the broom away in the closet. "She's always doing something kind for me—for instance, typing all my employment applications when I was looking for a job. I'm the world's worst typist, and Adele is good at it, and she said she didn't mind. She wouldn't have had to do that."

Connie closed her math book and slid her paper between its pages. "Why is Adele such a grouch? Why doesn't she come out of her room? Does she stay in there all the time?" she asked.

"No, she doesn't stay in there all the time, but she's sometimes not so happy," Lisa said, and she sat down across the table from Connie and told her an abbreviated version of Adele's life story. "So you see, Connie," she concluded, "Adele has lost everyone who was important to her."

Connie thought about this for a long moment. "It must be like when my parents went away and left me with Nina. I felt like they had died," she said.

"I think it *is* something like that," Lisa said quietly. "Maybe you can understand better than anyone how Adele feels."

"I do. But you know, she'll never get to feel better if she doesn't come out of her room," Connie said seriously.

"You're right. After dinner I'll go talk with her," Lisa said.

"I'd like to thank her for cleaning my brush and my shoes. Do you think she'd like to have one of the pictures I drew of the zoo? I brought one of them here with me— it has monkeys in it."

"She might," Lisa said cautiously.

"I'll go get it," Connie said, jumping up and running to her room. When she came back, she was carrying a cleverly done crayon drawing of three comical monkeys sitting on a rock; Lisa laughed when she saw it because she remembered the scene, and Connie had caught the monkey's expressions perfectly.

"We'll tack your picture to the refrigerator for now," Lisa said, producing two magnets from a drawer.

The drawing of the monkeys was in place when Jay arrived, and he laughed at it, too. When Jay and Connie set up the checkerboard in the den, it was in a mood of hilarity that Adele could surely hear, and after Jay and

Connie settled down to their game, Lisa wasted no time in knocking on Adele's door.

"Come in," Adele said. When Lisa opened the door, she found Adele sitting on a rocking chair by the window.

"I wanted to see how you are," Lisa told her, perching on the edge of the bed.

"Not much sense in that," Adele said with the air of a martyr. She looked as though she had been crying.

"Connie thought you might like to have this picture. She drew it after we all went to the zoo," Lisa said, producing the picture of the monkeys and unfurling it for Adele's benefit.

Adele studied it. "She drew this?" she said.

"Yes, isn't she a good artist?" Lisa replied.

"Pretty good," Adele said without much interest.

"Here, I'll stick it on your mirror," Lisa said, getting up and walking to the dresser. Adele didn't say anything while Lisa affixed the picture in the frame beside a grade-school photo of Megan.

"Connie said to tell you thank you for cleaning her brush," Lisa said.

"It was nothing," Adele said.

"To her it was. She's not used to anyone doing nice things for her."

"I'd have done it for anyone. When is she leaving, anyway?"

"She'll be staying with us until her father comes to get her, which will probably be in June or July."

"It's only February," Adele said glumly.

"She's a cute little thing, Adele," Lisa said. "She's also fun and talented and easy to have around. She's not any trouble."

"As long as she doesn't wake me up too early, we'll get along fine."

"She wasn't noisy in the morning, was she?" Lisa asked.

A long silence. "Well, no," Adele admitted.

"I'm glad to hear that," Lisa said. She stood up and forced herself to speak in a bright and cheerful tone.

"Jay's here. He and Connie are playing checkers, and I get to take on the winner. We'd love to have you join us if you'd like, even if you only want to watch," she said.

"I'm fine right here," Adele said obstinately.

"Well, keep it in mind," Lisa told her. Adele said nothing as Lisa went out and closed the door behind her.

Connie was chortling with glee when Lisa walked into the den. "I just made one of my men a king," she told Lisa, her eyes dancing.

Lisa sat down close to Jay. He smiled at her, his eyes lighted from deep within. "Well?" he said.

"Adele is—resting," Lisa said.

"Oh. I see," Jay replied.

"Resting from what? From being sad?" Connie asked as she waited for Jay to make his next move.

"In a manner of speaking, I suppose so," Lisa said, trying not to smile.

"Well," Connie said, "if I was Adele, I'd read a good book. That cheers me up sometimes. You know how a book kind of makes you part of its world and takes you out of the one you're in? That's good, especially if you don't like your own world very much."

Jay slid one of his men over to another square, and Connie bent over the board in concentration.

"Should I try to talk to Adele?" Jay asked Lisa in a low tone.

Lisa shook her head. "It wouldn't do any good, at least right now."

Connie, her tongue between her teeth, made her move. "Did you give Adele my picture?" she asked Lisa, glancing up.

"I certainly did," Lisa said.

"Good," Connie said. "Jay, it's your move."

Adele did not come out of her room for the rest of the evening. Connie won the first game, and Lisa won the second. While Jay and Lisa played, Connie wandered to a bookcase and browsed through Lisa's collection of books.

"What are you doing, Connie?" Jay asked her.

"Choosing something for Adele to read," Connie called over her shoulder.

"I don't think—" Lisa began, but Jay nudged her foot under the table.

"Let her," he mouthed silently.

Jay won handily this time, then Lisa and Jay sat together in the darkened living room while Connie gathered up her schoolbooks from the kitchen table. In a few minutes she walked into the living room and turned on a lamp.

"I'm going to bed now," she said. "I found a good book in your bookcase that I'd like to read, Lisa. It's called *Little Women*. Do you mind if I borrow it?"

"That was one of my favorite books when I was about your age," Lisa said. She recalled that Megan had given it to her for her eleventh birthday, just before she'd moved back to West Palm Beach from Stuart.

"Another thing I'm going to do is write Adele a note and leave it in the book of poems I picked out for her," Connie said. She hesitated for a moment. "Lisa, do you mind if I hug you?" she asked falteringly.

Lisa held her arms open. "You know you may have a hug whenever you need one," she said warmly, and Connie flew to her, burying her face in Lisa's shoulder.

Jay smiled at Lisa over Connie's shiny head.

"Don't I get a hug, too?" he asked Connie.

"Sure," Connie said, obliging happily. Afterward she scampered away toward her room, humming a song under her breath.

Jay slid his arm around Lisa. "Connie's adjusting well, don't you think?" he asked.

"Absolutely," Lisa said. "It's Adele who is making the problem."

"The real problem," he said, bending over to nibble on her earlobe, "is that I want us to be together. Alone."

"I wish you wouldn't joke," she said, pulling away in irritation. "What if Adele never relents about Connie? How can the three of us go on living together for the next several months if Adele is no more than a shadow presence?" She focused troubled eyes on his face.

"Lisa? Do you have a pencil sharpener?" Connie asked coming to the end of the hall.

"I'll get it," Lisa said, standing up and gracefully stepping over Jay's feet, and he sat back and considered Lisa's problem.

What *would* she do if Adele decided to make their lives miserable? Quite possibly, there was no good answer.

And with all these worries swirling around them, distracting them and gobbling up their time, how were he and Lisa ever going to find space for themselves?

## Chapter Ten

That night a cold front settled in, and the next morning Lisa put on a wool skirt and found a warm cardigan that would fit Connie, who had brought no winter clothes from Nina's house.

Lisa wished that people who thought there were no seasons in South Florida could experience a morning like this one. She turned on the car heater and shivered until warm air flowed out of the vents. This morning the river was gray and sluggish, its saw-grass fringe shrouded in wispy shreds of fog. On the road to Yahola, the naked cypress trunks, which would be wreathed in tender green foliage in the spring, loomed as stark silhouettes in front of the rising sun.

The cold didn't seem to daunt Connie, however. This morning she seemed bright and chipper.

"I left the book I chose for Adele next to the bathroom sink," Connie said before they reached the mission. "She can't help but find it. She'll look down while she's brushing her teeth, and—surprise!—there it is!" Connie giggled at the idea.

"Maybe a few surprises would be good for Adele," Lisa told her with a smile. "She doesn't have enough excitement in her life."

"We'll just have to fix that, won't we?" Connie said, and Lisa laughed out loud at the mischievous expression on Connie's face. If only Adele would loosen up, she couldn't help falling in love with Connie.

Connie thumbed quietly through one of her schoolbooks, and Lisa marveled that the world could go on spinning, that everything could look the same but not be the same and that no one knew that she had fallen in love with Jay Quillian.

This was not one of the days when Jay was scheduled to work at the school, nor was it a day when the dining hall would serve a meal. Lisa caught up on menus, planned the next week's shopping and taught a nutrition class that afternoon. It was a busy day, and she had little time to think about Adele. When she did, she quickly put the thoughts out of her mind. She didn't like to think about Adele's antagonism.

That afternoon she and Connie were riding home from Yahola when Lisa thought of a peace offering. Adele loved chocolate éclairs from the supermarket bakery; Lisa sometimes stopped and bought several on the way home from work. The parking lot at the supermarket didn't look particularly crowded today, so it wouldn't take long to run inside and out again. Lisa turned in and pulled her car into a parking space.

"Why are we stopping here?" Connie wanted to know.

"Oh, Adele loves to eat chocolate éclairs. I thought we'd buy some."

"Can I go in the store and get them? All by myself?" Connie asked.

"Well—"

"I always shop for Nina," Connie said.

Connie looked so eager that Lisa smiled. She counted out five dollars from her wallet and gave them to Connie:

"Ask the woman behind the counter to put the éclairs in a box, not a bag," she called out the window.

"I will," Connie called back.

Lisa sat back to wait, thinking about Jay. She hoped he'd come over tonight; she'd thought about him so much during the day that she could hardly wait. Her reverie ended when Connie returned sooner than Lisa had expected. She was carefully balancing a white cardboard box in both hands.

"I got six éclairs, two for each of us," Connie announced.

"Just put the change in my wallet," Lisa told her.

"There wasn't any," Connie said.

Lisa raised her eyebrows. "No change?" she repeated. The way she calculated it, she should have received eighty cents back.

"Nope," Connie said, avoiding her eyes.

"They must have raised the price," Lisa said, but she soon forgot about it when Connie began to relate a long-winded tale about something that had happened on the playground that day.

Adele wasn't around when they came in, and Lisa and Connie made tacos for dinner, chattering all the while. For dessert they ate their éclairs, which Connie pronounced "scrumptious," a new word that she'd recently learned from Sister Clementine.

Later, when Adele still hadn't left her room, Lisa took her an éclair, and although Adele's eyes lighted up when she saw it, she still hadn't relented about Connie. It was with a feeling of despair that Lisa left Adele's room; she hated the division in this household.

As she passed Connie's open bedroom door, she heard Connie singing in the shower, a jaunty Mexican song, and her first thought was that Connie's singing might disturb Adele.

*Let it,* she thought defiantly, and she went into Connie's room to wait for her to get out of the shower so she could ask if Connie needed any help with her homework.

Connie had left her jeans lying on the floor, and Lisa, feeling motherly, automatically picked them up. As she was folding them, a piece of paper fell out of one of the pockets.

Lisa's first thought was that it might be a homework assignment, but when she unfolded it, she saw that it was the receipt for the éclairs. Her eyes leaped to the total; four dollars and twenty cents. She had been right, after all—she should have received eighty cents in change!

She stared at the receipt, wondering why Connie had lied. It was a small amount of money, it was true, but it wasn't the money that upset her. It was the fact that Connie had lied.

Slowly she put the jeans in a drawer and sat down on the edge of the bed to think. A glint of silver winked up from one of Connie's sneakers. Lisa slowly bent and picked up the shoe; when she upended it, exactly eighty cents—three quarters and a nickel—fell into her lap.

Lisa felt sick. The evidence was too clear to ignore. Connie had lied about the change and had hidden the money in her shoe. But why? Did she need money for something?

No. Sister Maria had been quite clear on Sunday when they had all talked to Connie about the new living arrangements. The mission would provide Connie with an ample allowance. And if she needed more money, all she would have to do was to ask Sister Maria.

The shower and the song stopped, and Lisa steeled herself to confront the child. When the door opened and Connie saw Lisa, her face lighted up with a bright smile that immediately began to fade as soon as she saw the strained expression on Lisa's face. Connie's own expression became wary and guarded. She tightened the knot of the belt on her bathrobe and walked nonchalantly to the dresser, where she began to drag a comb through her wet hair.

"Connie," Lisa said quietly, "we'd better talk."

Connie whirled around, her eyes bright. Too bright, Lisa thought.

"Oh?" Connie said. "What about?"

Lisa held her hand out and opened her fist. The money gleamed coldly in the lamplight. "This," Lisa said.

When Connie didn't speak, Lisa said, "I found it in your shoe. And this receipt fell out of the pocket of your jeans."

Connie stared, her face expressionless.

"Well?" Lisa said quietly.

Connie lifted frightened eyes to Lisa's. There was a long silence.

"What are you going to do to me?" Connie finally asked. Her voice trembled.

"Do? Why, I expect an explanation," Lisa said firmly.

Connie's face crumpled. "I—I kept the money be-cause—because—" Connie said, and tears welled in her eyes.

"Connie," Lisa said kindly, "come sit beside me." She patted the bedspread.

Reluctantly, Connie sat. She wouldn't look at Lisa, and Lisa reached out and turned Connie's head toward her.

"You can hit me if you want," Connie said brokenly. "I don't care."

"I'm not going to hit you," Lisa said. "All I want you to do is explain why you lied. You told me there was no change for the éclairs."

"I don't know," Connie said, lowering her head. She stared at the rug.

"Do you need money? If you do, we should speak to Sister Maria about an advance on your allowance," Lisa said.

Connie wiped a tear away with the back of one hand. "I'm so ashamed. Please don't tell Sister Maria," she whispered.

"Well, why did you keep the money? Why did you lie?"

"When Nina sends me into a store to buy something, I always tell her it cost more than it really did. I keep the money in an old stuffed rabbit. Look," she said, and she pulled a decrepit toy rabbit out from under the bed and tugged some of the stuffing out of its stomach. A cascade of nickels, dimes and quarters rained down on the bedspread, accompanied by a flurry of one-dollar bills.

"Why do you need the money?" Lisa asked in mystification.

"To go to my father. When he wants me, that is."

Connie began to scoop the money up and stuff it into the rabbit.

"Oh, Connie," Lisa said helplessly. "Surely your father will send you the money when it's time, or Sister Maria will loan it to you, or Jay or I will give it to you. You don't need to steal."

Connie bit her lip, and Lisa sensed that she was holding back sobs. "I can't count on other people," she said. "Only on myself. And I don't have many ways to get the money, and I want to be with my father more than anything else in the world. He wrote me a letter, but he didn't say if he could pay my way to meet him, and money's always a problem in our family. It always was." She pulled a tattered piece of notebook paper out of her pillowcase and handed it to Lisa.

It was the letter that Carlos Fernandez had written to his daughter, and after Lisa skimmed through it there was no doubt in her mind that Carlos was as eager to be with his daughter as she was to be with him. True, the letter didn't mention how Connie was to be reunited with him, but it made it clear that there was a lot of love between father and daughter.

Lisa waited until the money was safely back in the rabbit before she set the letter aside and folded Connie in her arms. Connie, unable to hold back any longer, broke into a torrent of tears. Lisa rocked her for a long time, crooning comfort into her ear.

Finally the crying stopped, and Connie disentangled herself. Lisa handed her a tissue from the box beside the bed, and Connie blew her nose.

"I must look awful," Connie said.

Lisa smoothed a stray lock of coal black hair back behind Connie's ear and tried to smile. "I've seen you look better," she admitted.

"It's way past my bedtime," Connie said.

Lisa glanced at the clock. "So it is," she agreed. "I'd better let you get to sleep. One thing, Connie—don't lie to me again. You can say anything to me as long as it's true, but no more lies. Understood?"

"Understood," Connie said slowly. "You really mean that, Lisa? I can say anything to you?"

"Yes," Lisa said. "But I can't tolerate dishonesty."

"Okay, Lisa. I'm sorry I kept the money."

"I would have given it to you if you'd asked," Lisa said.

"I'll give it back right now," Connie said, reaching for the rabbit.

"I don't want it," Lisa said, staying Connie's hand. "And remember, when the time comes to go to your dad and you need money, we'll see that you get it. There's no need to steal."

"All right. Good night, Lisa," Connie said.

"Good night, Connie," Lisa said, going out and closing the door behind her. She leaned against the wall, feeling wrung out and completely devoid of energy. She hadn't known that dealing with Connie would take every bit of resourcefulness that she possessed.

Later, when Jay called and Lisa told him about the incident, he was flabbergasted. "I never would have expected this of Connie," he said. "Never in a thousand years."

"I really don't care that she kept the money," Lisa said. "It's the lie that upset me the most. I can't stand it when people lie to me."

Jay didn't say anything for so long that she thought he must have dropped the phone.

"Jay?" she said.

He cleared his throat. "Yes, well, I know how you feel," he said lamely.

"What I mean is, if Connie could lie to me about this, what else could she lie about?" Lisa said in a troubled voice.

"Exactly," Jay said, and although he had been going to suggest that he come over, he decided that it wouldn't be a good idea.

"I'm going to bed," Lisa said. She sounded discouraged, disheartened, upset.

"I'll talk to you tomorrow," Jay told her, and he hung up gently. Afterward he sat in his darkened living room, staring at nothing and wondering about everything.

A WEEK WENT BY; Connie caused no further problems, and Lisa began to relax again. Jay came over every night, lending support and bringing gifts. He brought Connie a toy monkey on a stick because it reminded him of the picture she had drawn for Adele, and he brought Lisa a steering-wheel cover for her car because she had complained that the steering wheel felt too cold on chilly mornings. He gave Connie a new set of paintbrushes and Lisa an outlandish ponytail holder with neon ribbons trailing from it. He even brought Adele something, a box of mints. It had no effect, however. Adele never came out of her room when Connie was in the house.

Finally, when Lisa had given up hope that things at home would ever improve and when Connie had stopped asking curious questions about "the lady in the bedroom," they came home for dinner one night during a cold snap and found a pot of stew simmering on a back burner of the stove.

Adele walked briskly into the kitchen. "I thought stew might taste good on a chilly night like tonight," she said matter-of-factly.

Lisa set down the bag of groceries they'd brought and took off her jacket, which she hung on the back of one of the kitchen chairs. Connie stood and gawked at Adele until Lisa gave her a gentle nudge.

"Why don't you set the table, Connie?" Lisa suggested,

"I'll put my schoolbooks in my room first," Connie said.

When Connie had gone, Lisa said, "It's good to see you out and about, Adele."

Adele stirred the stew. She said nothing.

Lisa tried again. "You'll like Connie if you give her a chance," she said.

"I don't want to get attached to her. She'll be leaving, won't she?" Adele said.

"Eventually she'll leave, but in the meantime she needs a lot of love and attention," Lisa argued.

"All right, all right," Adele said. "Would you mind making a salad? This stew's been ready for half an hour." Lisa thought Adele's expression softened when Connie came in and began to set the table, but she couldn't be sure.

The stew was delicious. "How do you make this, Adele?" Connie asked.

Adele chewed slowly before swallowing, and Lisa held her breath. She didn't think she could bear it if Adele was rude to Connie. But Adele only said, "Oh, it's just a matter of a little of this and a little of that."

"A little of what and a little of *what?*" Connie persisted.

"A little carrot and a little potato, and I always add some dill. I *like* dill," Adele said thoughtfully.

"I don't know what dill is," Connie said.

"You don't?" Adele said in surprise.

"Nope. It sounds like your name. A *dill*," and Connie laughed.

Lisa was surprised to see Adele's mouth turn up at the corners. "I have some dill seeds in the garage," Adele said.

"It's something that grows? In the ground?"

"It's a plant. We could start some seeds in a flower pot," Adele said.

"Connie could set the pot in her window where it will catch the sun," Lisa suggested quickly.

"Oh, wow! And grow a plant? Of my own?" Connie wriggled with delight.

"Well, I don't know if you'd want to grow a plant," Adele said, and it seemed to Lisa as if Adele was about to slip back into her uncommunicative state.

"Connie helps Jay in the garden at school, and she's painting pictures of vegetables to decorate the dining hall at the mission's community center," Lisa said desperately.

"Did you like the picture I gave you?" Connie demanded of Adele.

"I—I liked it fine," Adele said reluctantly, picking at her meat.

"It's my favorite because I liked the monkeys at the zoo. And the elephants. Have you ever seen a flamingo, Adele?"

"A flamingo—why, yes, when my second husband and I went on our honeymoon to Nassau in the Bahamas we went to a show of some sort, flamingos parading around. It was lovely. Very lovely," Adele said. For a moment she looked like the old Adele, the one Lisa remembered before Megan's accident.

"I could draw you a picture of some flamingos to go with the monkey picture. I'd *like* to draw a flamingo picture. How about if you show me how to plant the dill

seeds after dinner and I draw you the picture tonight? Is
that a fair trade?''

Adele wrinkled her forehead at Connie. ''I don't
think—'' she began, but Lisa interrupted.

''I bought some potting soil just the other day,'' she
said. ''I can clean up the kitchen while you show Connie
how to plant the dill seeds.''

''Oh, good! I can hardly wait!'' Connie beamed and
Adele shifted uncomfortably in her chair, clearly aware
that there was no getting out of participating in the evening's activities short of throwing down her fork and
stomping back to her bedroom.

The phone rang. ''Oh, Lisa, may I answer the phone?''
Connie hopped up and bounced restlessly on the balls of
her feet.

''Go ahead,'' Lisa said.

Connie ran into the kitchen, grabbed the phone off the
hook and in a moment said, ''Hi, Jay! I kind of knew it
was you. Are you coming over? You are? Oh, good!
Here's Lisa.''

Lisa took the phone eagerly from Connie's out-
stretched hand.

''What's on the agenda for tonight?'' he asked.

''Adele and Connie are going to plant some seeds, and
Connie is going to draw a picture of flamingos,'' she said.

''Adele and Connie? Have I missed something?''

''I'll explain later. Anyway, tonight I happen to be
free,'' she said.

''How free? Can we go skinny-dipping in the river?''

''Where do you get these ideas?'' Lisa asked.

''They occur naturally whenever you come to mind. If
you're not interested in swimming, how about if I bring
Hildy over and we all go for a walk along the river road?
Would you mind?''

"No, and I'm sure that Connie would enjoy it," Lisa said.

"I hope Hildy will. She's perked up in the last day or two, so I think the exercise will do her good. We'll see you in an hour or so."

"I'll tell Connie," Lisa said.

"I love you," he told her.

And she said, "I do, too."

"Can't you say it?"

"Not at the moment," Lisa said cautiously.

"At a later moment, then. And I expect you to show me just how much."

"I hope you won't be too disappointed," she said, watching Adele out of the corners of her eyes. Adele had begun to stack the plates at the table, but Lisa knew she was avidly listening to every word.

"I'm never disappointed with you. 'Bye," he said, and the dial tone buzzed in Lisa's ear.

"Tell me what?" Connie said close behind her, and Lisa, taken by surprise, jumped.

"Jay will bring Hildy over and we can all go for a walk," Lisa told her.

"I love Hildy. She's almost like a real person. Better, maybe," Connie said with a happy grin. She went to help Adele clear the table, and Lisa began to rinse the plates.

"Hildy can count better than most people," remarked Lisa.

Adele raised her eyebrows. "A dog that does arithmetic?" she said skeptically.

Lisa explained, and Connie laughed. "Hildy can't add. I know how Jay does it," she said.

"How?" Adele asked, sounding interested.

"He holds the dog biscuit in front of Hildy's face, and after she barks the correct number of times, he drops his hand just the littlest bit, and Hildy knows to stop barking," Connie told them gleefully.

While Lisa was still mulling over this revelation, Connie confronted Adele.

"Aren't you going to show me how to plant the dill, Adele?" she asked.

"Well, I thought maybe tomorrow," Adele said.

"You said before that you'd show me tonight. Tonight, tonight, tonight!" Connie said playfully, grabbing Adele's limp hand and pulling her toward the door that led to the garage. Adele let herself be propelled along, scarcely protesting, and when the door swung shut behind them, Lisa could have sworn that Adele was holding back laughter.

Lisa listened to the two of them in the garage for a moment, decided that Connie's banter was exactly what Adele needed and hung her apron up behind the kitchen door. With Connie and Adele keeping each other busy, she hurried to her room and chucked her work clothes in favor of jeans and a black turtleneck topped with a favorite sweater.

She stopped for a moment to stare at herself in the mirror. She looked like the same person that she'd been a few weeks ago, but she certainly didn't feel the same. She was in love. She loved Jay so much that to be apart from him caused her to ache physically, created a hollow in her very soul, made her conjure up constant thoughts of him.

She heard a car door slam outside, ran to the window and saw Jay trying to coax Hildy out of the back seat of his car. She hurried to let them in, but Connie had seen them too. They both stood at the door, waiting while Jay urged Hildy along, and when at last they were inside,

Connie knelt on the tile floor, burying her face in Hildy's silky fur.

Jay captured a quick kiss and smiled down at Lisa. "I thought we could ask Adele to go on our walk with us," he said.

At the sound of her name, Adele appeared in the entrance to the kitchen. She was carrying two clay pots full of dirt.

Connie jumped up. "See, Lisa? See, Jay? Adele and me planted seeds in these pots and we're going to put them in the sun and water them so they'll grow. It's better than our garden at school because they'll be inside. Come on, Adele, let's put one in your window and one in mine."

Adele didn't say a word. She merely shrugged and followed Connie down the hall to their rooms, an amused expression on her face.

"Well, that's something," Jay said, pulling Lisa into his arms and kissing her properly this time. Hildy sighed and lay down across their feet, resting her chin on her paws.

"Mmm," Lisa said, slipping out of the circle of his arms as Adele and Connie reappeared. If Adele's look was suspicious, Lisa pretended not to notice.

"How about it, Adele? Would you like to go for a walk with us?" Jay asked.

"Well, I—"

Connie danced around them. "Please go! It'll be dark and scary and Lisa and Jay will want to walk beside each other and whisper, and you and I could walk together."

"You could walk with Hildy," Adele told Connie in a small voice.

"Hildy may be able to do arithmetic, but she sure can't talk to me. Oh, Adele, please?" Connie was irresistible as she eagerly waited for the answer.

A ghost of a smile flickered over Adele's lips. "All right, I'll go. Is it cold out?" she asked.

"Most of the cold wave has passed through, but you'll still need a sweater," Jay said.

After they had all put on something warm, the four of them stepped out into the cool night air. Overhead the stars shone in sharp brilliance and the moon flickered through the pine branches. An uncertain breeze wound around the house and blew the soft green scent of the water into their faces; Lisa and Jay smiled at each other, a secret smile sharing their own special happiness, and Hildy even managed a few frisky steps before settling down to a more sedate pace.

Connie pulled Adele along until they were walking ahead of Lisa and Jay, and Jay took Lisa's hand. The road was deserted; houses here were far apart, and the only indication that anyone else lived nearby was the glow of incandescent lights along the edge of the river.

Connie ran back to them. "Let me take Hildy's leash," she begged. "I promise I won't let her get away from me."

Jay handed the leash over. "I'm not worried about that," he said. "It's been a long time since this old dog has wanted to get away from anyone."

"Especially me," Connie said with a great deal of satisfaction. "Hildy *loves* me."

Connie and Hildy soon caught up with Adele, and Jay and Lisa deliberately lagged behind.

"What happened with Adele? She seems much better," Jay said.

Lisa explained, and Jay laughed. "I didn't think she'd be able to hold out forever," he said.

"I did, but, then, there's no figuring Adele's moods. She seems quite taken with Connie," Lisa told him. She took his hand and wound her fingers through his.

He pulled her close long enough to kiss her temple. He would have liked to do more than that. Perhaps later; maybe they could steal a few moments together after Adele and Connie had gone to bed.

Up ahead, they saw Adele and Connie stop. It was so dark that they couldn't see what was happening; perhaps they were merely waiting for Lisa and Jay to catch up.

But then Connie knelt, and as Jay was beginning to wonder why he couldn't make out Hildy's shape, Connie called, "Lisa? Jay? Come here! Hildy's lying down in the middle of the road, and we can't make her get up!"

# Chapter Eleven

The cold fluorescent lights in the waiting room of the veterinarian's office showed no mercy; they illuminated the anguish in Jay's eyes and turned Lisa's honey gold complexion an unbecoming yellow.

"How long has Hildy been in there?" Jay asked impatiently after a futile look at his bare wrist. He had forgotten his watch when he'd left home earlier.

Lisa glanced at her own watch. "Thirty minutes, more or less," she said, shifting uncomfortably on the hard plastic seat.

"Thirty minutes. It seems like hours," Jay said.

Lisa reached for his hand. "Surely Hildy will be all right," she said.

"I don't know," Jay replied. He expelled a long sigh. "With all her health problems, I'm not too optimistic. Maybe I shouldn't have taken her out for a walk tonight. She wasn't eager to go anywhere."

"She looked better by the time we got her here," Lisa said encouragingly. "I'm sure of it."

"Do you think so? She licked my hand when I helped the doctor lift her onto the table. I thought that showed some of her old spirit," Jay said. He leaned forward in his chair, frowning and staring at the floor.

They must have waited another half hour or so before the door to the waiting room opened. They both looked up, trying to read Dr. Stillion's expression. The vet, a round, ruddy man with a kindly light in his eyes, rested a heavy hand on Jay's shoulder.

"I'm sorry, Jay," he said. "Hildy's gone. I did all I could."

Jay stared at him for one long, black moment before burying his face in his hands.

Lisa slid an arm around Jay's shoulders and bent her head close to his.

"I'm all right," Jay said quietly. He stood up.

"Like I said, Jay, I tried. Her old heart gave out, that's all," the vet said.

"Hildy was a good friend," Jay said, half to himself.

"Sometimes the best thing to do when you've been together as long as you and Hildy is to get another dog right away," said the vet.

"I'll think about it," Jay said vaguely, but Lisa knew that at that point, all Jay wanted was to get out of there.

They stepped out of the vet's office into a sharp-edged wind cutting suddenly around the corner of the building. Jay shoved his hands deep into his pockets, and they walked silently to his car. Once inside Jay sat with his hands resting on the steering wheel, staring straight ahead. It wasn't until Lisa's eyes adjusted to the dim lights in the parking lot that she realized that tears were streaming down his face.

Without a word, she turned to him and gathered him into her arms. He lowered his forehead to her shoulder, and she stroked his hair. He made no sound, but she felt his hot tears through the thin fabric of her turtleneck.

After a few moments, he said, "I need a handkerchief," and she pulled a tissue out of her pocket and handed it to him.

"How am I going to get along without Hildy?" Jay said helplessly. "She's been my best friend, the only one who's stood by me through—well, through a lot of things." His eyes were dry, but his expression was bleak.

"It isn't easy to lose a pet," she said. How well she remembered when her own dog died; she'd hardly eaten anything for a week.

"Losing Hildy is like a death in the family," he said, his voice sounding hoarse and strained. He dug the heels of his hands into his eye sockets, and Lisa's heart ached for him.

"I don't want to be alone," he said heavily. "Can you come to my place for a while?"

Connie was with Adele; they seemed to be hitting it off well. There was no reason why Lisa shouldn't be with Jay.

"I'd like that," she said.

Jay started the engine and backed the car out of its slot. His movements were deliberate and overcontrolled.

"Did you know that I found Hildy when she was a puppy? That she was abandoned behind the used car lot where I worked when I was in high school?" he said.

"It's hard to imagine Hildy when she was small," Lisa said.

"I loved her from the very beginning. Sometimes I felt that she was the only friend I had," Jay said pensively. This was the truth; in the aftermath of the accident when he was seventeen, his buddies had denied that they'd asked him to buy more beer. His mother had acted as though she wished he'd never been born, and his aunts had whispered about him behind his back.

He'd been desolate when he'd had to leave Hildy behind when he went to the University of Florida. After his freshman year there, he'd lived in an off-campus apartment and had been able to bring Hildy to join him. That was when he'd finally begun to pull himself out of his depression over the accident.

He didn't talk about any of that; it didn't seem like the right time. He drove directly to his town house, but when they stood in Jay's darkened living room, the place seemed empty without Hildy, empty and unnaturally quiet.

After switching on a light, Lisa went into the kitchen and, without asking, poured Jay a glass of iced tea. She came out and handed it to him.

"Do you feel like eating anything?" she asked.

He shook his head and sipped the tea. It tasted bitter. He grimaced and set the glass down on the dining room table.

"I feel exhausted," he said.

"Let's lie down for a while," she said, leading him into his bedroom.

He felt blurry-eyed and overwhelmed with grief. He hoped that Lisa wouldn't want to make love, which was a fair measure of how upset he was. He sat down on the edge of the bed, noting in the mirror over the dresser that he looked as stupefied as he felt. His eyelids were swollen and red, and his feet felt like two lead weights.

Lisa bent down and untied his shoes as she would have untied a child's. She slipped them off, then tugged his socks off after them.

"Lie back," she said in a soft voice, and he was only too glad to follow her instructions. He stared up into the darkness. *Hildy,* he thought. *Hildy is dead.*

Lisa lay down beside him and curved her small body around his. It fit in all the right places, and he rested a hand over hers where it nestled on his chest. It was a comfort, such a comfort, having her there. His eyes drifted reluctantly closed, he slipped into a state of half consciousness and he must have slept after that, because he lost all sense of time and place.

When he woke up, at first he didn't recognize the solid warmth nestled against his right side, but after a few seconds, he realized that it was Lisa. Then he remembered—Hildy was gone.

"Jay?" Lisa said, her voice a mere whisper in the darkness.

For an answer he rolled over on his side and drew her close.

"I'm glad you're here," he said.

Her lips were soft upon his, and tentative, and gentle. At first he held back, feeling inept, thinking that on this night, he could not be interested in making love. Her lips persisted in their ministrations, sweetly seeking, opening to his like a spring flower to the dew. He felt himself responding, much to his surprise, and after a few minutes the world went away.

It was so good to hold her, to feel her compact body pressed close to his. He couldn't feel happy on this of all nights, but he felt a glimmer of pleasure blossoming in the far regions of his consciousness. She ran her fingers up his arm, along his neck, across his lips. He closed his eyes, swirled down and into the feelings, swam up and slid his leg across her body, drawing her even closer with the firm pressure of his thigh.

Certainly this way of making love wasn't filled with the sense of overwhelming passion; this was something else.

This was nurturing, and comfort, and succor. It was a gift.

He was awash in gratitude; it felt strange to be kissing Lisa with any feeling other than unbridled lust. But as her hands began to move more purposefully across his body, his feelings evolved into something else. He rolled over, taking charge, thinking how kind she was, how sweet, and how lucky he was to have found her.

His hand reached up and found her breast and he lowered his head and touched his lips to the fabric of her shirt. Her nipple felt like a small, hard berry beneath his tongue. Slowly he slid his hand under her shirt and curved it around the swell of her breast.

She said, "Wait," and shimmied out of her clothes with a fluid motion that he found unbelievably titillating so that, suddenly eager, he gathered her breast into his mouth and teased the nipple with his tongue. She moaned, and when he stroked open her thighs he realized with surprise how ready she was.

Her desire for him excited him even more. Her hands worked feverishly at the buttons on his shirt, and her fingernails scraped his skin as she tried to find the zipper of his pants.

Then he was free of his clothes, the cool air a balm, and his legs were entwined with hers, and she was staring up at him, her eyes glazed with a kind of luminescent wonder. For a moment he hovered over her, taking in her face flushed with love, her breath coming in bursts, thinking that never had he been so mesmerized by a woman, and then he plunged into her again and again until she begged for release.

But he stopped, began kissing her again, drawing the brightness of her soul into his and feeling himself transported by the joy of it, and his feelings for her were so powerful that they transcended even his grief.

She arched beneath him, her body in perfect tune with his, and his hands adjusted beneath her hips to urge her on. He would have stopped again, but he was incapable of it. She was a fire in his veins, pulsing, convulsing until he couldn't bear it any longer and he exploded into her.

Her whole body clenched around his, her damp skin melded with his, and then he found her seeking mouth and drank from its sweetness until they fell apart, weak and sated and gasping for breath.

Afterward, they lay quietly in each other's arms, half sleeping, half awake, stirring occasionally to kiss and from time to time touching each other with fitting reverence.

She slept, stirring only when Jay got up and went into the kitchen. When she heard him rustling quietly, she got up and put on his bathrobe, which she found hanging on a hook behind the bathroom door. She paused at the entrance to the kitchen and waited for him to turn and greet her, but he was preoccupied with the teakettle. He was wearing nothing, and the dim hood light over the stove illuminated the ripple of the muscles in his back, the indentation of his waist, the contours below. Her heart overflowed with love for him and with gratitude for the happiness he had brought into her life.

She padded silently up behind him, opened the robe and wrapped it around him. He leaned into her for a moment, perfectly still, then turned within the confines of her embrace, breasts brushing against back against arm against chest.

"Oh, Lisa, my dearest love, how did I ever live without you?" he whispered in her ear, and his hands reached around and lifted her to him, his arousal evident. She wound her legs around him, wanting more, feeling him hot against her, floating feather-light in his arms. The robe fell away, leaving them skin to skin, breath to breath, and then he was inside her again, his mouth moist against her cheek.

He gasped with pleasure, shuddered, and she felt her own body tremble and convulse in ecstasy. Her tears were wet against his neck as the keening of the teakettle began. It whistled for a full two minutes before he impatiently reached behind him and shoved it from the burner.

They stood trembling in each other's arms until Jay picked up the fallen robe and slowly and deliberately draped it around her shoulders.

Lisa lapped the robe in front and retied the belt, still shaken by the suddenness of their lovemaking. She had always wanted a relationship that encompassed the entire love spectrum—the right man for her would be father, mother, child, friend and an I-like-you-even-when-you're-being-a-bitch kind of lover. The one thing she had left out was passion, and now she couldn't imagine how she had overlooked such an important ingredient in the relationship.

"I don't suppose you're in the mood for a cup of tea," Jay said, and at the comical expression on his face, she broke into laughter and so did he.

He caught her around the waist in a loose embrace. "Well," he said, "if you don't want a cup of tea, the only other thing I have to offer you is a marriage proposal."

She thought she hadn't heard him correctly. "What?" she said.

"Marry me, Lisa. I can't go on like this, sneaking moments away from Adele, keeping our feelings a secret from the nuns at the mission, living apart. Marry me."

She *had* heard him correctly. He wanted her to marry him. She covered her mouth with her hand, gazing up at him in disbelief. She saw only his kind, gentle face, his eyes alight with amusement.

"This isn't a simple fling, Lisa. We're crazy in love with each other, and there's no point in denying it," he said.

"You sound—you sound as though you're arguing your case before a jury," she whispered.

He laughed. "Do I win my case?" he said.

"You're not joking? You're serious?" she said, scarcely daring to believe it.

He kissed the tip of her nose. "Completely serious," he assured her.

She threw her arms around his neck. "Yes! Yes, yes, yes!" she cried.

He picked her up and whirled her around as he might have swung a large doll. "You mean it? You'll really marry me?" He'd asked her on impulse; he hadn't expected her to reply in kind. He'd thought that women needed time to think such things over.

But she nodded, her cheeks red, her eyes bright.

And he laughed with happiness and swung her around again until she was dizzy with love and excitement.

"When?" he asked. "When will we get married?" He wanted it to be soon, the sooner the better, before she could change her mind, before his past intruded.

She thought for a moment, her eyes dancing. "Well, we'll have to reserve the church," she said. "And we'll want to choose bridesmaids and groomsmen, and I'll have to order a cake. And there's the matter of picking a china pattern, and crystal, and I already have my mother's sterling silver, but I'll need a dress, and it has to be the most beautiful dress in the world, and—"

"What about my work? Is there any way a busy law practice can survive such a wedding?" he asked doubtfully.

"I don't know about the law practice, but school at the mission will be over the last week in May."

"You haven't mentioned a ring. I want to buy you one that you'll like. No—make that two, an engagement and a wedding ring. Shall we go together to pick them out?" he said, pleased that she looked so happy.

She rested her cheek against his chest. "I love surprises," she said. "I'd like you to choose it."

"Are you sure? A wedding ring is a pretty personal thing, you know. You'll have to wear it every day for the rest of your life."

"Every day for the rest of my life. That sounds wonderful, Jay. And that's exactly why I want you to choose it."

"When should I give you the engagement ring?" he asked.

"Just before you want me to broadcast the news. Until then, let's keep it a secret. It's so much more special that way," she said, smiling up at him.

IT WAS VERY LATE before Jay finally drove her home.

"Somehow I'll have to tell Connie about Hildy. I wonder how she'll take it," Lisa said as they turned onto the river road. Here houses became fewer and farther between; their lights hid like secrets behind thick shrubbery.

"It'll be a blow," Jay answered. "She loved Hildy."

"If only Connie didn't have so many changes in her life to deal with right now, she'd probably take the news of Hildy's death much better. As it is, it's just another thing she's going to have to learn to accept."

"Connie is a survivor, Lisa."

"I forget that sometimes. She seems like a normal little girl who has never had to face any hardships."

"How does someone who has faced hardships look, Lisa?" Jay asked her. His expression was blank.

"I think of Adele whenever I think of a person who has dealt with adversity," she said slowly.

"She may have dealt with it, but I don't think she handled it very successfully. She's had some hard times, I'll grant you that, but so have a lot of other people. I don't think we can classify people into two groups, one that has seen hard times, the other that hasn't. All of us have had problems," he said.

Lisa thought about losing her best friend and about her parents' deaths occurring so close to each other; she knew she looked like no more than a girl, but she'd felt her share of pain.

"And you?" she asked quietly as they were turning into her driveway. "What kind of misfortunes have affected you?"

He braked to a stop, turned his head and gave her a long measured look.

"Remind me to tell you about it sometime," he said before he got out of the car.

She didn't know what he meant, and anyway, such a random comment seemed to have no bearing on her present happiness. They were engaged to be married, and she was so caught up in the blissfulness of the idea that nothing else seemed important.

CONNIE TOOK Hildy's death harder than even Lisa had expected.

Lisa provided only vague answers to Connie's anxious questions about Hildy until after dinner the next night, when she quietly sat down on the edge of Connie's bed and gently broke the news that Hildy had died.

"Why? *Why?*" Connie cried, slumping across the bed and beginning to sob as though her heart would break.

"She was old, Connie, and—"

"But she didn't *seem* so old," Connie sobbed.

"She had trouble walking, you know that, and she was hard-of-hearing and had heart problems. Jay is sad, too, and so am I, but it was Hildy's time to go."

Connie only buried her face in a pillow and wept.

Adele came out of the adjoining bathroom. "Is there anything I can do to help?" she asked.

"I told Connie about Hildy," Lisa said. She stood up, and she and Adele watched helplessly as Connie's small supine body continued to be wracked with long shuddering sobs.

Adele lifted a finger to her lips. "I'll take care of her," she whispered, waving Lisa away. When Lisa left, closing the door behind her, Adele was sitting on the bed, bending over Connie.

The incident had shaken Lisa; she didn't like to be the bearer of bad news. She picked up a book and tried to read but couldn't concentrate because she kept watching the clock. Jay had said he would be working late at his office tonight and would call her later, but now she wanted to ask his advice about Connie. She had known that Connie would be sad about Hildy's death, but she hadn't been prepared for such utter desolation.

She waited for a while, but when Jay didn't call, she decided to phone him at his office. Maybe she'd ask him to come over for a late supper, or perhaps she could take him a sandwich and sit down to eat it with him in his office, where they could chat privately.

Jay's office phone rang five or six times, and finally his answering service picked up.

"Mr. Quillian left the office some time ago," the operator told her.

"Will he be back tonight?" Lisa asked, thinking that perhaps Jay had only gone out for a bite to eat.

"Sorry, he didn't say," was the breezy reply, so Lisa left her name and hung up.

She dialed his town house, but he wasn't there, either. Thoughtfully she walked back into the living room, wondering what Adele was finding to say to Connie all this time, wondering where Jay was and feeling lonely and out of sorts.

Finally she gave up on the book she'd been trying to read and went to listen briefly at Connie's closed bedroom door. When she heard the soft rise and fall of Connie's and Adele's voices, she decided not to interrupt.

Outside, the darkness was scented with the damp green smell of the river. The night was warm and there was no wind. She zipped the hooded sweatshirt she wore up to her neck and wandered down to the small bench her father had built for her beneath the pines. There she sat for a long time, moodily watching the river run past and wondering where Jay could possibly be.

MEANWHILE, JAY was barreling south on I-95 for no good reason at all.

He had been working in his office when he had suddenly slammed the folder of briefs shut and decided on the spur of the moment to go for a ride. The office had seemed much too confining for his present restless frame of mind.

Probably he should have headed for Lisa's house, but for some reason the prospect of jollying Adele, shoring up Connie and trying to get Lisa to himself for a few private moments was totally unappealing.

Lisa would be full of plans; she would want to know things like whether he preferred gladiolas and chrysanthemums to roses as decorations for their wedding and where they should hold the reception, which to him were tiresome questions.

Not that he didn't love Lisa as much as ever—it was just that he would feel uncomfortable speaking of the trivial. He had heavier, weightier matters on his mind, and he didn't know how to tell her what they were. In fact, he was beginning to feel like a first-class fraud, and tonight, only one night after deciding to forfeit his bachelorhood, he needed some space. This struck him as ironic, but what could he do about it? He couldn't lie to himself, not anymore.

Green interstate highway signs loomed up in front of him one by one: Palm Beach Gardens, Lake Park, West Palm Beach. At every one he speeded up almost imperceptibly, until he was driving well over the speed limit. He had no idea where he was going; he didn't want to go home, that was for sure. Without Hildy the town house felt too empty.

It was hard to explain to other people what Hildy, the only constant in his life, meant to him and why. He had an idea that Lisa understood, but she couldn't know all that was on his mind and in his heart. He still hadn't had the guts to tell her about the accident, and the accident was the reason that he had come to depend on Hildy as his only friend.

Lisa loved him; she was going to marry him. She thought she knew him. But what would she say when she found out that he was directly responsible for the death of another person?

Of course he would tell her eventually, and he didn't think that it would make her stop loving him. How could it? Neither one of them had eyes for anyone else since the day that they had first met.

But.

In the back of his mind always lurked the accident.

Sure, back in 1979 when it had happened he had been a stupid seventeen-year-old kid, smug enough to think that a few beers wouldn't affect his response time behind the wheel of a car. That didn't make it any better. A girl had died because of him.

He had paid the price and would pay it for the rest of his life. He had served time in jail, which was bad enough, but it was the counseling and community-service work that had made him a different person. He'd never forget all those kids his own age whom he'd lectured about drinking and driving or the way they had stared at him when the tears began rolling down his face as they inevitably did whenever he spoke about the accident in front of a group. And he still recalled the pain of their questions afterward, innocent questions that broke him up all over again, such as "Did you ever meet the family of the girl you killed?"

The answer to that one was no, he hadn't. On the advice of his lawyer he hadn't attended the girl's funeral, and her family hadn't come to the courtroom when he was sentenced.

He'd continued to atone for his mistake in many ways, but mostly through his work with disadvantaged kids after he'd fulfilled his community-service sentence, and he'd gained a lot from those needy kids. He'd put the bad part of his life behind him, and since he'd seen the inner workings of the court system, he'd decided that he'd like to devote his life to the practice of law.

Now he had a good practice, a nice place to live, and he had gained some inner peace. He'd sublimated his natural desire for a home and family by working with the kids at the mission, but in the past few weeks, he'd realized that they were no substitute for a passionate woman who would share his life. Hildy had been the last vestige of his early life, and she was gone. As much as he'd miss that mutt, maybe it was for the best.

Tonight he should have at least called Lisa. He knew she had expected him to call her tonight as he had every other night; she would be missing him.

His foot eased slightly off the accelerator. Is this what being engaged was all about? Was he going to feel as though he had to be with Lisa every free moment?

It was a sobering thought, but he'd better face it: that might be what he was in for. Last night, only minutes after his proposal, she had told him what kind of wedding they were going to have, and next she'd be wanting to haul him around to look at china patterns.

He saw the Palm Beach Mall coming up on the left, and he eased into the off ramp for Palm Beach Lakes Boulevard. Maybe he'd stop at one of the department stores and take a look at a few china patterns himself. It couldn't hurt. Perhaps he'd even be able to muster enthusiasm for all the fuss that Lisa seemed to think should accompany a wedding.

The clerk in the china department barely looked up from what she was doing when Jay walked in. He studied the plates lined up against the wall, the names of their patterns written on tasteful little cards clipped to the fronts of the shelves. He liked the clean spare lines of the pattern called City Lights, hated the dismal one called

Grey Vogue and wondered if anyone ever chose the overblown one named Floradorable Lavender. He certainly hoped that Lisa wouldn't.

And then there was silver, and crystal, and stainless-steel flatware. He passed a girl who looked barely old enough to have graduated from high school; she was disagreeing with her mother over whether to pick out a casual china pattern as well as a more formal one. The two of them seemed to be enjoying the argument, going at it for all it was worth.

Jay grimaced to himself; none of this seemed important enough to argue about, but apparently it all went along with getting married, especially for women. He would never have pegged Lisa as the type to go overboard about china and crystal, but she had mentioned it right along with her plans for the wedding, which had surprised him a lot.

"May I help you?" asked the clerk, who had put aside her paperwork and found him as he wandered somewhat aimlessly through the aisles.

"No, just looking," he told her. On a large table nearby he saw carefully arranged place settings bearing calligraphed cards proclaiming that the choice was that of Miss Vanessa Drake or Miss Hinda Celine Levinson or Miss Denise Michele Spurgeon. It occurred to him that he didn't even know Lisa's middle name.

"If you need a gift for someone, we may have the couple signed up in our book," the clerk said helpfully.

"I doubt it," he said, starting to walk away.

"Well, you never know. Brides come in here and sign our bridal register before the engagement announcement appears in the newspaper, you know, so that people who are sure they will be invited to the wedding can order a special piece of their china or silver in plenty of time for it to arrive before the big day.'' She followed him along planting her small feet determinedly in his footsteps.

An engagement announcement! Jay had never considered that Lisa might want to announce their engagement in the newspaper, but the way she'd talked about the wedding, he was sure she would. And why not? She had lived in this area all of her life, and it was only natural that she'd want to share her good news with friends both old and new.

''You might like to take a look at our lovely collection of candelabra,'' the clerk persisted. ''It's right over here.''

''I'm not interested,'' Jay said, heading for the escalator. He bounded down the steps to the first floor two at a time, eliciting alarmed looks from the other riders.

Downstairs he suddenly found himself in the fine jewelry department, where he stared blankly into a case of diamond engagement rings winking and blinking under the bright lights.

What was wrong with him? Was he feeling pressured? Did he want out only one day after proposing to the most wonderful woman in the world? Had he turned into one of those people who get married after they fall in love because action seemed necessary, and they couldn't think of anything else to do?

With a sickening sense of colliding with reality, he thought all of those things might be true.

''Would you like to look at a ring, sir?'' inquired an unctuous voice somewhere behind him.

''No,'' he said, and bolted blindly for the door.

# Chapter Twelve

Connie had long since sobbed herself to sleep, Adele had departed for her room and Lisa was beginning to be concerned because Jay was not answering either the phone at his office or the one at home.

After yet another fruitless attempt to reach Jay, Lisa slammed down the phone in her bedroom and scooped her car keys off the top of her dresser. It was late, but she was too worried about Jay to let this slide by; it wasn't like him to disappear so completely from view.

She sped along the winding river road, switching off the radio when the music became too distracting. She drove past Jay's office first; it was located in a one-story building off Indiantown Road, and at this hour, there were no cars in the parking lot. Her quick drive-by yielded nothing, so she headed toward the development where he lived.

She slowed her car at the guardhouse at the entrance, but the guard only looked up briefly from his crossword puzzle and, smiling in recognition, waved her quickly through. She braked under the palm tree beside Jay's town house, noting with relief that Jay's car was parked in its usual parking spot. When she knocked, however, no one answered the door. She stood in the small courtyard and looked up at the window of his studio; no light burned there, either. Finally she decided that he wasn't going to answer her knock on the door, and she went and got in her car, feeling troubled.

She drove slowly past the guardhouse, then backed up. The guard glanced up from the puzzle.

She rolled down the car window. "Jay Quillian's car is at his town house, but he doesn't answer when I knock on the door. Do you know if he left?" she asked.

"Sure, he went for a walk about a half hour ago. Headed toward the beach. I wondered about it when I saw you come through a few minutes ago—I thought you must have just missed each other."

"We did," Lisa said before pulling her car into one of the parking spaces reserved for visitors.

This late at night there were no skateboarders on the path beside the beach; in fact, aside from one lone dog walker ahead of her, no one was walking along the ocean path. Jay was down on the beach, she decided, so she headed straight for the steps to the sand.

She looked for his solitary figure silhouetted against the sea, but she saw no one. She stood indecisively for a moment, then turned her resolute footsteps northward. It was the way they had walked that first night together when he had kissed her.

Tonight the surf was up, and great white-tipped breakers crashed upon the sand. Overhead a curved moon tilted out of the darkness. The scent of iodine, borne upon the steady wind, made Lisa's nostrils twitch.

She almost didn't see him sitting on the driftwood log and might have passed him by if he hadn't jerked his head up in sudden recognition.

He cleared his throat. "Lisa?" he said.

"Jay! I've been worried about you," she said. "I called your office and you weren't there, and I called your town house, and—"

"You were worried about me?" he asked. He was still sitting, and she stood in front of him, feeling out of place and out of sorts. He might think she'd been spying on him and she didn't want him to think that.

"Well, of course I was worried," she said testily. "I thought something might have happened to you."

"I can't recall the last time someone was worried about me," he said, sounding bemused. "Come and sit down, Lisa." He edged over on the log to make room for her, and hesitantly she joined him. He was idly toying with a piece of driftwood that he had picked up somewhere, and something was clearly wrong.

"Is it Hildy?" she asked gently. "Are you still thinking of her?"

"Yes, it's going to take me a while to get over her death. I tried working tonight, but I just couldn't pay attention to a bunch of briefs. Not only because of Hildy, Lisa. Because—" He stopped. He couldn't finish what he was going to say; he couldn't tell her how worried he was, that she wouldn't, couldn't love him if she knew the truth—that he had killed someone.

He tossed aside the driftwood twig and reached over to take her hand. Lisa was good, kind, beautiful and desirable. He loved her.

"You have a lot on your mind right now with deciding to get married, and Connie's problems, and losing Hildy," she said. He saw that she was determined to be understanding, even though he knew she couldn't understand at all. Someone like Lisa, so sweet, so loving, couldn't know what he'd been through.

Her eyes were brimming with trust, and he looked away, ashamed that she was making excuses for him.

"Yeah," he said, feeling like a heel and a fraud. She thought he was wonderful, and he wasn't.

"I know one way to make the problems go away," she said, and when he looked back at her she was smiling up at him, her old elf self, and he was sickeningly aware that he had been deceiving her all along. He should have told her the truth before she fell in love with him, and then she could have made up her mind about whether to move ahead in the relationship. But when had they not been in love with each other? It seemed to him that he had loved her from the moment he'd first seen her.

He pulled her close and drew her head onto his shoulder. She kissed his neck, and he sighed. She was so warm and alluring, so lovely. And she was so in love with him.

"I love you, Lisa," he said, striving to keep the panic out of his voice.

"Then why are we sitting out here on this damp beach?" she said.

It was a lighthearted remark, but he could not reply in kind. Instead he pulled her close so that she wouldn't see the anguish in his eyes.

ONE NIGHT about a week later Connie sat at Lisa's kitchen table and circled ads in For Sale—Dogs, Cats, Pets column of the daily newspaper.

"Here's one—'Free to a good home, female chow,'" Connie read out loud. "That sounds like the kind of dog that a dietitian might own, not a lawyer. What kind of dog is a chow, anyway?"

"Large," Lisa said. "But not as large as Hildy."

"Chows have black tongues," Adele added. "We had a chow once when I was a girl."

"Black tongues—ugh," Connie said. "Here's another one. I wonder if Jay would like a dachshund."

"Too small," Lisa said, vetoing it.

"Maybe a golden retriever puppy," Connie suggested, circling another ad.

"That sounds more like it. Yes, Jay would definitely like a golden retriever," Lisa decided. "Let me see that, Connie." She read the ad herself. The owner, who lived in Jupiter, had advertised four puppies for sale, and there was an address where they could be seen by appointment.

"Can we go look at them, Lisa? Please?"

"I suppose you could call and make an appointment if you like," Lisa said.

"Oh, good. Jay's so lonely without Hildy. I hate to think of him living at his town house all by himself," Connie said.

"We could give him some of the hangers in my closet," Adele said.

Lisa blinked. "What?" she said.

Connie took it upon herself to explain. "Oh, it's funny. Adele says that she has a coat-hanger farm in her closet. That the hangers in her closet multiply. That they breed in there. She says she's never lonely because she has all these hangers, and I think it's the funniest thing! I never heard of hangers keeping anyone from being lonely!" She dissolved into giggles.

"I recall that you were going to help me by adopting some of my hangers, Connie," Adele said, standing up. "I'll give you the pick of the litter to keep in your own closet if you'll come along right now and get them."

"I was going to call about the puppies," Connie said.

"I'll do it," Lisa offered.

"Tell them we want the pick of the litter," Connie instructed her airily as she and Adele hurried off, and Lisa smiled.

Connie's effect on Adele had been nothing short of miraculous. Ever since Adele had so skillfully comforted Connie after Hildy's death, they could often be found together. Adele was knitting Connie a red sweater, and she had even driven Connie to her own hairdresser for a haircut yesterday. They were good for each other. Connie had brought out Adele's innate tenderness and had freed the joyful spirit that had been imprisoned inside Adele for so long.

And if Adele was smiling more, why was Jay smiling less? These days, when they had not yet announced their engagement, when they had told no one of their plans to marry, when they should be wrapped in their own private bliss, why did Jay seem to want to put distance between them at times?

Last Sunday afternoon at the beach, for instance. She and Jay had taken Connie with them, and Connie had been sitting far away sketching when Lisa had brought up the subject of a guest list for the wedding. She told Jay that she was sure that her sister Heather would come, and she would invite her great-uncle Richard to walk her down the aisle. They deserved to be told the date of the wedding, since all of them lived far away and would need to make travel plans. Lisa thought she'd telephone them soon.

She had mentioned casually that surely Jay's mother and stepfather and their two children would want to come from Albuquerque for the wedding, and she had suggested that perhaps Jay should phone them later that afternoon and tell them of their engagement.

"Now? Today?" he had said, alarm written all over his face.

"Of course. They're your family, Jay. Why shouldn't they be the first to know we're getting married?" she had countered.

He looked off into the distance, squinting against the hot sun. "Naturally I thought you'd want to tell Adele and your sister before we told anyone else," he said.

Lisa rolled over on her stomach and pillowed her cheek on her hands. "Not necessarily," she said. "I can telephone Heather anytime, but I don't know when I'd tell Adele. It's 'Connie this' and 'Connie that,' almost as though she's infatuated with the kid. She hardly pays attention to me anymore," Lisa had said with a laugh.

"Is that a complaint I'm hearing?" Jay said.

"No, only an observation. Adele and Connie seem to supply to each other exactly what they both need. Connie needs Adele's nurturing, and Connie has restored Adele's sense of humor," Lisa had said.

At that point a child had raced by in pursuit of a Frisbee, spraying them with sand, and their discussion never returned to the topic of telling his family about their engagement. She couldn't help puzzling over Jay's reticence, but she forgot about it after a while. She had other important things to think about, such as when to break her good news to Adele. Adele liked Jay; Lisa was sure of that. But how would she react when Lisa told her they were going to be married?

The opportunity to tell Adele of their plans luckily presented itself a few days later while Adele was conducting an elementary swimming lesson in the river. Adele told Lisa, much to Lisa's surprise, that she had worked as a water-safety instructor before her marriage. It was the first time Lisa had ever heard of it, but when she had suggested that Adele begin to teach Connie the rudiments of staying afloat in the water, Adele had responded with enthusiasm. She had even gone out and bought herself a new swimsuit, a one-piece job with a pert little skirt.

Lisa had gone swimming herself early that morning, and she sat wrapped in a giant beach towel on the bench under the pines at the water's edge while Adele drilled Connie in the dead man's float.

Although Connie came up sputtering once or twice, she learned the float and was even mastering the simple frog kick, before Adele laughingly claimed that she was getting tired and needed a rest.

"Here, wrap yourself up in this—it's chilly here in the shade," Lisa said, tossing a towel in Adele's direction as she waded out of the shallows.

Adele mopped her face and brushed a few sodden locks of hair out of her eyes. "It's been so long since I've been in the water, I've almost forgotten it all," she said, sitting beside Lisa on the bench and lifting her face to the sunlight that streamed through a space in the web of blue-green pine needles overhead.

"I'd never know it," Lisa said with affection. "You and Connie looked like two tadpoles when you were teaching her the frog kick."

"One tadpole, one tired old frog," Adele said, but she was smiling when she said it.

"Speaking of frogs, I think I've finally kissed the prince," Lisa said.

"Kissed the— Oh, you mean Jay! It's getting serious then?" Adele's eyes were lively with enthusiasm, and Lisa took heart. Perhaps this wasn't going to be as difficult as she thought.

"I'm in love with him, Adele. And he loves me. I've never been so happy in my life," Lisa said quietly.

"I knew it. I suspected it the first time I saw you together on the morning when he came over and I taught him to make crepes. The way the two of you were laughing when you were looking for the vase in the garage was a sure clue. I'd never heard you laughing with anyone like that before. Oh, Lisa, I'm so pleased. He's a wonderful man."

"I think so, too. Adele, I was worried about telling you. I didn't think you'd be happy," she said.

Adele turned sober eyes upon her. "At one time, maybe I wouldn't have been as glad for you. But now I see that you need someone else in your life, someone to bring you happiness. I wasn't doing that. I was only making things harder for you. I wish—"

"Shh," Lisa told her softly, putting an arm around her shoulders. "I'm glad things are better for you now."

"It's Connie," Adele said. "You were right about her, and I'm going to miss her terribly when she goes to be with her father. I was thinking—Ginny at the gift shop works full-time and needs someone to pick up her daughter after school when it's in session. Next fall after Connie's gone, I could do it. The little girl is younger than Connie, but she's a darling child, and she could stay with me every afternoon until her mother picks her up after work. What do you think?"

"I think it's a wonderful idea. You're so good with children, Adele."

"Maybe so," Adele said, watching Connie as she practiced floating. "Maybe so."

Lisa glanced at Adele out of the corners of her eyes. "Are you ready for one more surprise?" she asked.

Adele caught her bottom lip between her teeth and stared for a moment, then broke into a smile.

"You and Jay—you're going to get married!" she said.

Lisa laughed out loud. "You guessed! How did you know?" she exclaimed.

"The look on your face gave it away," Adele said warmly. "I couldn't be happier for you, Lisa. When is the date?"

"We don't know yet. We've discussed living at Jay's town house, but even though you'll lose me as a housemate, you aren't going to lose the house. You can live here as long as you like, get another housemate or not, whichever you prefer, and you'll be a frequent guest in our home."

"I don't know what to say," Adele said helplessly. "I'd always thought that if you ever got married, I'd have to leave this house, and I do love it. This seems—this seems like more than I deserve, Lisa. You're so kind."

"I'll feel good about your living here. You'll take care of things the same as I would," Lisa said.

"Adele! Adele!" Connie called from beyond the reeds. "Am I doing this right?" She was demonstrating a jerky elementary backstroke.

"No, your rhythm is all wrong. Your legs and your arms are supposed to come up at the same time—wait a minute and I'll show you," Adele said.

"By the way, we haven't told anyone else that we're getting married yet," Lisa told Adele hastily as Adele chucked her towel and strode into the water.

"Don't worry, your secret is safe with me," Adele called over her shoulder.

Lisa tipped her head back and breathed deeply of the river-scented air. Well, she had done it. She had told Adele, and Adele was happy for them.

Tomorrow she'd call her parish priest. She'd reserve the church for a Saturday morning in the middle of June and then she'd call Jay and tell him the date.

She shrugged off the nagging feeling that Jay wasn't ready to get married. They loved each other as they'd never loved anyone else, and they couldn't wait to get married.

So why did she feel so insecure? Why did she feel that they weren't really sharing their lives?

SHE HAD RESERVED the church, Jay reminded himself that weekend. The least he could do was buy her an engagement ring.

He idled outside a few jewelry-shop windows, studying the situation. He finally decided that Lisa would like a diamond solitaire, and he wanted to buy one as big as he could afford. The wedding ring would be a simple narrow gold band.

He chose a lovely oval-shaped diamond. He could imagine the ring on Lisa's small finger, sparkling in the sunlight and telling the world that she belonged to him.

He loved Lisa with all his heart and soul; he had trouble with all this marriage business, that was all. The emotions engendered by the idea of a big wedding were mind-boggling. For instance, he knew that his mother would find it difficult to return even for so short a time to the West Palm Beach area, a place that would always be filled with bad memories for her. His stepfather, who had given Jay his last name and loved him like a son, would probably feel the same way.

And then there was the matter of friends. Whenever Jay ran into his old buddies around town, the ones he'd partied with in high school, they usually acted embarrassed. Not that they didn't like him; they did. They just didn't know what to say. Their lives and his had diverged sharply after Jay's sentencing. They'd gone on drinking, and he had never taken a drink since the day of the accident. His old friends didn't even know what to call him these days, Jamie or Jay.

The fact was that his engagement announcement in the paper would stir up all the old trouble again. People would say, "James Quillian...James Quillian," and they'd scratch their heads for a few moments, until they remembered that he was Jamie Watkins, that he's changed his name and made a new life for himself, but the life he'd begun since the accident wouldn't count with a lot of these people. What would count was that he had killed a girl once and that he'd gotten off almost scot-free.

Damn! How long was that part of his life going to follow him around? Just when he'd allowed himself to think that he was free of it, the shame of his past jumped up and slapped him in the face. His new and wonderful relationship with Lisa was something just for him, the first happiness that he had dared to allow himself in a long, long time. He couldn't shake the feeling that it was wrong to feel so much pleasure, that he didn't have the right to be happy. He had denied himself this kind of fulfillment all his adult life.

He had mostly kept his own counsel since he'd come back to Florida after law school. Most of the important people in his life today didn't know about his past, and that was the way he wanted it. Except for Sister Maria, the nuns at Faith Mission didn't know; the children he taught didn't know; Lisa didn't know.

And that was the problem.

Lisa knew that he liked granola brownies, making love on lazy Sunday afternoons, canoeing with her on the

Loxahatchee, and her, not necessarily in that order. Lisa, to whom honesty was key, knew every important thing there was to know about him except that he had once killed a woman.

And he couldn't bring himself to tell her.

ON SATURDAY Lisa and Connie went to Yahola so that Lisa could teach a nutrition class and Connie could work in the art room. That afternoon on the way home they stopped briefly behind a converted school bus letting off passengers on the outskirts of the settlement.

"We have an appointment to go look at those golden retriever puppies next week," Lisa told Connie as they waited for the bus to move.

"We do?" Connie said, clearly delighted. "What day?"

"Friday," Lisa said. The bus increased its speed and lumbered onto a shell rock road bisecting the highway; Lisa was finally able to push on the accelerator and make tracks for home.

"I wish we could go see the puppies tonight," Connie said.

"Well, we can't. They won't be ready to leave their mother for another week, and besides, Jay and I are going out to dinner," Lisa told her.

"Tonight I'm going to show Adele how to make tortillas for supper. She buys them straight out of the frozen-foods case. Yuck," Connie said.

Lisa cast a sidelong glance at Connie. She wondered if Connie had any inkling of the seriousness of her relationship with Jay; she wondered if they gave themselves away when they were around her. He was always trying to steal a kiss when Connie's back was turned.

"You want to know a secret?" Lisa asked Connie.

"I love secrets," Connie said. "Tell, tell!"

"You have to promise not to tell the Sisters at the mission or your cousins until I say you can," Lisa told her.

"I promise," Connie said solemnly.

"Jay and I are engaged to be married," Lisa told her.

Connie's eyes grew wide, and a smile spread across her face. "You're going to get married? Really and truly married?" she squealed.

Lisa laughed at her expression of delight.

"As really and truly as two people can be," she affirmed. "We're going to be married on the third Saturday in June."

"Does Adele know?"

Lisa nodded, and Connie jiggled up and down on the seat. "She knew and she didn't tell me! Oh, am I going to get her when we get home!"

"Don't be too hard on her, Connie. I asked her to keep it a secret."

"But how could she not tell? I deserve to know. I was there on your first date—wasn't the day we went canoeing on the river your first date? Wasn't it?"

"Almost. I guess we could count it as the first," Lisa said, smiling again.

"What about a ring? Aren't you supposed to get an engagement diamond?"

Lisa lowered her voice to a conspiratorial whisper. "He told me to wear something special when we go out to dinner. I think he might give it to me tonight," she said.

Connie clapped her hands at this. "No matter how late you get in tonight, Lisa, come into my room and show me. I hope it's a be-yootiful diamond."

"I'm sure it will be lovely," Lisa said. She could picture it in her imagination: a flawless, pristine diamond, not too big, not too little. She could hardly wait to begin wearing it.

She could hardly wait to become Mrs. James Quillian.

THAT NIGHT Jay thought that Lisa looked especially beautiful, her hair knotted on top of her head but trailing in careless wispy tendrils all around. The glow of the candle on their table polished her skin to mellow perfection. The filmy white dress she wore made her look like a bride, and a surge of emotion flowed through Jay when he thought that soon she would be his wife. It was hard to shake the feeling that he of all people did not deserve such complete happiness.

The restaurant was special, a place where they could watch the moon rise over the marina, and the tables were set with starched white tablecloths and napkins and fresh flowers in plump silver bowls. They ate pâté for an appetizer and fresh red snapper for a main course; the vegetables were crisply steamed. They ate slowly, enjoying the ambience, the charm and the intimacy.

A trio played for after-dinner dancing, and when they danced, she felt feather-light in his arms. The diamond ring burned a hole in Jay's pocket; he could hardly wait to give it to her, to see her eyes become enormous with pleasure and to brim with happy tears, to have her throw her arms around him and tell him how much she loved him.

When the music stopped he looked at her, said, "Let's get out of here," and she didn't even speak, just nodded and looked at him with those enormous eyes. He threw some money down on the table and then they were outside hurrying to his car.

"Let's go for a walk on the beach," she suggested impulsively as they drove out of the parking lot. "It's a full moon."

"That brings out all the crazies," he said.

"Like us?" she said, moving close to him, and he laughed and kissed her because he *was* crazy, crazy about her.

He drove to the same spot where they often walked on the beach and parked the car in one of the parking spaces near the wooden steps to the sand. They had to pass a group of chattering teenagers to get to the steps, but when they reached the beach, it was deserted. Lisa steadied herself with a hand on his arm and bent down to pull off her shoes, and Jay took off his shoes and socks, too. He paused to roll up his pants legs, and Lisa, suddenly playful, danced tantalizingly out of reach at the edge of the surf until he chased her and caught her in the circle of his arms.

"I love you, Lisa," he said, holding her tight against him. "I love you so much. Has any other couple ever loved this much?"

"I suppose every couple asks themselves that question," Lisa said more thoughtfully than he had expected.

"Hmm," he said. He released her but caught her hand in his.

"Maybe the real question should be 'Has any other couple known each other as well?'" she said.

He darted a quick look in her direction. She looked supremely happy and satisfied, and he wondered if she'd recently talked to someone who had known him long ago. Who could it have been? His mind ranged over a list of acquaintances and old friends, but he could think of no one. No, she was probably just glorying in their relationship, congratulating herself on their getting to know each other so well in such a short period of time. And they had. Except . . .

"Lisa," he said quietly and with great gravity, "I feel as if I've known you all my life. Maybe it's always that way when you find another person who feels the same way you do about so many things. We have a mutual interest in the mission and in Connie, and—well, I could go on and on."

"Oh, *do*," she said in that impish way of hers. She hadn't yet caught his serious mood.

"I have something I should tell you. I probably wouldn't have to, and it won't be as important to you as it is to me, but I want to get it out of the way. I don't want you to hear it from somebody else."

Her eyes were clear and puzzled. "What in the world are you talking about, Jay?" she said.

"Something happened a long time ago, something that changed my life. I didn't mean to do it, and I've been paying for it ever since," he said evenly.

She stopped walking, and her face froze. "You make yourself sound like a criminal," she said.

He captured both her hands in his and gazed down at her. "I am," he said. "I killed a woman."

Her mouth opened, but no sound came out. Her eyes widened in incomprehension and disbelief, and she inhaled a deep breath, an inrush of surprised air. "I don't believe you," she said, her eyes searching his face.

"It was an accident," he said rapidly, wanting to make the rigid expression on her face go away as soon as possible. "I'd been drinking with my friends at a graduation party when I was only seventeen years old, and my car skidded through a red light in the rain and hit another car, a sports-car convertible. The girl who was driving the sports car died. It was an *accident,* Lisa," he said when he saw the look of horror in her eyes.

"Megan," she said in a very small voice.

"What?" he said, clearly disconcerted.

"Megan. That's how Megan was killed, in the same way. The boy who killed her got almost no sentence at all—the judge sentenced him to weekends in jail and community-service work." She pulled her hands away from his and stood staring at him.

"That's what my sentence was," he told her. "It's how I got interested in kids and art. I taught my first art class to a group of disadvantaged kids in Gainesville when I was at the University of Florida. I was trying to make up for—"

"No," Lisa said clearly and distinctly. She had added the numbers up in her head. Jay was twenty-eight years old, and Megan had been killed almost twelve years ago. Jay's birthday was next week. That would have made Jay seventeen years old in June of 1979, exactly the right age to be the driver of the car that had killed Megan.

"Lisa—"

"You're *him.* You're the one who killed her. My God, how can you be?" She sank down on the sand exactly where she stood and wrapped her arms around herself, shivering visibly.

"Lisa?" he said, kneeling beside her. He'd never seen her like this.

"I don't feel so okay right now. My stomach hurts. Oh," she said as though she couldn't breathe.

"Lisa, I—" he said, and he touched her shoulder in supplication.

"Stop," she said. Her mind whirled. She was trying to piece it all together, and suddenly the pieces tumbled into place. But how could it be? What weird coincidence had brought the two of them together? How could she have fallen in love with the man who had killed Megan? She had no doubt that Jay was that person; it must be true. A wave of nausea swept over her, and she stumbled to her feet and reeled away from him in revulsion.

He followed her, caught her by the wrist and whipped her around to face him. Her hair blew around her ashen face, and her eyes were hard as agates.

"I don't know what you think," he said desperately, and she knew that he hadn't caught on yet.

"*Megan,*" she cried. "You killed her. But your name—it's all wrong, and I don't know, I don't know *how.*" Her eyes beseeched him, and all of a sudden he understood. Adele's daughter, the one who had died young—her name had been Megan. And the woman he had killed had been named Megan, too.

At first he was too numb to speak and all he could do was gaze in astonishment at the contorted features of the woman he loved.

"I was James Watkins then," he said at last. "My stepfather adopted me later."

Lisa's eyes widened, and she wrenched away from him and stumbled back toward the steps to the parking lot.

"Lisa, wait," Jay called after her, but his heart had fallen to the pit of his stomach and his voice hadn't found its full timbre. A wave of self-loathing swept over him, threatening to cut off all his air.

"Go away," she cried, and he tried to hold her in his arms, to make her talk to him, but she was beyond talking: she was beating her fists against his chest; she was hysterical.

There were people in the parking lot above them and she was out of control; now she was heading toward the ocean and he grabbed her and pulled her back. A wave broke too far inland, slamming against their knees before catching them in its ebb, and the sand eroded beneath their feet. The water surged around their ankles as he struggled with her, trying to hold her up when she would have collapsed.

She summoned every bit of her strength and lurched away from him, this time, thank goodness, in the direction of the shore. The water sucked at his feet, holding him back, and he cursed it and tried to reach her. Lisa was already hurtling past the debris at the high-tide mark when he caught up with her.

"Lisa, don't do this! We need to talk!" He was aware of the people above them in the parking area—what if they heard, what if they saw? They would think he was assaulting her.

She kicked at him, broke away, and he did the only thing he could think of. He brought her down with a football tackle.

She struggled beneath him for a few moments, then gradually her flailing stopped and she lay beneath him gasping. When he felt all the fight drain out of her, he relaxed and sat up. She lay in the sand, her skirt wet and clinging to her legs, her face swollen with crying. But reason had returned to her eyes, and for that he was grateful.

"If we could just talk," he said heavily.

"I never want to talk to you again," she said clearly and distinctly, recoiling from him. He was halted by the steadiness of her gaze.

"Lisa, I'm a different person now," he began.

"You killed my best friend, and I'd kill you if I could," she said in the most cold, dispassionate voice he'd ever heard. She stood up and found her shoes and purse in the sand, but now she didn't run. With an eerie calm she walked up the steps to the path and the parking lot beyond, with Jay trailing after her, unable to say anything as long as they were around the other people.

Two pay phones stood nearby, and she marched up to one.

"What are you going to do?" he asked as she picked up the phone directory.

She looked up a number. "I'm calling a cab," she said.

"For God's sake, Lisa, I'll take you home," he said.

She ignored him until she'd completed the phone call. Then she walked to the road and stood slightly apart from the talking, laughing group by the steps, some of whom kept glancing at them curiously.

"Lisa, will you please come get in my car? I promise I won't say one more word about the accident, about Megan. Please let me take you home." Her thin wet skirt was wound around her legs, but she didn't move. He himself was barefoot. He didn't care.

Hostile and stony-eyed, her back ramrod straight, she continued to ignore him, and in five minutes or so the taxi arrived. She yanked the door open as soon as it slid to a stop, and he touched her arm.

"Get your hands off me. I never want to see you again," she said, and when he realized that she meant it, his hand fell away and she slammed the taxi door behind her.

He watched the cab drive away, and a kid wearing baggy surfing shorts walked by and said, "Hey, I know how ya feel. Tough luck, buddy."

"Yeah," he said, turning his head quickly so the kid wouldn't see the tears in his eyes. "Tough luck."

## Chapter Thirteen

"You didn't wake me up last night, Lisa! Let me see your diamond ring!"

The mattress bounced, and Lisa opened her eyes to see Connie on her hands and knees, her earnest smiling face only inches from Lisa's in the strip of sunshine penetrating the curtains.

"Mmfgh," Lisa said, pushing Connie away and struggling to a sitting position.

"You're not wearing it. Lisa, didn't you get the engagement ring?" Connie had backed off and was staring at her with an expression of perplexity.

"No, I did not. What time is it?"

"Seven-thirty. Adele and I are going to Mass in a few minutes. Want to come along?"

"When did Adele start going to Mass again?" Lisa asked.

"This morning. But you didn't tell me about the ring."

Last night came back to Lisa in all its revolting detail, and she slumped back onto the pillow.

"I'm not going to marry Jay. I never should have mentioned it," she said.

"Not marry Jay? Ohhhh," Connie said in one long disappointed exhalation, the light fading from her eyes.

That alone would have been bad enough, but the tears that followed were even worse. They coursed down Connie's plump cheeks in wide rivers, and Lisa wanted to crawl under the covers and never come out.

Instead, she slid out of bed and walked stolidly to the tissue box on the dresser, where she yanked several tissues out.

"Here," she said to Connie as she handed them to her. "I wish I could explain, but I can't. It's just not right for us to get married, that's all." She climbed back on the bed and clasped her hands around her legs, resting her forehead on her kneecaps as she pictured that awful scene on the beach in her mind. Had she really hit him? Had he really tackled her? Taking her sore shoulder into evidence, it was obvious that he had.

"But Lisa, everything that Jay says will happen *always* happens, absolutely everything," Connie said in a bewildered tone.

Lisa lifted her head. "Not this time, honey," she said gently.

"Did I hear you say you're not getting married?" Adele asked in consternation as she hurried into Lisa's bedroom.

"That's right," Lisa said as the telephone rang.

Connie picked up the receiver from the phone beside Lisa's bed. She listened for a long moment to the speaker on the other end of the line. It was clear that she didn't know what to say.

"If it's Jay, I'd better take it," Adele said after a keen look at Lisa's tear-swollen and stubborn face, and Connie silently handed the phone over to Adele.

Adele adroitly stepped into the breach. "Well, Jay," she said, "right now I'm the only one here who's not all teary-eyed. I don't know what's going on, but Connie and I will be late for Mass if we don't leave in a few minutes. Lisa?" Adele shot a look at her, and Lisa vigorously shook her head no.

"I'm afraid that Lisa doesn't want to speak with you. No, I don't know anything about it, but I can't make her talk if she doesn't want to talk. Okay. All right. Goodbye, Jay," Adele said. After she'd replaced the receiver in its cradle, she said, "I think he's crying, too. Has the world become one big waterworks this morning? Will somehow please tell me what on earth is going on?"

"I guess you could say I broke our engagement," Lisa managed to say.

Adele rolled her eyes. "I don't know what the story is, but I suddenly feel in need of spiritual renewal, and it doesn't look like I'll get it here. Come along, Connie. We'd better go to church as planned."

"I'll get my rosary," Connie said disconsolately, and, eyes downcast, she left.

"Are you sure you're all right, Lisa?" Adele asked in a kindlier tone.

"I—I just want to be alone for a while. I can't talk about it yet," Lisa said.

"When you're ready, I'll listen. Look, Connie and I may go to a restaurant to eat brunch after church," Adele told her.

"Go ahead. I'm fine," Lisa said, but she was aware that she didn't look fine. She was relieved, however, that Adele took her at her word. After giving Lisa an encouraging pat on the shoulder, Adele left, closing the door softly behind her.

Lisa buried her face in her hands. How was she going to tell Adele that Jay was the person who had killed Megan? And yet she would have to tell her. There was no way to get around it; Adele liked Jay so much that she would expect an explanation for the breakup.

On the way into the bathroom she passed her lovely white dress from the night before crumpled into a damp heap in the corner. She picked it up and threw it in a nearby wastebasket. She would never want to wear it again.

As she stood in the shower with the sharp needles of spray beating down upon her, she wondered if there had been any possibility that she could have known who Jay Quillian really was. Had there been any clue, any way to find out? He hadn't talked much about his childhood, but a lot of people didn't. Now that she thought about it, perhaps he had been a bit evasive about certain things, but she had always put it down to an impatience with small talk or an unwillingness to talk about something unimportant.

She stepped out of the shower, dried herself, and became aware of a heavy pounding on the front door. Wrapping herself in the towel, she ran to the bedroom window and saw the unwelcome sight of Jay's car parked in her driveway.

She backed away from the window and sat down on the edge of the bed, struggling to think. She didn't want to see him or talk to him; she wanted him to leave. The barrage of blows to the front door continued unabated, until her head began to throb. She finally got up and pulled on a shirt and a pair of shorts. Surely Jay would go away if she never came to the door, but then she realized that Adele had left the garage door open and that Jay could see her own car inside.

Jay commenced ringing the doorbell. She drowned out the sound by turning on the hair dryer, but by the time her hair was dry, her hands were shaking so much that she could barely put on her lipstick.

"Lisa? I know you're in there!" she heard him shout, and she clung to the bathroom vanity, closing her ears against his familiar voice and wondering how to escape.

She glanced at the clock in her bedroom. Adele and Connie might be gone for hours, and she couldn't stand any more of this harassment. She pulled herself together and hurried to the front door. When she threw it open, Jay's fist was raised for one more blow, and she involuntarily flinched.

Slowly he dropped his hand and his fingers unclenched. She thought she might faint at the sight of him; she felt extremely light-headed. She clutched at the edge of the door and hung on with all her might.

The impact of seeing him wearing the same clothes he'd worn last night, all rumpled and dirty, hit her hard. His eyes seemed sunken into his skull; the whites were bloodshot.

"Lisa," he said. "We have to talk."

"There's nothing to talk about," she said icily. "Will you please go away and leave me in peace?"

He looked at the ground; he looked at the sky; he looked everywhere but at her. Finally he said, "We're engaged to be married and you don't think we have anything to talk about?"

"*Were* engaged. Big difference," she said.

"Lisa, I love you. I love you with all my heart. Surely we can find some way to work this out," he said desperately.

"I could never marry the man who killed my best friend," she said.

"I didn't mean to do it. It was a long time ago." He stopped talking and slumped against the column holding up the porch. It was only then that she noticed that he had a blood-soaked rag wrapped around his other hand.

"What happened?" she cried involuntarily.

"Got mugged in the parking lot at the beach," he mumbled.

"You got *mugged?* Last *night?*" she asked.

"Not right after you left. Later. I went back down to the beach to get my shoes, sat down on the steps and stayed there until everyone else went away. It must have been three or four in the morning when a couple of punks showed up, started waving a broken beer bottle at me and demanded my wallet. They got it, but not without a fight. Thank goodness they didn't find your engagement ring in my suit pocket. Not that it matters to you, I take it."

Lisa ignored the bit about the ring. "Are you all right? You'd better come in. You look weak and sick," she said. She stood aside while he stepped inside.

"I'm sick all right, but not because of my hand," he said.

"You'd better let me look at it," she said.

"Nice of you to be so solicitous when last night you said you wanted to kill me," he reminded her, but he held out his hand. She spared him a murderous look before unwrapping the cloth that bound it.

"This cut looks terrible, Jay. I'd better wash the sand off, at least, and put on an antibiotic. I can't believe you didn't take care of this sooner."

"I've been driving around all morning. I didn't want to go home. No Hildy and no you. I didn't think I could stand it."

"You should have gone to a doctor. Come with me," she said, all bustling efficiency, and she led him through the quiet house into her bathroom where she kept a small first-aid kit.

He sat on the edge of her bed while she doctored his hand. He looked around him curiously. "I've never been in your bedroom before," he said. "It's pretty."

She ignored this, but when she'd finished bandaging his hand, she said, "You'd better go now." She self-consciously busied herself with the first-aid kit.

"That's *not* all, Lisa. Not by a long shot." He stood up and, with an air of deliberation, took the first-aid kit out of her hand, setting it gently on the bed.

"Jay—"

"Lisa, I'm not the same person that I was when I was seventeen years old. I've changed, and for the better. I've paid my debt to society. Can't you understand?" he said.

"You've paid your debt to society, but how about to Megan? Can you give her back her life, Jay?"

He winced. "Of course I can't. But I've paid and I've paid. Because of all that community service work I did, I've found a niche working with kids who don't have much of a chance in life. Maybe, just maybe, I've given children like Connie and Mike, Ruy, Felipe and Alejandro a little bit of what they need to make it. I hope I've helped to save a few lives."

Lisa waved him away impatiently. "You're full of baloney, Jay. Now will you leave, or must I? I don't care to be in the same room with you." When he didn't move, she walked around the bed and out of her room. He caught up with her halfway down the hall.

"It's no small thing to give disadvantaged, high-risk children an opportunity to express themselves, to vent some of their frustrations through creativity," he said heatedly.

"Oh, you're a real saint, all right," Lisa said through gritted teeth. She hurried into the kitchen and found her purse, realized that all her money was in her wallet on the dresser in her bedroom and headed down the hall again, with Jay in hot pursuit.

"Lisa, I look the same as I did yesterday, I act the same and I love you as much as ever. Why should my admission make things different? I wanted to be up-front and honest about myself. Can you at least give me credit for that?"

"No," she said, dumping her wallet into her purse.

"Haven't you ever made a mistake, or are you always perfect?" he asked in desperation.

Her eyes pinned him for a brief moment. "I never killed anyone," she said, taking off down the hall again.

"How long do I have to go on paying for a mistake I made when I was seventeen?" he asked, following on her heels at a fast clip.

"Until you bring Megan back to life, and even you, the self-proclaimed savior of I don't know how many children at the Faith Mission, can't do that," she said, fishing her keys out of the side pocket of her purse. She rushed through the kitchen and out the door to the garage, where she opened her car door and got in.

"Lisa!" he called after her as she backed out the open garage door and turned. "Wait!"

She slowed the car and rolled down the window. He ran over to where she waited, a hopeful look in his eyes.

"By the way, Jay, Adele doesn't know you killed her daughter. She'll be home in a couple of hours, so why don't you wait around and tell her all about it? That'll save me the trouble," Lisa said.

When she drove away, he was standing in her driveway staring after her as though his heart were broken.

LISA DROVE AROUND for an hour or so until she'd calmed down, then headed for Yahola. She had things she could do at the mission today; the books needed balancing, and it would be quiet in her little office off the kitchen without Sister Clementine and Sister Ursula raising their usual clatter.

The kitchen and dining hall were deserted, as she'd known they would be, but Lisa stared at the account books blankly for a long time before she bent her head over them and began to work. Concentration did not come easily; it was a struggle. After a while she pushed the books to the far side of her desk and rubbed her eyelids with a thumb and forefinger. She had hardly slept at all last night, and now she kept seeing Jay's haggard face in front of her eyes, kept hearing his despondent voice in her ears. She wasn't sure why, but she felt guilty for saying so many sarcastic things to him. Her guilt didn't change things; she couldn't marry him.

How could she marry Jay Quillian now that she knew who he was? But should she *try* to come to terms with what he had done? *Could* she?

She had thought that she'd loved Jay more than it was possible to love anyone. He had been everything she had ever wanted in a man and more. When she thought of how tenderly he touched her, about the soul-stirring kisses they had shared, she couldn't believe that he was a killer, that he had killed her best friend.

Yet he had admitted it himself, and she couldn't ignore the fact that he had concealed his past from her. What other secrets did he have? How could she ever trust him again?

Tears of hurt and disappointment filled her eyes and slid slowly down her cheeks, pooling into small damp puddles on the desk top. All their dreams of marrying, establishing a home, having kids...all gone now. He had killed their dreams just as he had killed her best friend all those years ago.

Suddenly she was furious with him. In a healthy fit of anger she picked up the stapler from her desk and threw it with all her might against the wall. It left a gouge in the paint, which made her feel better, but only momentarily.

In a minute or two she was overcome with despair and she slumped over her desk, burying her face on her folded arms. She felt as though a cold hand around her heart were squeezing the tears out one by one.

WHEN LISA ARRIVED HOME later, she found herself in the middle of an unexpected battle.

She noted with relief that there was no sign of Jay, but she heard Connie's and Adele's raised voices in the kitchen when she was still in the garage.

"I don't want to go see Nina," Connie said. When Lisa went inside, Connie was sitting at the kitchen table, her arms folded across her chest, and she was scowling at Adele.

"You know you're supposed to go on alternate Sunday nights. It's an agreement Sister Maria made with Nina," Adele said patiently. She was stirring a package of cherry Jell-O, Connie's favorite kind, into a bowl of hot water.

"That's right," Lisa told Connie, sitting down on a chair beside her. "I remember that you agreed with Sister Maria that you would visit Nina every other Sunday if you could live with me."

"That was before I had time to think it over," Connie said.

"Think what over?" Adele said, sliding the Jell-O into the refrigerator.

"How mean Nina is to me and the boys."

Lisa and Adele exchanged glances, and Lisa decided to try again.

"She wasn't mean last time, was she?" Lisa had been relieved to learn from Connie when she'd come home from Nina's two Sundays ago that nothing had gone wrong; Nina hadn't been friendly, but she had left Connie alone to play with the boys.

"You don't know Nina. The way she looks at me is pure meanness," Connie said darkly.

"Jay will be here to pick you up and take you to Nina's in half an hour," Adele reminded her.

"He will?" Lisa said.

"Yes," Adele confirmed. She said in an aside to Lisa, "He's not coming in the house, he says."

Lisa stood up. "That's good," she replied. She turned back to Connie. "Connie, go get ready. No nonsense. You're responsible enough to live up to your agreement, and that's what Adele and I expect you to do."

"I can't stand Nina yelling at me," Connie said unhappily.

Lisa's heart softened toward her. She gave the girl a quick hug. "If she yells at you or is mean to you, we'll talk it over with Sister Maria, okay? But this time, you really must go, and besides, you want to see the boys, don't you?" she said.

"I guess so," Connie said slowly and reluctantly.

"Now run along," Lisa told her. "Adele and I have things to discuss."

Adele sat down at the table. "Jay sounded awful when I talked with him early this afternoon," she said, taking in Lisa's puffy eyelids.

Lisa sighed. "I saw him this morning, Adele. He came over while you and Connie were at church."

"Isn't there some way—"

"No," Lisa said, and she felt the set of her jaw stiffen. She didn't relish telling Adele what she was going to tell her after Connie left; the thought made her feel slightly queasy.

"I'm ready to go," Connie said, marching into the kitchen with an air of resignation.

"And you look very nice, too," Adele said in approval of Connie's new skirt and blouse, which Adele had helped her choose on a recent shopping trip.

"Can I wait here for Jay? I'll be able to see his car through the window when he comes down from the driveway," she said.

"Sure," Lisa told her. Connie sat down on a chair and began to swing her legs back and forth.

"Do you remember what the sermon was at church today?" Adele asked after a time.

Connie thought for a moment. "About forgiving people," she said.

"Right. I thought it was a good sermon, didn't you?"

"Kind of. Well, yes, I did," Connie said.

They heard Jay's car in the driveway, and Connie jumped up.

"You might think about forgiving Nina for the way she's treated you," Adele said gently, clearly catching Connie by surprise.

Connie seemed to think this over. "Uh—maybe I will. Lisa, is it okay if I talk to Jay about why you're not going to get married?" she asked.

Lisa passed a weary hand over her eyes. "I wish you wouldn't," she said.

"Okay. Maybe you'll tell me later, right?" Connie asked hopefully.

"Maybe," Lisa said.

Lisa held her breath until Jay's car was gone and then she looked bleakly at Adele.

"Maybe you'll tell me right now, right?" Adele said, trying to mimic Connie for effect, but her effort fell flat.

"I'll tell you," Lisa said. "But I wish I didn't have to." And then she leaned over the table and told Adele all the details about Jay Quillian and how he had wrought havoc in their lives.

IT WAS ABOUT ten o'clock that night when Jay brought Connie back from Yahola, and although Lisa heard him walk Connie to the door and make sure she was safely inside, she stayed in her bed until she was sure he was gone. She and Adele had both retired early; Lisa was exhausted, and Adele was still distraught.

"I can't believe that Jay Quillian could be the same person," Adele had said over and over after Lisa had told her. "I simply can't believe it."

But Lisa finally convinced her, and then Adele had slipped into a morose mood and retreated to her room.

After Jay had brought Connie home and after Lisa had gone into Connie's room and been assured that she had enjoyed her visit with her cousins and that Nina had been civil if not affectionate, Lisa listened outside Adele's door and finally pushed it open slightly.

"I'm awake," Adele said in a subdued tone, and Lisa went inside, shutting the door behind her. The small lamp on Adele's dresser was lighted, and the room was quiet and dim. Adele had changed into her nightgown and her favorite old bathrobe, and she was lying on the bed.

"Sit down," Adele said, indicating the rocking chair where she herself often sat beside the window. Lisa sat; she began to rock. The motion was soothing.

"Connie is about the age my grandchild would be if Megan had lived and had a baby right after she got married. Megan wanted babies more than anything in the world," Adele said. Her voice was quiet and wistful.

"I know," Lisa said. When they had been in high school, Megan's idea of an exciting way to spend Saturday mornings was to visit the hospital's newborn nursery and stand in front of the big glass window marveling at the babies, all the babies, so sweet and tiny in their little bassinets.

"Is Connie all right?" Adele asked.

"She says she is," Lisa told her.

"How about you?" Adele asked.

"I wonder if I'll ever be all right again," Lisa said ruefully.

"I know the feeling," Adele said. It was quiet for a time, and finally it was Adele who spoke first.

"Do you still love Jay?" she asked.

Lisa stared out the window at the night. Insects trying to reach the light inside buzzed at the glass.

"How can I love him?" she asked brokenly. "He killed Megan."

It was silent for a long time. "That wasn't my question," Adele reminded her at last. "I asked if you love him." She spoke gently and thoughtfully, as though she had considered the words for a long time.

Lisa took her time answering. "I don't know," she whispered finally. "I don't know."

Another pause, and then Adele said in a small voice, "How can we expect Connie to forgive Nina if we're not willing to forgive Jay?"

They stared at each other, listening to the insects beating their wings against the window in frustration.

LISA DIDN'T SEE or talk to Jay all week. At the mission he was invisible. At home, she refused to take his calls. She would have gladly forgotten that she'd ever known the man if it hadn't been for Connie.

"Aren't we going to give Jay the new puppy, Lisa?" Connie asked plaintively on Thursday after the dinner dishes were put away.

Lisa set aside the newspaper she had been reading. She had forgotten that she and Connie had an appointment to see the golden retriever puppies the next night.

"I don't want to see him," she said. She had been adamant about this.

"But he's having a *birthday*," Connie said. "How can we ignore his birthday?"

"It would be easy for me," Lisa muttered, lifting the paper so that it hid her face.

"Well, I want to give him a present. How much will the puppy cost? I could pay for it with the money I saved in my stuffed rabbit," Connie said.

"The puppy won't cost much, but I don't think you have enough money."

Connie's face fell. "Oh. Well, maybe Sister Maria will give me an advance on my allowance. I *have* to give him the puppy, Lisa. Jay is so lonely without Hildy. But how will I get to see the puppies and pick one out? I don't know where the place is, and how would I get the puppy home all by myself? And how will I give it to Jay, and—"

Lisa slapped the paper down on the table. "I'll take you to buy the puppy, Connie," she said with a sigh. "I told you that we could, and I won't go back on my word. I'll even make up the difference if you don't have enough money."

Connie thanked her with a swift hug. "Oh, good. Now we have to decide if we want a girl or a boy puppy. Do you think—"

Lisa tuned out Connie's excited ramblings and told herself grimly that somehow she would live up to this commitment, that she wouldn't poison Connie's mind against Jay, that Connie was lucky to have Jay and that she would never interfere with their relationship. But it was hard to hold her tongue. It was very hard.

The next night, Lisa drove Connie to see the puppies. In spite of herself, Lisa fell in love with the puppy that Connie picked out for Jay. It was a female with curly taffy-colored fur, big chocolate-brown eyes and a lively disposition. She ended up paying most of the price of the dog herself, since Connie's savings wouldn't cover it. It was worth it, she told herself, for Connie's sake, because Connie fairly bubbled with happiness all the way home.

That night Connie spent the night in Lisa's room, the two of them curled up with the puppy on Lisa's bed. The puppy only whimpered once or twice during the night, and since it wasn't housebroken, they were pleased that it only had one accident, and that one on the tile floor of the hallway, where it could be cleaned up easily.

"When will we take the puppy to Jay's house?" Connie wanted to know immediately after breakfast.

Adele eyed Lisa. "Don't look at me," she said. "I promised the piano tuner that I'd be here today when he comes to tune the piano."

After Adele had left to walk up the driveway to check the mailbox, Connie announced, "I'm going to give the puppy a bath so she'll be clean and smell good when we take her to Jay," and she changed into her swimsuit and took the dog outside, where she washed her in a big washtub that Lisa kept in the garage. Afterward the two

of them romped in the grass while the puppy's fur drie
in the warm sunshine.

"It looks to me as if you got wetter than the puppy,
Lisa remarked when Connie came back inside carryin
the dog in her arms.

Connie laughed and dodged the squirming puppy'
pink tongue. "I'll put a shirt and some shorts over m
swimsuit and then I'll find a bow to put around the pup
py's neck. She needs a name. How about Goldie?"

Lisa laughed. "Not original, but it's appropriate
You'd better call Jay and tell him that you're bringing
present for his birthday. And you can take Goldie int
Jay's town house by yourself. I *don't* want to see him,
she called after her.

"All right," Connie called back.

Lisa heard Connie talking on the telephone, and whe
Connie returned to the kitchen, she studied her closely
"You *did* tell Jay that I'm not coming in, didn't you?
she asked.

"I told him," Connie said.

"We'll drive up, you'll take the dog inside, wish Jay
happy birthday and come right back out again. Agreed?

Connie hesitated. "I wish—" she said unhappily.

"Connie, we've been over this before. I don't want t
see Jay. Okay?"

"Okay," Connie said, and she was subdued all the wa
to Jay's town house. After Lisa parked outside, Conni
struggled to contain the wriggling puppy, which wa
adorned with a ridiculous pink-and-green bow for th
occasion.

"Are you sure you won't go in with me?" Conni
asked one last time before she got out of the car.

"Positive. Don't take too long, Connie. I'd like to eave as soon as possible," she said, forcing herself to smile.

Connie disappeared through the gate, and Lisa let herself slump forward. Somewhere a rotary sprinkler was slapping water against a cypress fence, and it was one of the sounds she remembered from that first day when she and Jay had made love. The sound brought back bittersweet memories: it was on that day that she'd known that she wanted to marry Jay. There had been no doubt in her mind.

Why didn't Connie hurry? She had been gone an interminably long time. Lisa didn't want to be here, and she didn't want to think about any of this.

Tears filled her eyes and fell onto the leather steering-wheel cover—the cover that Jay had bought her when she had complained that the steering wheel was too cold on chilly mornings. It was exactly the kind of thoughtful gesture she had learned to expect from Jay. If only—but what was the point? She would never marry him now. Maybe she would never marry anyone.

She didn't see him approach the car; she never heard his silent footsteps on the lush grass. But when she lifted her head she saw him standing in front of her car and gazing at her through the windshield.

She looked around for Connie, who was nowhere in sight. Where was she, anyway? She fumbled with the car key in the ignition, but then Jay opened the door on the passenger side and sat down in the seat next to her.

His face was pale, his eyes were sad and there were blue rings beneath them. His cheeks were concave; he had lost weight.

"I couldn't let you go without seeing you first," he said. "Please don't blame Connie."

"Where—where is she?" Lisa stammered.

"She's in my kitchen drinking a chocolate milk shak and introducing Goldie to her new home. She's a nic dog, Lisa. Thank you."

"It wasn't me. It was Connie," she said, starin straight ahead. She couldn't bear to look at him, to wi ness what their breakup was doing to him.

"Lisa, we need to talk. I can't go on like this. Withou you, I have nothing. Without you, my life is meanin less. My work, the mission, even Connie can't fill th void in my life," he said.

"We have nothing to say to each other," she said.

"I love you. I believe you love me. We have plenty t say," he said heatedly.

At that moment Connie came out of the courtyar "Goldie went to sleep, and I drank all of my shake. Can we go swimming in the pool? I want to show Jay how can do the backstroke."

Lisa sprang out of the car. "Connie, I told you to com straight out after you gave Jay that dog. I told you didn't want to stay here long," she said angrily.

"It's not Connie's fault," Jay said. He angled his ta frame out of the car and walked around to where sh stood. "It's my fault for giving her the milk shake. Can Connie play in the pool here for a little while? She's s eager to show off her swimming." His eyes pleaded wit her, and Connie bit her lip and looked as hurt and pa thetic as possible.

Lisa was exasperated. "You two go swimming," sh said. "I'll come back later to get Connie."

But Jay took one of her arms and Connie grabbed th other.

"Jay! Connie!" she said, nearly in tears again, bu over her voluble protests they marched her to the poo nd deposited her in a lounge chair, after which Connie umped in the pool, sending a gush of water flowing over he sides so that Lisa had to pick her feet up fast to keep er shoes dry.

Jay sat down beside Lisa, watching her closely. He vished he knew where all this was heading, but for now, maybe it was enough to reestablish contact. Maybe there vas hope.

"See, Jay? Did you see me float?" Connie said, spiting water out of her mouth.

"I sure did, doodlebug. Keep it up."

"You'd better call me *water*bug," Connie said, hurning toward the other end of the pool.

"I've missed you," Jay said quietly when Connie was out of earshot.

Lisa stared straight ahead. For some reason, all she could think about was Adele saying, "How can we expect Connie to forgive Nina if we can't forgive Jay?" And Lisa knew that Adele *had* forgiven Jay. She had seen t in Adele's eyes.

"I've thought about everything in great detail," Jay said, studying her face, her beautiful face. "I know it must be a shock to you that I'm the guy who killed Megan, but it was a long time ago. It's the worst thing I've ever done in my life, I admit it. I've been living in the shadow of that one terrible, thoughtless act ever since, and so have you. Some ironic destiny has recently brought us together, but in reality we were connected long ago, in the effect that Megan's death had on each of our lives."

She looked at him, emotions shifting rapidly across her face. "Jay—" she said, looking uncomfortable.

"What I'm trying to say is that it's time to step out from under that shadow, Lisa. Together."

She could not bear—absolutely could *not* bear—a[ny] more of this. She leaped up and began walking rapi[dly] toward her car, but Jay caught up with her on the oth[er] side of the thick hibiscus hedge screening the pool fr[om] the street. He grasped her by the shoulders, his han[ds] strong and firm, and turned her slowly so that he cou[ld] see her face.

"Step out of the shadows, Lisa. Walk in the sunshi[ne] beside me. Forever."

She looked squarely into his desperate eyes and saw t[he] love written there; his expression was earnest and plea[d]ing. He loved her, and she, in spite of everything, st[ill] loved him. He didn't deserve her punishment. If lovi[ng] was giving, then it was also *for*giving. And, suddenly, [in] a burst of understanding, she knew that she had alrea[dy] forgiven him. Holding on to her hurt and resentme[nt] would prove nothing except her own stubbornness, a[nd] if she let this wonderful man go, how would she ev[er] forgive herself?

"Forever?" she said, her voice quavering.

"Forever," he replied, scarcely daring to breathe, a[nd] then, seeing the wonderful accepting light spring into h[er] eyes, and the tears, he circled his arms around her a[nd] gathered her to his heart.

# Epilogue

*June, 1991*

The last few wedding guests had finally been seated in the church. Lisa's sister, Heather, as maid of honor, and the bridesmaids, and Connie as the very excited junior bridesmaid had already started their measured march down the long aisle in time to the strains of the traditional wedding march. Lisa was wearing the beautiful satin wedding gown made so long ago for Megan; Adele had insisted on altering it to fit her. Now Lisa waited at the door in the vestibule poised to begin.

*To begin.* In a few moments she would become Mrs. James Quillian, Lisa Quillian. She gazed at the beautiful oval diamond of her engagement ring and felt giddy with the promise of a new life.

Suddenly her eyes swam with unexpected tears of happiness. The scene before her—the pastel dresses of the guests waiting so expectantly, and the shimmering pink roses filling the air with their scent, and the priest in his vestments beyond—blurred her vision. She blinked back the tears. Jay wouldn't want to see her crying on this their special day.

Sunbeams slanting through the wide clear window behind the altar touched upon the profusion of pink roses, reminding her poignantly of the flower dolls that she and

Megan had made together on that summer's day so long
ago when they had vowed to be each other's maid of
honor. *If only Megan could be here,* she thought wistfully.

Megan, with her sweet and generous spirit, would have
wanted Lisa to be happy. And today, on her wedding day,
wearing the dress that Megan had never had the chance
to wear, Lisa was happy, happier than she had ever been
in her whole life. Together, she and Jay had found a sense
of purpose. They would go on giving of themselves to
those less fortunate, to Connie and to other children like
her, and they would do it in memory of Megan.

*And as long as Megan is remembered by those who
loved her, she can never really die,* Lisa thought.

Her silver-haired great-uncle Richard, looking courtly
and distinguished in his wedding finery, smiled down at
her. "It's time," he said, tucking her arm through his.

Slowly they stepped forward as the big pipe organ
played the triumphant trill heralding the appearance of
the bride.

In front of the altar, Jay waited, his expression exultant, his eyes shining with love and admiration as he took
in Lisa in her long satin gown and veil of silk illusion.

"I love you," Jay whispered as she joined him. Lisa
felt a surge of pure joy at the words, and her smile was
radiant.

Giving him her hand, trusting him with her life, she
stepped forward into the warm blaze of sunshine spilling
across the altar, and together they left the shadows behind forever.

# H A R L E Q U I N
## *American Romance*®

Be a part of American Romance's year-long celebration of love and the holidays of 1992. Celebrate those special times each month with your favorite authors.

Next month, we pay tribute to the *first* man in your life—your father—with a special Father's Day romance:

## JUNE

| S | M | T | | | E | S |
|---|---|---|---|---|---|---|
| | 1 | | | | | |
| 7 | 8 | | | | | 13 |
| 14 | | | | | | 20 |
| 21 | 22 | | | | | 27 |
| 28 | 29 | | | | | |

FATHER'S DAY

**#441**
**DADDY'S GIRL**
**by Barbara Bretton**

Read all the books in *A Calendar of Romance*, coming to you one per month all year, only in American Romance.

If you missed #421 HAPPY NEW YEAR, DARLING; #425 VALENTINE HEARTS AND FLOWERS; #429 FLANNERY'S RAINBOW; #433 A MAN FOR EASTER; or #437 CINDERELLA MOM; and would like to order them, send your name, address, zip or postal code, along with a check or money order for $3.29 for #421 and #425 or $3.39 for #429, #433 and #437 (please do not send cash), plus 75¢ postage and handling ($1.00 in Canada), *for each book ordered*, payable to Harlequin Reader Service to:

**In the U.S.**
3010 Walden Avenue
P.O. Box 1325
Buffalo, NY 14269-1325

**In Canada**
P.O. Box 609
Fort Erie, Ontario
L2A 5X3

Please specify book title(s) with your order.
Canadian residents add applicable federal and provincial taxes.

COR6

## *Harlequin*®

# JANELLE TAYLOR

# *Valley of Fire*

**HARLEQUIN IS PROUD TO PRESENT *VALLEY OF FIRE* BY JANELLE TAYLOR—AUTHOR OF TWENTY-TWO BOOKS, INCLUDING SIX *NEW YORK TIMES* BESTSELLERS**

VALLEY OF FIRE—the warm and passionate story of Kathy Alexander, a famous romance author, and Steven Winngate, entrepreneur and owner of the magazine that intended to expose the real Kathy ''Brandy'' Alexander to her fans.

Don't miss VALLEY OF FIRE, available in May.

# BIG SUMMER READ

## Summer Reading At Its Best

In July, Harlequin and Silhouette bring readers the Big Summer Read Program. Heat up your summer with these four exciting new novels by top Harlequin and Silhouette authors.

**SOMEWHERE IN TIME by Barbara Bretton**
**YESTERDAY COMES TOMORROW by Rebecca Flanders**
**A DAY IN APRIL by Mary Lynn Baxter**
**LOVE CHILD by Patricia Coughlin**

From time travel to fame and fortune, this program offers something for everyone.

Available at your favorite retail outlet.

BSR

OVER THE YEARS, TELEVISION HAS BROUGHT
THE LIVES AND LOVES OF MANY CHARACTERS INTO
YOUR HOMES. NOW HARLEQUIN INTRODUCES YOU
TO THE TOWN AND PEOPLE OF

One small town—twelve terrific love stories.

GREAT READING...GREAT SAVINGS...AND A FABULOUS
FREE GIFT!

Each book set in Tyler is a self-contained love story; together, the
twelve novels stitch the fabric of the community.

By collecting proofs-of-purchase found in each Tyler book, you can
receive a fabulous gift, ABSOLUTELY FREE! And use our special
Tyler coupons to save on your next TYLER book purchase.

Join us for the fourth TYLER book,
MONKEY WRENCH by Nancy Martin.

*Can elderly Rose Atkins successfully bring a new love into
granddaughter Susannah's life?*